TOUCHED SERIES, BOOK 2

CENTAUR LEGACY

NANCY STRAIGHT

Book design by Inkstain Interior Book Designing
Available electronically from all major bookstores.
Printed in paperback in 2012.
ISBN-13: 978-1481153225

BOOKS BY NANCY STRAIGHT

MYTHOLOGY

TOUCHED SERIES

Blood Debt
Centaur Legacy
Centaur Rivalry
Centaur Redemption

Think Centaurs can't be sexy? Think Again!

PARANORMAL ROMANCE

DESTINY SERIES

Meeting Destiny
Destiny's Revenge
Destiny's Wrath

How many lifetimes are enough with your soul mate?

THRILLER/SUSPENSE

BREWER BROTHERS SERIES

His Frozen Heart
Fractured Karma
Shroud of Lies

Award-winning series!

CHAPTER 1

Beau Strayer – Camille's oldest half-brother, Charleston, SC

I needed to make the call: a promise was a promise. I was hoping to get his voicemail, but no luck; he picked up on the third ring. The voice who answered said, "Daniel's Orphanage. You make 'em, we take 'em."

I looked at the phone to make sure I'd dialed the right number. "Uh, Daniel, it's Beau."

"Shit, I didn't recognize your number. Sorry, man."

Daniel was a good friend of Cami's. He'd been driving the whole family crazy trying to get in touch with her the last couple months. As a way to get him to back off, I told him that as soon as I heard anything about Cami, I'd call him. I chuckled, "How many people hang up on you when you answer the phone like that?"

He grunted. "Usually only friends stay on the line. What's going on?"

I took a deep breath and let it out slowly, "She was here for a couple hours last night."

Daniel shouted, "She *was* there?! Where's she now?"

"She flew out last night."

"Where to? Back to San Diego?" His voice was hopeful. The two were close. Cami had only stayed with us for a week, but most of the funny stories she had shared involved Daniel. When Daniel didn't hear from Cami for a few days, he flew here to Charleston to find her. Cami's grandmother had kidnapped her and taken her to her estate in Florida. Daniel went into a psycho rage when he arrived and Dad told him she was gone.

"No. Calm down a minute. I told you I'd let you know as soon as I heard anything. She escaped from Zandra's house last night. She stopped by here when I wasn't home. I didn't actually see her, but my mom and dad did. They chartered a jet for her, and she was gone before I got home from work last night."

"Where is she?"

"I'm not sure. She's got someone with her, so she's okay."

Disbelief engulfed his voice, "How do you know if she's okay if you haven't seen her, Beau?"

"My dad wouldn't lie to me. Zandra doesn't have her anymore."

"And you believe him?" Daniel growled.

Daniel had taken a swing at my dad the night he came looking for Cami. It was actually more than a swing; he punched him square in the jaw. They had no love for each other; worse yet, both were suspicious of the other. Before I dialed, I knew that Daniel would need more of an explanation than I could give him. "I know you don't care for my dad. I can understand why you think that, but he's one of the good guys. He loves Cami and wouldn't let anything happen to her."

I could hear the doubt in his voice, "Don't hand me that line of shit. She was kidnapped, and he didn't do anything about it."

I caught myself shaking my head at the phone. "Daniel, your dad talked to you, right?"

A heavy sigh echoed back at me. "I know what I am, Beau. But thanks for reminding me that I'm just a lowly human."

"I didn't mean it like that. I don't think that way. Neither does Cami. But you know why Dad was a jerk to you?"

"It's not up to him to decide who Cami's friends are."

"No, you're right. But I saw it when you were here that night, and I hear it in your voice now. Cami is a lot more to you than some pal." I paused, hating to say it, but he needed to know. "She's found a full-blooded Centaur. She's off the market, man."

His response was sharp. "She was locked up for months! I've heard how this works. I'm sure she got free last night and your dad shoved some guy on her. That's bullshit. Cami would never agree to it. She doesn't take to people trying to run her life."

"You've got it all wrong, Daniel. The Centaur she's with helped her escape. He wasn't chosen by Dad. Cami picked him. They flew out last night."

"Where?" The wariness in his voice returned. I started to think this call wasn't such a great idea after all.

"I don't know where they went. I promised you if I heard anything, I'd call. She's safe."

Daniel's voice quieted; I wasn't sure if he was talking to me or himself. "I was there you know. I went to Florida. The old bat wouldn't let me see her."

If Dad couldn't get Cami out of Zandra's grips, why would Daniel even try? He had to be clueless as to who Zandra was. The direct descendant of Chiron and Daniel tried to get tough with her? He's lucky he's still breathing. Rather than tell him he was an idiot, I said, "No, I didn't know. When? And what would have possessed you to do that?"

"I had to do something, Beau. I couldn't just sit on my hands and pretend everything was fine. I had to try."

He couldn't see me, but I nodded at him anyway. Pangs of guilt enveloped me. Daniel had gone on a suicide mission and survived. I hadn't even tried to go after her. Not against Zandra. "Does your dad know?"

Daniel chuckled, "Oh yeah, he knows. He threatened to disown me if I set foot into *his* world again."

"Your dad's protecting you by telling you to stay away from Centaurs. There are things you don't understand."

Daniel snickered, "That's the funny thing: the whole time I was growing up, Dad pretty much said his family didn't exist. Now I find out there's this other whole bunch of relatives who he talks to all the time, but I'm not good enough even to warrant an introduction. Screw 'em. I don't want to meet any of 'em, anyway."

While I was trying to figure out what to say, he added, "It wasn't 'til a year ago that I even found out about the Centaur thing, you know? Dad doesn't want me anywhere near the pure-bloods." He was trying to play it off like it was funny to him, but I could hear his bitterness when he said the word, "pure-bloods."

"Daniel, I know it's hard. Centaurs have been living this way forever. It isn't you. It's just tough to shake thousands of years of tradition. Look, I'm going to be in the same boat as your dad soon. I doubt I'll see much of my family after a year from now. I'm sure it's hard on him."

"That's the dumbest thing I've ever heard. So, just because a female Centaur doesn't choose you, you're suddenly a lower class, not worthy to mingle with the pure-bloods?"

"You have to understand, it's just our way. Like it or not, it's your way, too. Most half-bloods don't know anything about Centaurs. Your father could get in a bunch of trouble for telling you about Centaurs. The more you know, the greater your risk."

"Risk from what? If I told anyone, they'd put me in a straight jacket. Besides, Cami and I are just friends. I'm not her boyfriend. I never have been, but I'll be damned if I'm going to sit on the sidelines and let something happen to her again."

My twenty-ninth birthday was last weekend. I didn't want to wait around another year. I didn't want to become one of those pathetic

Centaurs – promising anything and being united with a Centauride whose hand was forced by her family. I couldn't bear the thought of being married to somebody who only did it out of obligation. A plan began to form in my mind. Would I have the strength to put it into action?

I could leave. I could start a new life now: maybe start my own financial consulting business, forget that I was a Centaur, and escape from all the pressures that came with it. I was ready to live my life, even if it wasn't the life my parents had always wanted for me. I took in a deep breath before I could chicken out and asked, "Hey, I was thinking of taking a trip out your way, but I don't know anyone. Any chance you'd be willing to hang out with me for a couple days? Maybe show me around?"

Daniel's voice was edgy, "Weren't you listening? I've got to make sure Cami's okay."

"She's not here. I don't know where they are, but Dad hooked them up with passports, so I'm guessing they've left the country. How about I come to San Diego, you show me around, and by the time you're sick of me, she'll probably resurface."

"Can't you just ask your dad where she went?" he pleaded.

I couldn't blame the guy, but what he didn't understand was that I'd already asked Dad a hundred different ways before I made this phone call. If Dad knew where they went, he wasn't telling anyone. "I already have, Daniel. If I stick around here, I'll go nuts. The way Cami talked about San Diego, I want to check it out. Maybe I won't miss her so badly if I'm there."

"That's the dumbest thing I've ever heard." He paused for a minute before he asked, "You sure this isn't some sort of Centaur hit squad thing?"

I couldn't hold my laugh in if I'd wanted to, "You watch too much television, Daniel. We don't have those, and if we did, would a hit squad call to tell you he's coming to see you?"

"Yeah, I guess not."

After Daniel and I hung up, I called the airport and bought my ticket.

This was the first step; a shiver ripped through my body, as if warning me not to go. I had wrestled with the decision to carry on my family's bloodline for months as it became more likely a Centauride would not choose me of her own free will. My family was more to me than the DNA we shared. Every happy memory in my life was tied to one of them.

The first time I got a hit in t-ball as a kid, Brent, still in diapers, had escaped Mom's watchful eye and met me at home plate. The other team's catcher didn't want to hurt him. Brent refused to move out of the way, so I got a homerun, and, from then on, Brent was my good luck charm.

I remembered teaching Bruce how to surf. I was only a year older than he was. He must have been around seven and was terrified of the ocean. I held out a board to him, he took it and said, "If I drown, Dad's going to be pissed at you." He didn't drown, and within a couple hours, he was giving me tips on how better to time catching the waves. Bruce was a natural, but any time someone complimented him, he always said, "Beau showed me that."

Ben was three years younger than I was. He'd always been a little on the shy side, but at all of my games, it was his baritone voice I could hear over everyone else's cheering me on. It was his shirtless painted body in the stands, shouting to me. I closed my eyes and could still picture it as if it were yesterday.

Bart's first word was "Mom," his second was "Bubba." I was "Big Bubba" to Bart until he was well into first grade. I'd been helping him with his homework one evening, and I signed the sheet he needed to take back to school the following day. When Bart saw my name, Beau Strayer, he asked, "What's that say?" I told him it was my name, and he got a sad look saying, "But, you're my Big Bubba."

Could I really just walk away from them? What would they think of me for not giving everything I had to finding a Centauride? Giving up on finding a Centauride meant I had given up on my family.

My eyes clouded as I remembered the last several phone calls sharing the news of recent betrothals. None had chosen me. I couldn't take one more rejection. I couldn't keep holding it together as my life unraveled around me. Leaving my family was more than just geography. If I went through with it and started a family with a human wife, my human family would never know my Centaur family.

I looked at the e-ticket staring at me on the computer. Monday morning I'd be on my way. I considered hitting the delete key, but a new emotion seeped into my consciousness: the idea to be free, to love who I chose to love, to have a career I wanted, to see the world through human eyes.

San Diego was as good a spot as any, and the transition might not be so hard if I had a pseudo-family to cling to. Now I just needed to find a way to break it to my family that I was done waiting; I was going to start a new life without them.

CHAPTER 2

Camille –On the airplane en route to Dublin, Ireland

Drake's ice blue eyes were watching mine as I wiped the sleep from my eyes. We were on the plane bound for Ireland. Our escape from Zandra's had gone more smoothly than I could have hoped. We were only at Will's house for a few hours when we heard she was coming after us, and we needed to get somewhere safe.

When Drake said we needed to find Hercules' arrow, I wanted to laugh. An absurd idea, but if there happened to be a sliver of a chance that we wouldn't have to worry about Zandra coming after us, I was all in.

I'd spent weeks believing Drake was dead. My grandmother Zandra was a devious and powerful Centauride who was accustomed to getting exactly what she wanted. She'd staged the death of Drake and Bianca, leaving me to believe the only way to escape her was to marry Gage Richardson. Gage and Bianca had been breaking Centaur rules for years by secretly dating when they weren't allowed to. Things got all mixed up way before I'd gotten into the picture: because of family pressures, Bianca was engaged to Drake but in love with Gage. Gage and Drake had been best friends right up until the engagement.

I didn't understand why Zandra did what she did. Maybe she had visions, maybe she didn't like choices I would make in the future, maybe she was just mean as a snake. Zandra must have known that her carefully laid out plan of betrothing me to Gage was going to unravel, so she did the unthinkable. She staged their deaths and led Gage and me to believe she had murdered them both. It would have worked if Drake's mom hadn't come looking for him when she did. That's how I learned he was alive; we were able to escape.

There wasn't anywhere I wouldn't be willing to go, so long as Drake was with me. My dad, Will, had chartered a private jet to take us to Ireland. I could get used to this: all of the seats were plush leather reclining chairs, a far cry from the few commercial planes I'd traveled on.

One other big bonus was this plane came complete with a bedroom. I would have been happy dozing in the comfy chairs, but I much preferred lying next to Drake. His body heat comforted me after the weeks of mourning I'd gone through. Unmarried Centaurs were barely permitted to touch in even the most formal of ways; lying in bed stretched out beside him was better than any gift I could have imagined.

His gaze held me. He looked uneasy. Something was on his mind, but after everything we'd both been through, I shuddered to think what it might be. My heart felt light; the pain that had been weighing it down for so long lifted as soon as we were free of Zandra's estate. My life was beginning to feel like my own again, and I didn't want the plane ever to land. I draped my arm over him. Absent any profound thoughts, I simply asked, "Did you sleep okay?"

A content grin appeared on his face, "I awoke to my dream, Cami. Shhhh, I may still be sleeping."

"Nice one. You're smooth. Keep talking like that and I'll do my impression of a puppy and follow you everywhere. Oh wait, I'm already doing that."

His smile broadened while his hand began caressing my arm. His touch was lulling me back into a restful sleep when he asked, "So, was it the sleep deprivation yesterday, the fact that you thought I was dead, or did you mean it?"

He didn't have to spell "it" out; I knew exactly what he was asking. Last night I'd confessed my feelings to Drake. I could feel my heart rate pick up speed as I remembered telling him I loved him and hearing the promise he'd made to me afterwards. "Insecure much?"

"Only with you."

I lightly caressed his back in slow circles with the arm that lay draped over him. "It wasn't the exhaustion talking. I love you, Drake."

He reached over and pulled me up against him, smothering me into his chest. His voice was tender and his grip on me tight. "The last time the subject came up, you were adamant that you didn't know me well enough to be in love with me. Before you have a chance to have second thoughts, what do you need to know?"

I wanted to laugh. He was right. He had sneaked into my bedroom at Zandra's house and asked me to choose him. I'd been so convinced that I didn't know him well enough to choose to marry him that I refused to let my mind know what my heart already felt. In my mind, I had to know everything about him, every obscure detail, before I could be in love with him.

At least that's what I'd thought before Zandra told me she'd murdered him. Then the reality of the situation hit me: Drake was kind, generous, protective, sexy, and he'd been willing to break his engagement with Bianca just for the chance that I might choose him.

To humans, breaking engagements was fairly common; it was *much* different for Centaurs. Breaking an engagement could result in a blood debt and could end a family's bloodline. I was threatened with paying the blood debt for my mother breaking her engagement with Kyle

Richardson. An arranged marriage between Gage Richardson and me had been brokered by his father and my grandmother; luckily, Gage didn't want it any more than I did.

For Drake to want to take a chance on me the way he did, while he was betrothed to Bianca was the same as putting his desire for me before his obligation to his family. If things didn't work out between us, he didn't have any siblings who would carry on the bloodline, and his family's blood would end with him.

That's not the kind of love you can stumble across at the beach. It was the rip your heart out, put everything you had to give into another's hands, and hope that they love you back. It seriously worked, because once we escaped, I didn't need years, or months, or weeks to decide. The details of his life up to this point were far less important than the man who lay beside me.

No matter what I learned, it wouldn't change how I felt. But there was so much about him I didn't know, and I wanted to know everything. Since he was giving me free range to ask anything, I let my interrogation begin. "You work for your dad; what do you do?"

"My father owns a residential construction business. I work wherever he needs me: laying foundations, hanging drywall, digging ditches, basically anything except plumbing and electric. The hours suck, it always feels like I need a shower, and I'm exhausted when I get home at night. Pretty glamorous, right?"

"Doesn't sound like much fun. Have you ever wanted to do anything else?"

"There are good parts, too. At the end of the day, I can see what I've accomplished. I think most jobs don't give you the satisfaction of ever really being done. If I worked at a bank, or in a store, or as a teacher, every day would be a lot like the previous day. I would never really finish anything and say, 'hey, look what I did,' so from that perspective, I'll always want a job building something. What about you?"

"I don't have a career or anything. I was a cashier when I lived in California, but I've been gone long enough that I'm sure I've lost that job. Any hobbies?"

"None that I can't live without. The weather's great in South Carolina from September through June, so I'm usually up for anything. You?" Drake's hand began caressing my shoulder. His touch sent shivers through me a second time.

"I'm used to California, so beach days in the summer, snow skiing in the winter, movies, dance clubs – nothing out of the norm. Daniel and I get together around each other's work schedules, and fit in whatever we have time for."

Drake's brows raised, "Daniel? Who's Daniel?"

I couldn't believe I'd never mentioned Daniel to Drake. "Daniel's my best friend. We've known each other since elementary school." I could see the questioning look on Drake's face – the same one I'd gotten from every guy I'd ever dated. I needed to elaborate before he'd jump to the wrong conclusion. "I can see it in your face, so I'll just answer now. No, he's not an ex-boyfriend. No, we've never been on a real date together. No, I don't have romantic feelings for him. And no, we've never slept together."

Drake looked like I'd offended him, "What makes you think I would need that kind of reassurance?"

"Every guy does."

Drake's eyebrows furrowed. "I'm not like other guys, Camille. I don't care if your best friend's a man, not unless he's devastatingly handsome, a rocket scientist, or a celebrity." He paused for a moment and added, "But for curiosity's sake, what qualifies as a 'real' date?"

"Daniel isn't hard on the eyes, but it's never been like that with us. We were always each other's automatic guest for friends' weddings, school dances, work holiday parties, that kind of stuff. I can't wait for you to meet him. I should probably call him. I wonder if there's a phone on the plane?"

I looked around the bedroom but didn't see one. As I moved to get out of the bed, a hand caught my wrist and pulled me back, leaning me back into the mattress. "Not so fast." Drake hovered over me on the bed. His mouth slowly closed the distance with mine. I'd kissed him since our escape, but this one was different. This kiss was slow, methodical, deep.

I felt his hand cup the back of my neck, my mouth molding to his. Having been denied contact for so long, Drake's kiss sent sharp shivers through my body. My hands instinctively began running up and down his silhouette. I was ravenous, hungry. . . starving for his touch.

The shivers morphed from tingles to full-fledged desire. I wanted to feel his skin against mine, for him to gather me in his arms and to stay lost there. Drake rolled onto his side, his icy blue eyes reflecting the longing I was sure my eyes were broadcasting to him. Drake brought his hand to my face and caressed my cheek with his knuckles. His voice was intense when he softly said, "There's nothing I wouldn't do for you."

I closed my eyes, savoring all the fantastic feelings ripping through me. I thought of what he had said to me last night, "Tell me your promise again, Drake."

I kept my eyes closed but could hear the smile in his voice when he leaned in close to my ear, feeling the warmth of his breath as much as hearing his words: "I promise to protect you. I promise always to put your needs before mine. I promise I'll never let you go to bed angry, and you'll never wake up alone. I promise to love you the rest of my life, and when this life is over, I'll spend my eternity in the pasture with you."

I wasn't sure if that was some Centaur creed or what, but I loved how it rolled off his tongue. Drake had promised eternity to me. My heart was pounding hard in my chest, my blood ablaze. I reached over, grabbed both sides of his t-shirt and tugged it over his head. Drake's eyes opened wide while the sight of him nearly took my breath away. My hands were drawn to his chiseled chest; his muscles screamed for me to press myself against them. Without hesitation, I stretched over his naked chest as a gravelly moan escaped his lips. I could feel his heartbeat pounding in sync with mine, his breathing labored, "Camille, we'd better slow down unless you think one of the pilots doubles as a priest."

I had nearly forgotten. I was so lost in the moment with Drake that it was easy to toss out a few of the Centaur rules that seemed stupid to me. I understood thousands of years of traditions wouldn't be able to dissolve in front of my eyes, but it didn't mean I had to like them. Drake had grown up as a Centaur, where acceptable behavior didn't include pre-marital anything; instead marrying as early as sixteen was encouraged. These practices were archaic to me.

I'd grown up in California, as a human. Mom had turned her back on Centaurs and all the rules that governed them. She had never once acknowledged that either of us was something other than a normal human, and she never discouraged me from any kind of dating.

I think I got some form of sex-ed classes in school every year from sixth grade up. Sure, most of the curriculum talked about abstaining, but in reality the teachers focused on safe-sex and pregnancy prevention. I had never put the premium on abstaining that Drake did, because no one I knew thought that way. On the flip side of the coin, none of my friends were willing, nor would their parents have allowed them, to be married at sixteen the way Centaurs did.

I was twenty-two, and marriage wasn't anything I'd ever given a second thought to. I loved him, I was sure I'd never want another, but I wasn't willing to elope with him. I had a feeling that as long as I clung to my desire not to be married, Drake would cling just as hard to his belief that "uniting" before marriage was off the table. I knew exactly where his beliefs came from and how far entrenched they were in his mind. Regardless of what I thought of them, I was sure he wouldn't miraculously change his mind here.

Drake detangled himself from me, "That wasn't much of an interrogation, but if that's the response I get: ask another question. I thought you'd want me to start at kindergarten and work my way forward."

Still distracted by his shirtless body next to me, I said, "Oh, all right. I've met your mom; since she's the reason we were able to escape, I already like her. What's your dad like?"

Drake's demeanor changed when he answered, "He's Centaur. Very set in his ways. He doesn't mix with humans, at all, not even in his business. Humans see houses he's built and try to hire him – he won't even return their calls."

"Really?" That statement made my heart skip a beat when I remembered what his mother had told me yesterday. "Your mom told me that you'd asked them about breaking your engagement with Bianca. She told me, at the time, she thought you wanted a human. How did that conversation go?"

"Mom basically told me to do what made me happy. . . Dad glared. I knew what his reaction would be when I asked; I was more hoping for my mom to be okay with it."

"But you didn't tell her you wanted to break it off to be with another Centauride?"

Drake's expression was shy, and I wondered if he was going to answer me at first. When he spoke, his eyes locked on mine, "I didn't know if you felt the same for me, Cami."

Having not grown up with two parents, the dynamics of two people with opposite belief systems sounded foreign. "If she had been against it, neither of us would be here right now, would we?"

"The fact that Bianca was still in love with Gage had a lot to do with me wondering if I could go through with marrying her – I'd thought that even before I met you. My parents are like most Centaurs: they didn't know each other that well in the beginning. They started a family and a life together, but love for each other wasn't one of their priorities. I wasn't sure how they'd feel about me breaking my engagement, regardless of the circumstances."

"That's sad."

"It's not happy or sad, Cami. It just is what it is."

"It's not sad that you almost married someone you didn't love? Someone you knew would never love you back? By standing up for yourself and breaking the engagement, you risked your parents disowning you. You don't think that's sad?"

A smile began to creep across his face. "When you put it that way, it's a little sad. But there are things we get to experience that humans will never know the pleasure of."

"Like what?"

"Like running so fast it feels like you're flying. Being united with another where words are no longer required because you are so attuned to them you can hear their thoughts and share in their joy. Those are things humans never experience, and I think that's sad." Drake looked away. He was searching for a subject change when he asked, "You haven't told me much about your mom. What was she like?"

Almost no one had asked me about her. Lots of people told me they were sorry for my loss, but no one would know why that loss was such a big gaping hole because no one knew her like I did. "She was intensely private. She didn't hang out with other moms. She wasn't on any school committees and only came to the school when she had to for conferences. She only had one friend that I knew of. She was always working, but Mom always had time for whatever was important to me."

I stopped for a second, remembering how she told me, "*Everything in life is your choice. Choose wisely.*" I'd heard that phrase from her my whole life, but I didn't understand its double meaning until after she died.

"I went through a phase where I told her I wanted to be a Marine Biologist – she worked it out so I could help a Marine Biologist from SDSU. After that lost some of its novelty, I decided I wanted to be a cop; she pulled some strings so that she and I could ride along with a cop a couple of weekends. Whatever I told her I was interested in, she found a way to help me do it. She's everything I ever wanted to be . . . I still want to be."

Drake was still caressing my cheek with his knuckles, "But she never told you about Centaurs?"

I shook my head, "Nothing. It's almost like, in her mind, she wasn't one. I guess I shouldn't claim to know her mind, but since I showed up in South Carolina, every Centaur kind of lets it run their lives – she wasn't like that at all."

Drake shook his head, "It doesn't run our lives. It's who we are."

"Only because you let it be who you are. My feelings for you don't have anything to do with you being a Centaur. You could be a human house painter, and I'd feel the same way." Drake looked away, and I worried I'd unintentionally struck a nerve.

I needed for him to understand, "I feel the way I do because you risked everything that was important to you, with no promise that I'd feel the same for you. When it was obvious Bianca loved Gage, you didn't try to guilt her into staying with you. You didn't try to force her to marry you. You were willing to let her be with Gage – you found a way to be happy for them. When I was teetering on the edge of folding in on myself from loneliness at Zandra's house, you appeared out of nowhere to back me off of the ledge."

A smile emerged at the memory, "Your crazy idea to sneak into my room, after everything I'd learned about traditions, rules, and acceptable behavior – that's not something a Centaur does." My fingers grazed his cheek as his eyes smoldered at my confession, "That was something a man in love does, someone who was willing to kiss his carefully laid out future good-bye. That's why I fell in love with you."

Drake wrapped both his hands on either side of my face and pulled my mouth to his. Just before our lips touched, "I'm glad you noticed, Love. I was running out of ideas."

As my thoughts swam wildly, I wondered how long kissing him would be enough? My whole body ached for his touch. I loved the way my body reacted to his. How long could I hold out before I was willing to give in and be married to him? Or would I be able to convince him to give in to the desire he felt for me?

CHAPTER 3

Camille – Dublin, Ireland

We landed in Dublin. One of the pilots, Chip, met us at the stairs before we could depart. "Mr. Strayer set up reservations for you; he just sent them to us." Chip handed me the piece of paper, "We'll refuel now. My number's on that sheet of paper. As soon as you're ready to go, send me a text, and we'll meet you here at the plane. Any idea how long you think we'll stay?"

Drake shook his head, "Sorry, Chip, it could be a day, or we may be here for several weeks."

"Understood. We'll need at least thirty minutes to file a flight plan and do a pre-flight check, so if you're going to be in a hurry, give us as much notice as you can."

It took all of three seconds to realize we needed to find some clothes. It had been cool in the evenings at home, but we stepped out of the airport into what felt like an icebox. *Icebox* is a relative term, but having never been beyond the balmy weather of the southeast and southwest

United States, the air was wet and cold. The low temperature coupled with wet air chilled me all the way to the bone: it was rainy and in the mid-forties, while we were dressed for eighty degrees.

We found our hotel, a clothes shop that specialized in wool coats and socks, a shoe store with a sub-zero guarantee on their hiking boots, and a bookstore that carried local maps. I had expected the Ireland I'd always seen in the tourist brochures. The dirt roads, emerald green pastures that went on as far as the eye could see, the cobblestone streets hundreds of years old, the clip-clopping of horse drawn carriages – wherever they shot those pictures, it sure wasn't Dublin.

Dublin had an energy all its own. Pubs lined street corners, roof-top bars blared dance music, and enthusiastic voices echoed to the passersby on the street. Cars littered the street with the same hustle and bustle of any major city I'd ever seen.

When Drake said we were going to be looking for the pasture of Thessaly, in my mind we weren't going to look for it on foot – I was wrong. We had bundled up to prepare for the next ice age and driven our rental car south of Dublin.

Once we were nearly an hour south of the city, we took a roundabout; eventually the pavement disappeared, and we found ourselves on a road with little more than one lane. Each time a car approached us, I squinted, hoping both cars would fit on the tiny road. Sheep seemed to own as much of the road as the cars, and fifteen minutes after we'd turned off the main thoroughfare, we found ourselves in our first traffic jam.

Rather than a mangled car blocking the road ahead, it was a flock of sheep that decided enough traffic had passed, and they were in no hurry to yield the right of way. Cottages with thatched roofs littered the countryside. The further we drove south, the more it felt like we were going back in time.

We were here to find my Uncle Zethus, who supposedly lived in the pasture of Thessaly and had an arrow with magical powers. I gazed out the window trying to remember the story Zandra had told me. A light caress on my arm turned my head. Drake kept his eyes on the road as his fingers nimbly wrapped around my hand. His thumb caressed the top of my hand, shooting tingles up my arm.

I loved the sensations he could give me with almost no effort on his part. As my mind wandered to the light touch on my hand, a question came to mind. "What do you know about the arrow?"

"Well, we know it existed a couple thousand years ago. Gramps said Chiron's family kept the arrow, but no one's seen it for a long time."

"I know it's the arrow that poisoned Chiron, but why's it so special?"

Drake didn't take his eyes off the road, "Hercules had been walking on the beach and found a ship wrecked high on the rocks. When he explored the debris, his uncle, Poseidon, rose from the sea, warning Hercules to leave the ship alone."

"Poseidon didn't want Hercules to touch the ship?"

"The crew had neglected to pay homage to Poseidon before they sailed. Poseidon sent a sea creature to the ship to remind them to ask for Poseidon's safe passage. The crew refused and slaughtered the sea creature. In retaliation, and as an example to others, Poseidon threw the ship onto the rocks for all the other sailors to see."

"Okay?"

"Hercules wanted to make his own arrows. He asked Poseidon if he could use the wood from the mast for the shafts of his arrows. Poseidon agreed, telling him a god's weapon should be born of a god's wrath."

"So the arrow was magical because of Poseidon's shipwreck?"

"Partly. Hephaestus was the god of fire, metalworking, and stone masonry. He made the arrows' tips. There were no sharper tips to be found on or off Mount Olympus. They could puncture a person's flesh just as easily as a pool of water."

I remembered back to the endless lessons in Zandra's garden, "Zandra told me something about the tips, but it wasn't how sharp they were."

Drake nodded, "Right, the poison. Hercules made a trip to Hades and dipped the tips in the blood of a Hydra. Not only could they slice through skin with no effort whatsoever, when they sliced, they deposited the most toxic poison available into the wound."

"And, this is what we're looking for? Nice. Why don't we just see if we can find some plutonium to walk around with? It might be safer."

Drake laughed, "Plutonium might be safer, but I'm not sure how much of a deterrent it would be for Zandra."

"If we are able to get the arrow, what're we going to do with it? We're not going to kill her. I mean, I don't have any love for her, but I don't want her dead, either."

"Just having it will be enough of a protection. It's Hercules' arrow. No harm can come to us if we have it – not from Zandra, not from anything."

We drove in silence for a few minutes. I didn't know how we would find the pasture, or even how we'd know when we found it. Lost in my own thought, I was jolted back to reality when Drake pulled the car into what looked like an abandoned gas station. A faded metal sign hung proudly advertising "Petrol," but from the looks of the place, no one had gotten gas there in a very long time.

I stood looking at the terrain in front of us. I'd always heard Ireland was the Emerald Isle and expected it to be lush and green in all directions. What we discovered was the terrain was rugged, areas were steep, and fields of rocks were far more prevalent than the grassy fields I had expected. We walked for over an hour across pastures, over rolling hills, through ravines, before I asked, "Drake, how are you going to know when we find it?"

He shook his head, "I'm not sure. Dad always said that the field was magical. I'd like to think I could feel the magic if we got close, or maybe *you'll* be able to."

I rolled my eyes. "Defective. . . remember?" He already knew I couldn't read thoughts, see the future, or anything else other Centaurides could do.

Drake stopped in his tracks, looked down at me and said, "You're not defective. You just haven't worked all the kinks out yet."

Smirking at him, "Kinks? You mean like I can't read minds, see futures, move objects. . . Those are kinks? Whew, here I thought there was something really wrong with me."

"You're such a smart ass, Cami."

I playfully grabbed his shoulder and leaned in toward him, "Just one of the many aspects of me you love."

A gruff voice echoed at us from off in the distance, "What are you doin' o' this way?"

I froze. It was the first person to notice us traipsing all over the countryside, and from his stance he didn't look pleased to see us. Drake picked up the pace and began walking faster toward the man, "Hello, I'm Drake and this is Camille. We're looking for some long-lost relatives."

The man had a light complexion and a forced smile. He wore a gray wool jacket hanging open over a flannel shirt, well-worn blue jeans and scuffed leather boots. He grunted. "Americans?"

Drake nodded. The man continued his interrogation. "Who might ya be lookin' for?"

"Chiron. Zethus Chiron. We were told he lived south of Dublin."

"Zethus Chiron?" The old man took a tobacco pipe from his mouth and spat at our feet. His eyes narrowed, and I was thankful they couldn't actually fire the daggers that were staring back at us. "He's been gone for years." The man turned his back on us and walked slowly in the other direction.

After I was sure he was out of ear shot, I asked Drake, "What do you make of that?"

He shook his head, "I don't know."

That pit in my stomach that I'd had while I was at Zandra's began to form again. Zethus was her twin. It wasn't a stretch to think he would be just as ruthless as she. "Maybe this wasn't such a great idea."

"It was one person, Cami." Drake took a step forward in the direction we'd been traveling, "At least we know we're in the right country."

Ireland was a whole different world from the United States. The never-ending pastures stretched on forever, and the rocky terrain caused us both to stumble. In my mind I had pictured pastures like I'd seen in northern California, lush and green. Ireland looked nothing like the nicely aligned fenced-in pastures flanked by roads skirting nearly every fence I had always seen in the US. We occasionally came across fences: most were made of rock, some had gates to go through, others had rock steps to easily climb over them.

I was still nervous from our first encounter with the older man when we came across an older couple crossing through a pasture perpendicular to us. The woman gave us a welcoming smile. I returned her greeting and asked, "Excuse me, we're looking for a distant relative. Do you know where we could find Zethus Chiron?"

The woman's eyes widened and her smile morphed into an angry grimace. She put her head down, reached over to her husband's coat sleeve, yanked hard, and scurried quickly back the way they had come without a word.

"Wait, wait! Please, won't you help us?" She neither answered, nor did she look over her shoulder in our direction. I stood there watching them speed-walk over the field, and that pit in my stomach began to throb. Drake sensed my fear, reached down and squeezed my hand, "We learned that we're close. We'll find him, Cami."

The words spilled out of my mouth before I could stop them. "So, what if he's just like Zandra? What if we've escaped one prison only to be locked up in another?"

Drake didn't answer me. I waited for him to reassure me that things would be fine, that these last three people we ran into were flukes. He didn't.

For the next few hours we kept up our pace and only came across sheep, goats, cattle and the occasional horse grazing. I looked at my watch; we'd been searching for almost six hours.

A person walked our way off in the distance. I planted my feet, waiting to see where he would go. The man continued toward us. He was younger, late twenties or early thirties, and he didn't seem to be in a hurry. As the man strolled up to us, he gave us a happy greeting as he approached. "Well, hello! Are you two los'?"

Since I had struck out with the couple we'd met before, I signaled Drake that it was his turn to try to strike up a conversation. "A little. We're looking for a distant relative. We were told that Zethus Chiron lived out this way, but we've had some difficulty finding him." That was an understatement.

Looking perplexed, the man asked, "Someone told you he lived ou' this way?"

I liked his question much better than the response we had gotten from the last three older people we'd talked to. "Yes, in this area."

"Not by anyone who knew anythin', that's for sure. No Chiron family's lived in these parts for as long as I've been alive."

I felt my heart sink. I couldn't make my eyes meet the man's when I asked, "Did you say you've never heard of Zethus Chiron? I was under the impression he was well known." No one had actually told me he was well known, but since Drake knew who he was and the first three people we asked seemed to have heard of him, I had to assume he wasn't a wallflower. Judging from the response we had gotten from the first three people we met – I had an idea of what his personality might be like, too.

The younger man shook his head, "No, I can't say that I've heard of him."

I forced a smile, "Thanks. Sorry to have bothered you."

"You weren't a bother, lass. You looked like you mighta' been los'. Sorry I can't help."

I looked at Drake; he wore the same defeated look that I did. We walked back in the direction we'd left the car. Drake's fingers curled around mine. His touch reminded me to put our adventure in better perspective. No one was chasing us, at least not that we knew of. We were together on a mission to save our future, and luckily, we were doing it together. Even if we weren't successful, this time together was a gift in itself.

We found our rental car and went back to the hotel. On the drive back I asked, "So, if that man's never heard of Zethus, maybe we aren't in the right place? The first people we asked were older, and one even sounded like he'd moved away."

Drake kept his eyes on the winding road, "Maybe, but let's give it a few more days. It was just one man. The others seemed to know him." He reached his hand over to mine and gave it a gentle squeeze.

I was glad he had more faith than I did. Even if we never found Zethus, spending time with Drake and spending that time away from all the crazy Centaur rules was something I couldn't take for granted.

We logged mile after mile on the winding roads on our way back to the city, and I savored each minute.

CHAPTER 4

Camille – Southern Ireland

By our third day ambling over the countryside, talking about our friends, families, dreams – I felt like there wasn't a person I'd ever known better in the world. Maybe Daniel, but even he had never been this open with me. Drake wasn't secretive about anything. He never tired of my questions, and the more I learned about him, the more I wanted to know.

Drake wasn't like the *Stepford-Centaurs* I'd met at my brother Bruce's wedding. He wasn't trying to be the guy I wanted him to be – but he was exactly who I had pictured in my future. When the massive earthquake had hit Haiti a few years ago, he didn't send a donation to help; he got on a boat and was digging people out of the rubble for days. Afterwards, he helped with reconstruction for weeks.

Drake was wealthy by human standards, but worked anyway. He said he liked the way it made him feel when a house was finished – like a piece of him would be around for the next hundred years.

A human neighbor's house burned down when a brushfire spread out of control. Their insurance company wouldn't cover the repairs. They were living in tents in their yard because of the damage to the structure. Drake bought the supplies and convinced his whole crew to give up several weekends making the house livable again. His father fumed about his crew helping humans, but Drake refused to back down. He volunteered for Habitat for Humanity two weekends a month and had a hand in building more than thirty houses. In a word, Drake was perfect.

Ireland's landscape was breathtaking; the rolling hills were grassy but didn't feel overgrown. It looked as if the land had somehow made a pact with the animals; it wouldn't provide them more food than they could eat, but none would ever go hungry. There seemed to be endless streams and lakes nestled between the shoulders of hills.

After cresting the top of another hill, we came across a deep valley and looked down into a lake that was completely still. It mirrored the sky perfectly, and I had to wonder if a bird had ever flown directly into the water, mistaking the mirrored clouds for the real thing. I stood at the top of the hill, mesmerized by the image in front of me – if there were a magical place, we had just found it.

Drakes fingers flexed around mine, "Cami, are you okay?"

He was still holding my hand, but I could sense his worry. I wondered if he saw it the same way I did? "What do you feel when you look out here?"

His gaze looked out over the still lake, just as mine had done. I felt his fingers constrict around mine. "I feel it, too."

When Drake told me we would feel the magic when we found it, in my mind I had pictured the rush the first time I'd seen a magician saw a lady in half as a child, or maybe when a friendly neighbor had pulled a quarter out of my ear and handed it to me. I expected that feeling of wonder that only a child can feel – the one that ingrains itself in your memory as if it's actually a part of your physical make-up.

This valley didn't feel like those things at all. It was energy, a sense of oneness, in a word – home. The terrain was vast; we had a clear view of the entire valley. We'd been walking for hours; I was hungry and exhausted, but all of that seemed to diminish – this was our destination.

I took a step forward, expecting Drake to be in lock step, but he held his position at the crest of the hill. "Not today, Cami. We've found it. We don't want to get lost in the dark. We'll come back tomorrow."

I'm sure the look I'd given him was confused because, well, that's how I felt. We belonged here. Couldn't he feel it calling to us, welcoming us home? Drake stepped behind me, pressed himself against me, while his arms snaked around both my sides and his chin rested on my shoulder. I could feel his breath on my neck, "It'll be here tomorrow, Love. We've found it. Let's get some rest."

I've never been an outdoorsy person. I had plenty of opportunities to camp growing up and found a good reason to avoid each one, but walking away from this place felt wrong. If this really was the pasture of Thessaly – I couldn't fathom why any Centaur would ever have left. The weather had been rainy most of the day. I didn't want to go back to civilization; not even the lure of a hot bath or dry clothes was much motivation to leave.

Drake looked down into my eyes, brushed a stray strand of hair behind my ear and said, "I promise, we'll be back tomorrow. It'll be dark soon. We've found it." He took my hand and gently tugged me back in the direction of the car. A twinge of dread began to seep into my consciousness, beckoning me to stay, but I reluctantly followed.

Still distracted by the strange pull of the valley we'd walked away from, I looked back over my shoulder to catch one more glimpse, and I wasn't paying attention to where I was walking. Drake was already twenty feet ahead of me at the car. I took two steps directly into a peat bog, was waist deep and sinking before I realized what had happened. "Drake!!"

He turned around and saw me stuck in the bog. He looked at the ground and saw the outline, carefully making his steps back to me. I tried to walk out of the muck and back to the solid soil I had just come from, but the more I moved, the further I sank. A feeling of panic gripped me. "Drake, I'm sinking!" I struggled to get closer to the side but felt the bog pulling me down further with every move.

His voice was calm, "Don't move, Cami. I'm right here." Drake kept his feet firmly on the ground while he reached out to me. I was only four feet from the edge, but I couldn't reach his hand; I had sunk too far.

Images flashed through my mind, not the comforting ones you're supposed to see when your life flashes before your eyes. I relived in a fraction of a second all the things that had scared me most in my life: the fear of the ocean's undertow pulling me hard out to sea, the first time glancing over the side of a twenty-story high rise, a brown tarantula staring at me from the banister on my front porch, riding a galloping horse on the beach that refused to stop. . .

I cried out, not sure if it was from the images or the fact that this peat bog threatened to swallow me whole. Beads of sweat peppered my brow while another ear-splitting scream escaped me.

Drake squatted down closer to the ground, extending his hand all the way to me. I grasped his fingers. "Okay, I've got you. Just relax. I won't let you go."

His fingers steadied me as I let him gently pull my hands to him; I took a step in his direction but lost my footing. I tried to pull my back foot free of the muck, but the bog was holding me, refusing to let go. I felt my fingers slipping. Panic overtook me as I tried desperately to free my foot, only to find out my struggle took me deeper.

"Oh, no you don't." Drake tugged the tips of my fingers in his grasp hard and got a better grip on my hands. "On the count of three, I'm going to pull. Are you ready?"

I nodded that I was, as the fear threatened to envelop me. I heard, "One. . . two. . . three." Still clasping just my hands, he pulled me smoothly free of the muck, out of the bog, and to his side on the ground. I lay on the ground, my pulse rapid, my hands shaking. I looked down at myself: the waterline had been just inches below my shoulders.

I grabbed hold of him as he cradled me on the ground. He stroked my hair and crooned, "You're okay, Cami. You're okay."

We had heard about the bogs and had been warned by the hotel staff to be careful of them. But they told us the bogs would be clearly marked and fenced off. This one was in the open. I didn't know how I could have missed it to begin with.

When described to us, I had thought they were a little like the swamps that surrounded Zandra's home, but after being in one, it was more like quicksand. I sat on the ground, wrapped in Drake's arms, thankful that he had reacted so quickly. His strength was as much of a surprise to me as finding myself free.

A friendly voice came from behind the car. "Welcome home. Was just coming to give you a hand."

The icy air intensified the cold I was already feeling. Drake stood up, cocked his head slightly to the side, but didn't return the stranger's greeting.

When the man was only ten yards away he asked, "So, which herd are you from?"

Shivers took hold of my body. I couldn't have spoken if I had to. Drake cautiously held out his hand to the stranger, "The Nash. And you?"

"Barber. We don't get many tourists ou' this way."

Tourists? Was he serious? I couldn't get my teeth to stop chattering long enough to say anything to him.

Drake grinned, "So, we've found it. This *is* the pasture of Thessaly?"

"Aye. That bog was meant to keep humans out of the pasture. Most don't like the feel of the place, so they turn around before the top o' the hill, but there are several bogs scattered near the crest of the hill as a precaution. Watch your step."

"Our hotel told us any bogs would be marked and fenced off. You're saying there are more?"

"These bogs were constructed with Centaur magic. They reposition themselves in front of humans and hold them tight until a Centaur comes to release them and send them on their way."

His words echoed in my head. I was a Centauride. Why had the bog positioned itself in front of me? Then doubt began to creep into my mind. Everyone just assumed I was a Centauride, but I couldn't do all of the things the others could do. Was I really William's daughter? Drake asked the question my lips wouldn't form.

"Barber, Camille is a Centauride. Why would it have held her?"

"I don't know, Nash. Maybe it didn't recognize her bloodline." Barber's eyes narrowed, as if he wanted to accuse me of something, but changed his mind. Instead of talking to me, he continued to address Drake, "She's part of your herd?"

Without hesitation, Drake answered, "Yes."

"Hmmm, I don't know. It used to catch the Tak herd, too, but they're long gone." The man glanced at me but turned his attention back to Drake. "Be on the lookout. There are more. If this one got her, pay attention to where she's walking. Could have just been bad luck. A few humans live in the pasture. They keep to themselves. Don't do anything to draw attention to yourself while you're sightseeing."

Drake nodded, "We won't."

The Centaur from the Barber herd gave a quick wave of his hand and walked away without another word.

When we got to the car, the shivers had turned to near convulsions. Drake found some clothes for me to change into in a backpack we had stuffed in the trunk for an emergency. As soon as he started the car, he had the heat blaring, handed me his jacket and asked, "Are you okay?"

I nodded my head through chattering teeth. Drake looked worried, "I know a way to get you warmed up." Drake leaned over to the passenger seat, wove his fingers into my hair and gave me the most passionate kiss I'd ever received. I'd heard the expression, "made my toes curl," but this was my first experience with the phenomena.

His hand slid down to my shoulder then glided down my side, our mouths locked tight as I felt sparks of desire raining all over my body. Within minutes I no longer cared that I wasn't wearing shoes or socks, that I smelled of decaying vegetation, or that I was soaked to the bone – none of it mattered. My heart was racing. Drake eased his lips away from mine, "I hope you're feeling warmer, because I feel like I'm on fire."

My hands grabbed the back of his head, pulling him back to me, "Don't stop."

Drake smiled shyly in response and gave me one more quick kiss. "Let's get you back to the hotel. This has been enough excitement for one day."

CHAPTER 5

William Strayer – Camille's Father, Charleston, SC

Camille and Drake had made it. They'd been in Ireland for three days, and as far as I could tell, their departure had gone unnoticed. I'd done everything I could for the two of them. They had passports, Euros, credit cards and each other. Just a few more loose ends to tie up and I was sure they'd be safe, for now. Gretchen tapped lightly on the door to my study. She almost never knocked. I waited for her to say something; her eyes were brimming with tears. I asked, "What's wrong?"

"Beau's packing." She was doing everything she could to hold back her tears. We'd always been such a close family, never once being away from each other beyond business trips. This would be the first time Beau would be away from home by himself. Even while in college, Beau commuted from home. She was taking it just as hard as I had expected her to.

I took a deep breath, "It's just a few days."

She shook her head, "He's leaving for good."

"For good? No, he just needs some time away. Cami's safe. He was pretty shaken up over Zandra's stunt. Now that we all know she's safe, he probably just needs to decompress, to relax. It's tough to do that here."

"No, Will, I feel it. He's leaving us."

"Do you want me to have a talk with him?"

She nodded as her eyes grew glossier and she pressed her lips together. She was letting her emotions get the better of her. I stood up and walked to the door of my study; as I walked past her, Gretchen reached out and grabbed my hand. I tried to reassure her, "It'll be fine. You'll see."

Beau's birthday had been last weekend. We wanted to go out for dinner to celebrate, but he said he didn't feel well. Even his brothers couldn't coax him out of the house. Gretchen had an uncanny way of seeing the future of the stock market, but she'd never been able to get a clear view of our sons' futures. I wondered if that was what had brought on the tears – the unknown.

I walked upstairs, and Beau was just zipping his suitcase. "Hi, Dad. All set. Sun and sand for a full week. I talked to Bart; he's going to cover my clients for me while I'm gone. If he gets too busy, Ben said he could pitch in, too."

That was just like Beau. He was the oldest, always the responsible one, setting the example for his brothers. "That's good news, son. Your mother's a little concerned. What prompted your vacation?"

Beau didn't look at me when he answered, "I don't know. . .it just seemed like a good time to go."

"Why don't you take Brent with you? I'm sure he'd like to meet some of Cami's friends, too."

"Brent can't stand humans. He's the last one I'd take with me."

"What about Bart?"

"Dad, I've already got my ticket. My flight goes in a couple hours. I'll be fine. I just need a break."

"It's just a ticket, Beau. If you'd given me a little more notice, you could have taken our plane. Or we all could have gone." Beau forced a smile at me. Gretchen was right; there was something he wasn't telling us.

"I tell you what; I don't want you on a commercial flight. Let me make some phone calls, and I'll arrange for a jet. You'll get there faster, and you don't have to worry about who'll be sitting next to you."

Beau shook his head, smirking at me. I imagine he thought I was just being over-protective. "Dad, I'll be fine. It'll be fun to be a human for a week."

I cringed. I tried not to let on how much I didn't want him to go. Part of being a Centaur is to know when to go out into the world. He didn't need to tell me; I could feel it in the air. He was done with our rules, our laws; Beau was ready for his own life.

I could never say it out loud, but in some small way – I envied him. The Centaur responsibilities could be stifling, and one misstep could have ill effects for generations. But Beau was my first born; he still had a year of eligibility.

He was stubborn. I had negotiated with another father for a wife for him; the whole deal was set, but Beau refused. He had some stupid notion that a Centauride had to choose him without pressure from her family, or he wouldn't accept. He told me I was not to "find" him a wife. If he were to carry on the bloodline, he would leave it to fate and not to my wallet.

"Understand, son. There is one thing you can help me with, as long as you're going."

"Sure, Dad. What?"

"Zandra's still in the area. She doesn't know that Camille has left, and I don't want her to dig so much that she finds where they've gone. I chartered a jet for Camille and Drake under a false name, and I gave the pilots cash."

"I'm not following, Dad."

"I'd like for Zandra to believe that Drake and Camille have returned to San Diego. The only way I can do that is if I charter a jet with a passenger manifest of two people flying to San Diego."

Beau nodded, "Sure, Dad. But I don't need to take anyone with me. You set it up, and I can hand them a little extra cash to change the passenger list from one to two. I'd rather take this trip solo."

"I understand. Give me an hour or so; I'll have the plane meet you at the Mount Pleasant airport." As I got a few feet away from his room, I had an overwhelming urge to turn back. If this was our good-bye, there were so many things I wanted him to know. I stood in the hallway arguing whether to go back. I decided not to. No matter what he chose, he would always be my son. If he chose to abandon the Centaurs and live a human existence, I wouldn't cut ties. The traditional rules only applied to Zeus's Centaurs – they did not apply to me or my herd.

All those times I'd cursed my existence, hiding my identity, blending in with the rest of society . . . I'd brought my sons up as if they were Zeus's Centaurs, but we were of the Lost Herd. We were not subject to Zeus's laws, and in the very near future – others would know us.

When Camille emerged, rumors began to surface; we couldn't stay hidden much longer. The fact that Camille had been conceived was proof of our existence. The plan to have a Chiron heir carry the Tak bloodline had been brilliant. At the time, I didn't understand why it was so critical to find Camille's mother, Angela. Now, the genius of our leader's plan was crystal clear.

When I'd been ordered to seduce Angela, I'd been told that if I were successful, I would be responsible for future generations living in peace with all other Centaurs. I wondered to what extreme Centaurs would go to eradicate the Lost Herd a second time, when doing so would mean the murder of the last Chiron Centauride. Their society would collapse around them if any harm came to Camille, yet if they allowed her to live, they would face the wrath of Zeus.

The Tak family would no longer be the Lost Herd. We would take our place, once again, leading the herds. Our Centaurs had always been the strongest. Rupert had been a vicious leader and only the strongest of his line were allowed to live. Centaurs from other herds who questioned his methods mysteriously disappeared or died.

The stories told of Zeus's anger with a Centauride from our herd, but hearing the stories of Rupert growing up – I wondered if he himself had been a threat to the gods.

Things would change, and the rules that bound our society would evolve. Camille was the key to everything: she would be the reason all Centaurs would be reunited. Somewhere hidden away was a fierce warrior, her twin. No matter what Gretchen tried, Angela refused to give her any information on Camille's twin brother. I need to find him before Zandra does.

CHAPTER 6

Camille – Dublin, Ireland

We took the elevator to our room. The red light was flashing on the phone, signaling a message waited for us. It was Will's voice: "Sorry, Grandma's not going to make it. She took a trip to San Diego. Hope you're having a good vacation."

I didn't understand the message at first; Drake must have read my confusion. "He called to tell us Zandra doesn't know where we are. She's looking for you in San Diego. We're safe here."

"Why didn't he just say that?"

Drake shrugged his shoulders, "I'm sure he didn't want anyone to be curious if the wrong person heard it."

Drake walked past me into the bathroom; I heard the shower turn on. I dug through the shopping bags brimming with clothes we had bought the first day we arrived and decided to put the clothes in the dresser drawers, so the housekeeping staff wouldn't think we were nomads. Tucked deep in the bottom of one of Drake's bags was a beautiful peach-colored, silk nightgown. I held it up and ran my hand behind the fabric; it was nearly see-through. I blushed at the idea of wearing this instead of my pajama pants and t-shirt.

I smiled to myself, thinking maybe I wouldn't have such a hard time getting him to abandon his traditions after all. The shower turned off, and I argued with myself whether to hide it in the bag and pretend I hadn't seen it, put it in the drawers with the rest of the clothes, or find a way to emerge from the bathroom wearing it.

Drake had bought me a white satin nightgown when we were both at Zandra's. It was beautiful, but not like this. This one would cover less of me, and what was covered would require very little imagination.

I felt even more connected to Drake than I had the night of our escape. I loved him while I was still captive at Zandra's, but after the last three days, I couldn't live without him. I balled up the peach nightgown in my palm, deciding it would not go back into the shopping bag or the dresser.

Drake stepped out of the bathroom, towel-drying his hair, without even looking in my direction, "Water pressure's great. Your turn."

I washed all the dirt and grime off of me, pulled my hair back in a loose braid and slid the nightgown over my head. When I looked in the bathroom mirror, my cheeks flushed a bright red. Brent would be furious with me if he saw all the Centaur rules we were breaking.

He had nearly come unglued when he found out I had been on dates and had a couple boyfriends growing up. Of my five brothers, Brent was the closest to me in age and was the most vocal with his disapproval of my upbringing.

I wasn't sure I wanted to walk out wearing the nightgown after all. The fabric was so sheer I felt completely exposed. Drake and I hadn't broached the subject of sex beyond our conversation on the plane. It wasn't much of conversation; it was him telling me we needed to be wearing rings before things went too far. I started to slip the nightgown off in favor of my sleep pants and t-shirt, but I stopped when I had it halfway over my head.

I thought of finding the pasture today, thought back to Drake's promise to me on the plane, how he'd saved me from being sucked under by the peat bog, and wondered if maybe he was just waiting for me to make the first move. If I knew anything, I knew he'd never take the initiative.

When I emerged from the bathroom, I walked out wearing the "barely there" peach-colored nightgown. Drake had the television on and glanced over at me. His eyes returned to whatever he'd been watching on the television, then the image of me registered on his face, and his head snapped back in my direction. He lay on the bed motionless, frozen. The look in his eyes was unmistakable – desire.

Drake's chest was bare; he lay on the bed wearing only a pair of nylon running shorts. His eyes drifted from my face to my toes, then back up, and settled slightly lower than my face. I'd always hated it when men stared at me; it made me uncomfortable, wondering what flaw they were zeroed in on. Drake's gaze didn't make me feel that way. There was turmoil raging in him, as longing was battling his conventional thinking, and the turbulence of these two shone through his eyes.

Centaur traditions had been all he'd known until I came into the picture. Dating was a supervised ritual; marriages were arranged and treated like mergers. Allowing a relationship to develop with all the insecurities and desires was something I had taken for granted, but it was a whole new world for Drake.

I knew how he felt about me; he'd risked everything he'd ever held dear to be with me. Drake ran halfway around the world for our future, yet he kept a barrier between us. When we got to the hotel, I was surprised that he hadn't insisted on separate rooms, or at a minimum – separate beds.

After finding the pasture today, I wanted to push my luck. I wanted to be intimate with Drake, but more than that – I wanted him to want it, too. I took a step closer to the bed, nervous because just days ago what I wanted had remained out of reach. Seeing him now, I wondered if I'd misjudged his Centaur resolve.

Drake could have used his Centaur speed and been at my side in a fraction of a second, but he didn't. He stood up slowly, stalking me as if a predator. Drake stopped only inches away from me, his eyes focused on mine. His hand rose slowly, as his palm lay gently against my face. I could feel his heart beating; it was keeping pace with the speed of my own. My shoulders were bare save for the flimsy straps holding the fabric in place. His fingers glided over my shoulders and down my arms as goose bumps materialized all over my body.

Drake's voice was strained, "You are exquisite."

I let out a heavy breath I'd been holding, "You're pretty sexy yourself."

"I wasn't expecting you to wear. . . that." He said the word with reverence, as if my choice had been a divine selection.

"You bought it for someone else?"

"No. . . I bought it for you. I imagined you in it, but my imagination didn't do it justice." He paused, and added as a confession, "I hoped you'd consider the eloping idea we'd talked about. You know, our first night together and . . ."

Heat spread all over me. I felt shy, looking at the floor instead of at his ice blue eyes, "But I'm wearing it now." I lifted my gaze to see his reaction.

Drake shook his head. "I didn't imagine I would be able to leave it on you very long." Our bodies were inches away from each other. I wanted to close the distance, but it wasn't me who had constructed the barrier. Drake had to want this, too.

I gently reached forward as my hand traced the chiseled lines on his chest, "It doesn't have to stay on."

"Cami, you are the most dangerous creature I've ever met." It sounded like a no, but he didn't move away, and his eyes never left mine.

"I'm not dangerous, Drake. But I've seen enough to know that sometimes you need to live in the moment. Sometimes it's okay to give in to what you want most." I took his hand that had been caressing my shoulder and brought it to my lips. I stood on my tiptoes, leaned my body fully into his and whispered in his ear, "I know what I want most. I chose you, remember?"

I had won. I felt my body flying through the air and all of Drake's weight pressed on me, as we both landed on the bed. His need was as primal as my own. All the pain from Zandra's house was gone. It was just the two of us. There was no distance between us, but I still wanted him closer. I wanted to melt into him.

His lips pulled away from mine. Thrill spread wide on his face, "So, tomorrow? We find a priest and make it official tomorrow?"

"Hmmmm?" I was so lost in the moment I couldn't get words out; if I could have, I would have told him to stop talking.

"Cami?" My eyes opened but my hands continued memorizing every inch of his body. "We find a priest tomorrow, you promise?"

"Drake, it's okay. Living in the moment, remember?"

I felt his body go tense. He slid to the side of me and stared directly in my eyes. The hurt was clear in his voice when he asked, "Are you ashamed of me or something?"

I couldn't help but smile at him, "Uh. . .no. Why would I be ashamed of the sexiest man alive?"

"But what you just said. . . what you want most. . . you weren't talking about marriage, were you?"

"Do we have to talk about this now?"

"No. Not if you don't want to." Drake did more than ease away from me. He slid off the side of the bed and walked around to the other side.

It felt like he'd just doused me with cold water. I couldn't hide the rejection I felt. Part of me wanted to leap over the bed and hold him without letting go, while the other part wanted to run to the bathroom and hide. I reached for the blanket on the bed and felt the need to cover myself up. Tears threatened to stream from my eyes, but I willed them away.

His voice was drained of all emotion. "I'm going to order something to eat. Did you like that Shepherd's Pie we ate at the pub today?" He picked up a menu and dialed for room service.

I nodded absently, wondering what the heck had just happened.

When he set the phone down, his attention went back to the television. I wondered how we'd gone from living in the moment to ordering a late dinner. I stewed about it for a couple minutes then asked, "That's it? We're not married, so suddenly you don't want anything to do with me?"

"You know how I feel, Cami. There's nothing I wouldn't do for you, but we can't just hop into *that* unless we're married."

"Why? You think Zeus will strike you down?"

He shook his head at me. "No. I just want the world to know you're mine in every way. If we aren't married, you aren't mine."

"I'm yours, Drake. I promise, I'm yours."

A half smile came to his lips. "Giving me your body's a great offer, but it isn't good enough, Cami. I want our souls bound, too. I can wait; I told you I'd wait forever if I had to. I meant it."

I had a tough time making eye contact with him; I wasn't sure whether to feel embarrassed for being so forward or devastated at his rejection. Drake gently lifted my chin, forcing me to look at him. "Cami, I get it. This is new to you. There's no rush. You've chosen me, and I couldn't be happier. When you're ready for marriage, we'll find a priest. Like I said, no pressure."

"Your mind's made up? There's no room for negotiation on this one? We're on a trip, you know: what happens in Ireland stays in Ireland," but Drake wouldn't budge.

His half smile turned into a grin, "I promise you, I've never had a better offer. You know how I feel. If you aren't willing to be my wife,

I'm not willing to be your lover." With a sultry smile he added, "I believe I would be an incredible lover."

Drake scooted down to the end of the bed, slid his hand down my leg and rested his hand on my ankle – an image of the two of us rocketed through my mind. It was more than an image: a shiny silver band was wrapped around my ring finger, I could feel his arms around me, I could hear the sounds of our love, I could smell his scent – it was one of the most erotic moments I'd ever felt. Drake let me savor the image for a couple minutes before he withdrew his hand from my ankle and the image in my mind evaporated. "Just say the word, Cami, and I'm all yours."

The flush on my face felt bright red. Just minutes before I was sure I'd get him to set his rules aside, and now I believed *he* to be the more persuasive of the two of us. "So let's say, for argument's sake, that I'm okay with getting married." He didn't even try to hide his excitement as a wide smile emerged. "When I get married, I want my family there. Why couldn't we go forward with the assumption that we'll be married when we get back to South Carolina and take advantage of being on a pre-honeymoon now?"

Drake cocked his head to the side as if he were considering it. "Let's say I agree, what's to say we don't end up in Athens, or Paris or Centauride before we get to South Carolina? I would have stolen your virtue beforehand, or your family may have already promised you to another. We'd both end up with broken hearts and a debt to pay. No, we make it official first."

His phrase, "stolen your virtue," hit me hard. I'd never pretended to be innocent. I wasn't promiscuous by any means, but I'd been with someone before. Why wouldn't he have assumed that? It wasn't the 1950's – people had sex. I was twenty-two, a fully functioning adult, so why did I suddenly feel embarrassed – maybe even a little unworthy?

I tried to tell myself there was nothing to be embarrassed about, but when I looked into his eyes, my voice wouldn't work. I got a glimpse of myself through his eyes; would I look the same with the imperfections he didn't know I had? I couldn't say anything, at least not tonight. My stomach knotted, and it felt like a bucket of ice had been poured on me.

I'd find a way to bring it up casually, tomorrow. I tried to keep my voice from giving me away, "Okay, well, I guess I'll get some sleep."

He eyed me suspiciously; he couldn't read my mind. Right now I wished that he could; I wished that he could see the truth, so I wouldn't have to say it and see his reaction to it. No wonder my brother Brent had all but freaked out when he found out I'd dated people. No wonder Centaurs all got married so young. I'm an idiot. I should have known, or at least asked the question.

This had never come up in any of Zandra's lessons when I was held captive learning the Centaur history. Maybe she didn't think to preach about pre-marital sex because it just wasn't done by Centaurs. Most married before they ever got the chance to learn anything about their partner. I wondered if I could even marry Drake if I'd been with someone else? He told me marriage unites two souls; could those souls be united if one was tainted?

"Cami, are you okay?" Drake leaned over to me and placed his hand on my forearm. I looked down at his hand and was suddenly scared. Could I lose him over something I'd done before I even knew about the rules? He squeezed my forearm gently, "Cami, talk to me. Tell me what's wrong."

I couldn't do it; my mind was racing in all different directions. What if, after I told him, he didn't want me anymore? What would I do then? I put my back to Drake, grabbed a pillow that I could hug close to me, and shut my eyes. "Nothing's wrong. I'm just tired. We've got a lot of walking to do tomorrow."

A soft knock at the door sounded before he could pull anything out of me, "Room Service."

I wasn't hungry. Drake ate then shut off the television and all the lights. He spooned in directly behind me and whispered, "Sweet dreams."

I'd tell him tomorrow. Conversation between us had been easy the last three days walking for hours. It would be much easier to bring up while we looked for Zethus. A single tear escaped, slid down my face, and landed on the sheet. If he rejected me, I could take his rejection better in the daylight, better in the open. If after I told him, he changed his mind, I wouldn't be strong enough here, in this room, all alone.

CHAPTER 7

Camille – The Pasture of Thessaly, Southern Ireland

Drake and I left the hotel early – like "before birds were chirping" early. By the afternoon, I was exhausted. My mood was gloomy from the constantly overcast skies and my inability to bring up the question that had been eating away at me since last night. I'd thought of at least five clever ways to insert it into our conversation, but each time I had an opening, I chickened out. I kept telling myself if he loved me, he'd understand. But a small part of me wasn't willing to risk losing him. I hadn't been this nervous about anything in my life; not even being kidnapped had instilled the kind of fear I had at the thought of Drake rejecting me.

By late afternoon I knew I had to stop obsessing over something I'd done that I couldn't undo. Either Drake would accept it or he wouldn't. I forced myself to pay attention to why we were here in the first place. During the course of the day, I think we had met every farmer and sheepherder in the whole valley. No one had ever heard of Zethus, and none gave us the reaction from his name like we'd gotten our very first day. No one seemed the least bit interested in the two of us traipsing around the countryside, either.

I had a blister the size of a quarter on my heel, but I didn't want to stop. I told myself if it popped, maybe it wouldn't hurt so badly, and the pain in my foot helped mask the ache in my heart. Drake was attuned to my solemn mood, and I could tell he wanted me to snap out of it when he said, "I'm bushed. You ready to call it a day and head back to town?"

I nodded, "We're running out of terrain. Maybe we were wrong. Maybe the pasture is bigger than we thought." I could feel we were in the right place, but it was disappointing every time we heard someone tell us they'd never heard of Zethus. Our search had been all through the area we believed to be the pasture of Thessaly, including three pubs along our route today.

Drake's resolve refused to waiver, "We'll find him."

I hated the doubt I felt about this place, but it helped to keep my mind off the question I really needed answered. "What if he's not here?"

Drake's mood kept pace with mine when he answered, "Then Zandra will eventually find us and take us back to her little house of horrors."

"I mean, what if Zethus is dead? Maybe he moved away? Maybe the people we met lied to us?"

"I don't know, Love. I feel like this is the right place. Since we got here, I've felt a connection to this place, but . . . I don't know. Let's head back to town and get a bite to eat." Drake wrapped his arm around me, and his touch eased some of the anxiety bottled up inside me.

As we topped a small hill on our way back to the car, we stumbled across a small sun-faded metal bed and breakfast sign pointing to a little stone house, literally in the middle of nowhere. Drake stopped once it was in clear view and said, "Listen, it's been a long day. We've got a change of clothes in the backpack. Why don't we see if they have a room here?"

Relief filled me. The house's exterior looked like it had been built by hand, one stone at a time. It set on a dirt lane with beautiful yellow flowers at least five feet high flanking it on both sides. I was exhausted, my heel throbbed from the blister, and I wasn't sure I could face our hotel room after last night. I wrapped both arms around him and laid my head against his chest, "You just made my day."

Drake's hands patted my back. "The sooner we ask if they have a room, the sooner we can get off our feet. Let's go."

There was a one-lane dirt road leading up to it with potholes big enough to hide a small sports car. We were still at least two miles from where we'd left our car, so they might think us strange arriving on foot. When we got closer to the house, I looked to see if a sign hung on the porch. The one we saw up by the road had seen better days; the lettering was . . . faded. I worried that this might no longer be a bed and breakfast.

Drake walked up the slate steps with me. I knocked on the door tentatively, and sure enough, an elderly woman welcomed us. "Well, hallo! Can I help you?"

Drake answered the cheerful woman, but something had changed in his voice. "Hi. We were. . ." He gently tugged my arm and angled his body so he was standing in front of me. Drake eased a step back, away from the woman, easing me back toward the steps. "We were wondering if we needed a reservation."

"How did you two find this place?" She asked in a kind tone, but her attention was on me and not Drake standing directly in front of her.

I peeked around his shoulder, not sure what to make of his actions. "We were looking for a distant relative, but got a little farther from town than we had planned. We were headed back but saw your sign. Do you have any rooms available tonight?"

The woman's smile was warm, "My family has lived here for generations. Who are you looking for?"

"Chiron. . . Zethus Chiron."

She eyed me suspiciously, her tone no longer welcoming. "Zethus has been dead for years. What did you want with him?"

My heart plunged. Four days of walking in the wet drizzle for absolutely nothing. I looked at Drake and saw the same defeat I was feeling. She had asked us both the question, but I answered, "I just wanted to meet him. My. . . a . . . grandmother had mentioned him."

The old woman was sharp. Her eyes narrowed when she asked, "Who are you?"

"I'm Angela . . I mean, I'm Angela Chiron's daughter, Camille Strayer."

An angry look shot across the old woman's hardened face, "I'd keep that name to yourself."

"Strayer?"

"Chiron! Zethus did no' win any popularity contests. He was more beast than man, and people in these parts do no' miss him. Your grandmother does no' have any friends here, either."

Drake took a more pronounced step protectively in front of me, "I'm sorry, maybe this wasn't a good idea. We'll be on our way. No disrespect was intended." Drake began backing away, keeping his body covering mine with his arms out to the sides. He gingerly backed down the few steps to the ground, blocking me the entire time. He refused to take his attention off the old woman. An unexpected downpour came out of nowhere, and in seconds we were completely drenched.

The old woman yelled, "You don't have the good sense to carry an umbrella? Americans! Get in here before you drown!"

I would have leaped forward when she offered, but Drake held his ground, still standing in front of me. "Ma'am, what is your family name?"

"It's shelter – get in here before I turn my back on you and leave you outside with the livestock!"

My teeth were already chattering, my blistered heel was throbbing, and I couldn't understand Drake's reaction to the old woman. I pleaded with him, "Drake, maybe just for a minute?"

Drake answered in a normal tone, but we were far enough away there was no threat of the woman hearing. "She's a Centauride, and she's not alone. This could be an ambush."

"It doesn't sound like she likes my grandmother any more than I do. It's not an ambush. Let's go inside. Please?"

Drake straightened his posture and projected his voice, "Ma'am, you are a Centauride. I can feel the other Centaurs near. Will you give me your assurance you mean us no harm?"

"If I meant you harm, you'd both be dead. Get in ou' of the rain." She turned her back on us and walked into the house.

As we made our way through the doorway and into the kitchen, I saw two blurs rushing our way.

The first stopped at Drake and flung him to the floor. Drake caught himself in mid-air, turning so that he would fall back first, then did this judo-karate-looking move and launched himself back into the air. His feet connected with the other man's chest and flung the unsuspecting attacker into the wall beside an ancient stove.

I was so in shock with what I was watching that I didn't realize someone had grabbed both my arms behind me and was applying pressure trying to get me to the floor. After being an unsuspecting victim of Zandra for the last three months, I wasn't about to let it happen again. I let my body drop easily to the floor, then did the strongest scissor kick of my life, and knocked my attacker's legs out from under him while I rolled free.

He was as surprised as I was when he landed right in the spot on the floor he'd tried to force me on to. I was on top of him faster than a heartbeat with my hiking boot at the base of his skull and my hands yanking on each of his ears, trying to pull them free of his head. No one in the room was more astonished with my action or speed than I was.

When I turned my attention back to Drake, he'd gotten the upper hand and had his attacker in a full headlock. Drake's muscular arm bulged, cutting off the man's oxygen while my prisoner screamed like a little girl. The old woman was on the opposite side of the room and held up one hand, speaking so quietly I wasn't sure if I'd actually heard her say, "Enough."

I looked at Drake, and he loosened his grip, allowing his attacker to get air but not releasing him. I did the same to mine, still keeping a clamp-like grip on my attacker's ears, but reducing the pressure. She gave us a forced smile, "They were merely going to search you for weapons. Given your skills, I think if you had weapons, you might have used them by now. Let them up, and I'll get some tea."

I looked at Drake and he nodded, allowing his detainee to go free. He reached his hand toward me, indicating that I was to let my attacker go free, as well. Drake's voice boomed in the quiet room, "We mean no one any harm. We're just looking for protection from Camille's family."

The old woman raised her brow, "Protection? Is there a bounty on her?"

"We don't know. We escaped a few days ago and thought the only Centaur who could help us was Zethus."

"Escaped? What were your crimes?" The old woman motioned to the table and chairs. My pulse was still racing, but Drake held a chair out for me to sit. He took the seat to my right, and the old woman sat on the other side of the rectangular table. The two men, who looked to be in their mid-thirties and way past pissed-off, stood tall on either side of her – glaring at us.

Drake was on a roll, so I made no effort to answer. "Camille was raised as a human. She was only recently introduced to her Centaur family. Her grandmother, Zandra Chiron, held her captive and arranged a marriage for her to the descendant of Winfield and Unice."

The old woman clasped her hand over her mouth in an effort to hold in her surprise. "She was trying to strengthen the Chiron bloodline, the same as she tried with Angela. But you two are married, are you not?" She eyed us suspiciously as if searching our thoughts, trying to break down our defenses.

We answered together, me saying, "No." and Drake saying, "Not yet."

Stronger than I felt, I explained, "While I was held captive by Zandra, a guard who was loyal to my father helped us escape. We're worried we won't be able to hide from her, so we are looking for her brother to see if he could help us. My father helped us make our way here. We meant no harm to you or your family."

The woman pursed her lips together and gave us a slight nod, "I believe you. How did you think Zethus would be able to help?"

For some reason, our plan no longer sounded absurd, so I told her the truth. "We wanted the use of Hercules' arrow."

The woman cackled at us, while smiles erupted on the faces of the two men standing just behind her. Her voice was full of humor, "That arrow doesn't exist. If it did, it would be so sought after that he who had it in his possession would be a target for every living Centaur."

Drake put his arm around me and squeezed my shoulder. He meant it to be a comforting gesture, but I couldn't be comforted. Zandra was probably already on her way to Ireland after us. There was nothing I could do about it but sit and wait or try to stay a few steps ahead of her.

As I felt my body repulse at the idea of coming face-to-face with her, the old woman said, "You two both look like you could use a good meal and some rest. There's a wash room through that door. Get cleaned up; I'll have dinner ready in thirty minutes. Once you both have a good night's rest, you may be seeing more clearly in the morning."

I wanted to believe her kind words. She was a stranger and yet she knew about my mother. She knew my grandmother. Would she alert Zandra that we were here? Would we really be safe for one more night?

CHAPTER 8

Camille – Bed and breakfast, Southern Ireland

Dinner conversation revolved more around me than I would have liked. I didn't have any real secrets, but was not all that comfortable being the center of attention. As the five of us sat together, it struck me odd that none of the three had shared their names with us. The older woman asked me, "So, how is it, Camille, that you were raised human?"

"My mother never told me about being a Centauride."

"Angela? She raised you to be a human? Not a Centauride?"

"Mom never married. She met my father, William Strayer, a married Centaur. . . briefly. She died a few months ago and told me who my father was. . . but not what we were."

The old woman was quick to pick up on the nuance that I'd shared, "You were born out of wedlock?"

I nodded. Both of the two men standing on either side of her exchanged a glance. I wanted to know what they were thinking, but I wouldn't be able to concentrate enough to listen to their thoughts while carrying on a conversation with the woman. To date I'd only been able to "listen in" with Phineas, and it was just the one time. She asked, "So how did she explain your abilities?"

I hated admitting this part, "It never came up."

"Listening to others' thoughts and talking to the spirit world never came up?"

"She never actually showed me how to do it."

"What about your grandmother?"

"She was more interested in teaching me Greek mythology than how to use the skills that every other Centauride seems to have at birth." Drake put a hand on my knee and gave me a reassuring squeeze. He knew I felt inadequate every time the subject of Centauride skills came up.

"So, you do not . . . "

I cut her off before she could finish her question, "It's sporadic." I didn't want her to know I was worthless as a Centauride. "My stepmother, Gretchen, offered to help me, but I haven't had much time alone with her."

"It's really much easier than that, my dear. You are tense; I can see it on your face. I can feel it in your demeanor. Relax your mind and listen to the voice that speaks to you from the inside. You need only accept who you are."

"I'm tense because from the moment I found out Centaurs were real, I've been jerked every which direction. My inner voice just keeps telling me to go back to being human and forget about everything."

She shook her head at me and shared a knowing smile, "No. Your inner voice guides you. 'Twas my inner voice that told me you needed me when you arrived on my front porch unannounced. It's my voice that tells me: you speak the truth. It's also my inner voice that tells me you have a long journey ahead of you. Listen to yours; it will tell you exactly where you need to be."

Drake confessed, "I convinced Camille to come to Ireland. It was a huge waste of time since Zethus is dead. We don't have any defense against Zandra." Drake, for the first time since our journey began, doubted himself.

The old woman nodded, "You are both fierce warriors. You are deceptively strong and quick. Any who attack you will not expect such a fight. Isn't that right, boys?" Her eyes twinkled as she good-naturedly jeered her two sons who had been rendered helpless in a matter of seconds by Drake and me. "Get some rest. You fall under my household's protection this evening. No harm will come to you while you rest. You have my word."

I offered to help with the dishes, but she wouldn't hear of it. Instead, the woman escorted us upstairs, to two awaiting rooms. My heart sank. After all of today's disappointments, I couldn't stand the thought of sleeping alone.

Drake held up a hand, "I'm sorry, Ma'am. Camille is my responsibility. Her father has entrusted her to my care."

Irritated at Drake's suggestion, she answered. "You know the rules, young Nash."

"Yes, Ma'am, I do. But I am sworn not to let her out of my sight."

The old woman's skepticism shone while she addressed me, "Miss Camille, our customs do not permit an unwed Centauride and Centaur in the same sleeping quarters."

I tried to mask my exhaustion, "We don't want to be disrespectful of your home. Thank you for your kindness. We will find our way back to town." I absently reached down and took Drake's hand in mine.

Her eyes moved to our intertwined hands, another obvious disregard for customs on my part. Clearly frustrated with my answer, "I told you, you both fall under my house's protection tonight. You will be perfectly safe here."

Drake's voice was gentle, "Ma'am, she has been through a lot. I won't leave her alone. Even just across the hall is too far for me to be sure of her safety."

Her brows furrowed and her lips pursed together tightly. She guffawed and asked the question she already knew the answer to, "No funny business?"

Without hesitation, Drake answered, "On my honor as her Centaur."

"Very well. It seems this arrangement has her father's blessing. Who am I to stand in the way?" She held open the door closest to us and motioned for us to go inside, then closed it behind us.

I had so many questions, like: How did Drake know they were Centaurs? How did we get the jump on the Centaurs who were both so much larger than we were? Could we trust the old woman? Why didn't she give us her name or introduce us to her sons?

I turned around, ready to ask him all these questions and more when he whispered, "Where did you learn to fight like that?"

I pushed on both his shoulders, trying not to laugh, "I went to public school in Oceanside, Drake." I softly punched him in the shoulder, "We make a pretty good team."

My face buried itself in his chest as his arms wound around me. I could feel his smile without seeing it. "I won't worry about you in a bar brawl, that's for sure. What possessed you to try turning the guy into Dumbo?"

I shook my head, still smiling at how impressed he'd been with my non-Centauride skills. "Everyone goes for the groin or the knees in a fight, but thirty-five pounds of pressure and you can actually rip someone's ear off. It's one of the most sensitive parts of the body."

Drake's hands were running the length of me. Those familiar shivers set my body ablaze when he whispered, "You're so hot when you're kicking the crap out of Centaurs."

"Funny. So, now that we know my great-uncle's dead and there's no arrow, what do we do next?" I didn't mean for it to sound negative, but

I hoped he'd have another idea.

"I'll send a text to the pilot tonight. We'll leave tomorrow morning."

"For where?"

"You're the Centauride, Camille. You're taking point."

"What?"

"You can't do any worse than I've done. Sleep on it. Something will come to you."

Talk about pressure. I must have stared at the ceiling for two hours, memorizing a water spot that looked strikingly similar to Sagittarius. I was becoming far too immersed in this whole thing. Since Drake was leaving it up to me, we were going to San Diego. If the U.S. Government couldn't find two hundred thousand illegal immigrants there, then there was a good chance Zandra wouldn't be able to pinpoint us, either.

I felt a wave of peace settle over me. I'd be home soon – my home. No more Centaur rules, Centaurides, crazy relatives – just awesome Carne Asada burritos, sunshine, sand, and Drake. After I'd made the decision, sleep found me quickly.

Drake held me tightly while we slept, his arm making an uncomfortable but welcomed pillow. My eyes opened to the pre-dawn light streaming in through the window. I felt Drake's muscles tense around me as he pulled me closer to him, and his voice, strong and unyielding, said, "Who the hell are you?"

I jerked the rest of the way awake. An old man sat in a chair just a few feet away from us. He didn't waste any time when he said, "Well, top o' tha marnin' to ya. Thought you two might sleep the marnin' away."

Drake sat straight up, pulled his shirt from the nightstand, and he was yanking it hard over his head when he asked, "What do you want?" Very subtly, Drake motioned for me to slide behind him.

"I should be asking you that question. Eadie says you're lookin' far me."

She had told us we would be safe in her home, but waking up to a strange man watching us didn't feel like much security. Ignoring Drake's hand still trying to move me behind him, I scowled, "Who are you?"

"Well – me friends call me Jeb, but me mather named me Zethus. I understand you two air lookin' for a family heirloom?"

Zethus's accent made it nearly impossible to understand him. Everyone we'd met had an Irish accent, but it was subtle. The only time we had really heard pronounced accents was in the few pubs we had stopped in, and only when there was drinking involved.

I sat up straighter, "You're my great-uncle, Zethus? But how? She told us you were dead."

"You aren't the firs' to come lookin' for me. She tells er'eyone I died. Wishful thinkin' on her part, if you ask me! No. . . you're the firs' that's looked for me in more than twenty years."

"I'm Camille. This is my. . . this is Drake. Your sister, Zandra, is my grandmother."

"How is the ol' bat?"

"She's actually pretty pissed off at me right now."

When he laughed, his whole face lit up. He was covered in wrinkles, deep set around his eyes. It looked like he hadn't seen a razor in weeks. He wore a cabbie hat and a tweed scarf, his skin looked like he'd worked hard his whole life, but his face was warm, and his eyes were the same brown as mine.

"Eadie says she tried to arrange a marriage you were no' in favor o' – she had bigger plans for you, did she?"

"She set up a marriage between Gage Richardson and me. Eadie said she was trying to strengthen the Chiron bloodline. What did she mean by that?"

"My fool sis'er dreamed up a plan that the Chiron blood with Winfield and Unice's could have a powerful effect. She's had a lot o' time on her hands since your mather disappeared. Ne'er could figure out where that lass went, probably for the bes'. So, lemme guess, you turn up out o' the clear blue, and Zandra swooped in an' locked you up."

He had put the whole situation together without me having to relive any of it. "She did. Once we escaped, I thought we'd be fine, but Drake and my dad think she's going to come after us."

Uncle Zethus turned his attention to Drake, "You're a smar' one. That deci'ful little bat will keep chasin' you. She gets somthin' stuck in her craw and there isn't any gettin' it ou'. What do you wan' from me?"

"Zandra's magic is much stronger than ours. If we had Hercules' arrow, we could protect ourselves."

He nodded, "Tell me somethin.' How did you and your mather stay hidden so long?"

There wasn't any reason to withhold information from him. "Aphrodite's magic protected us. Kyle Richardson gave his magic to hide us, but when my mom died, the protection went away."

He guffawed, "Well, isn't that ironic! The very magic Zandra was tryin' to give to you is what hid you from her all those years! An' since this handsome fella isn't a descendant of Winfield and Unice, he can't do nothing for ya. You sure know how to pick 'em."

I could hear the pleading in my voice when I asked, "So, will you help us?"

"I wish tha' I could, Darlin'. Too many Centaurs were power hungry. Didn't think I'd see a very long life with the arrow. Gave it to a bloke from the States."

"The states? You mean the United States?"

"Aye, he came to me o'er twen'y years ago, tellin' me he'd take care o' the arrow. He'd hide it from the Centaurs. He'd protect it."

"Who was he?"

"I forget his name. Said he lives by Crazy Horse."

"Crazy Horse, the Indian?"

"I knew enough to know that Crazy Horse was dead. But this fella says near Crazy Horse's Mountain. I handed it o'er and have no' seen him since. Crazy Horse was a powerful Centaur Warrior – but he adopted those Indians like they was his own. Seemed like a good idea for the arrow to be near his mountain. The fella needed it, so I handed it over."

"You don't remember the man's name or a way we can get in contact with him?"

"Robert or Roger. . . maybe, I don't remember. All I can tell ye' is he isn't a Centaur." Zethus paused as if there was something important he wanted us to know. "He's a man. He's go' that arrow. You tell 'em I sent you." Zethus stood up to leave the room, "Good luck to you. If that fool sister o' mine shows up here – I'll give her the what for."

When we were alone in the room again, I asked, "Did I hear that right? He gave the arrow to a man he didn't know, because the guy lived near Crazy Horse's Mountain?"

"That's what it sounded like."

"We're supposed to find the guy: no name, no description, no clue who he is, and tell him Zethus said we could have the arrow?"

Drake smiled at me, "Yeah, unless you have a better idea."

"We do this while we avoid my grandmother?"

"He didn't tell us that, but I think that's implied." Drake's smirk grew bigger. I was ready to give him a smart aleck comment back when it hit me. It didn't matter how much danger we were in, we were together. My blood debt should be forgiven – Bianca should have chosen Gage by now. None of those things seemed possible on Friday; now less than a week later, my life was nearly my own, other than the one little thing I still hadn't figured out how to tell Drake. Spending the night here and talking to Uncle Zethus helped put everything in better perspective.

As we emerged from the staircase, Eadie was waiting for us on the first floor. "You talked to Jeb, did you?"

"We did."

"Don't believe a word he says. He ain't been right since his sister killed their parents."

"His sister? Zandra? She killed their parents?'

"Aye, about thirty years ago. She was convinced they were hiding that fool arrow from her. Jeb tried to convince her that it didn't exist. She didn't believe him. If they had it, they took that location to the grave with 'em. He hasn't been the same since."

It sounded like Zethus had hidden the arrow from Eadie, too.

"Here, it isn't what you're looking for, but it protected my family against her. He wants you to have it." She handed me the ugliest broach I'd ever seen. It was a gold and metallic green spider with a torso that bubbled out and was the size of a full-sized locust. The spider had large bulging gem stone eyes, and I wanted to hand it back to her. When she pressed down on the spider's head, the abdomen opened to reveal a locket with hair in it.

"It won't protect you from any of her people, but it'll protect you from Zandra. This was Athena's locket."

I remembered this story from the endless lessons at Zandra's house. "Athena was the goddess of weaving. She got jealous of a mortal and killed her, but felt guilty, then brought the mortal back to life as a spider, right?"

"Yes. Arachne was the girl. Whoever's hair is placed in this locket cannot harm you. Zandra's hair is already in it."

"But, what will happen to you?"

"I'm an old woman. I don't need Athena's protection anymore. Be on your way. Sides, if Zandra shows her face here, Jeb won't be so kind. She won't leave this island unless it's in a box."

If things didn't go well, Ireland may be a place that we could set up as a safe haven from Zandra. I wasn't sure what to call my uncle, so I asked Eadie, "You keep calling him Jeb. I thought his name was Zethus?"

"Once his parents were killed by Zandra, he said he didn't want nothin' to do with the Chiron name anymore. Old timers around here still remember him in his younger days; he was a wee bit on the wild side and didn't take to humans living in Thessaly. After she killed 'em, he just up and changed his name and stopped goin' into town. Most folks assumed he died the day his parents did, others thought he moved away. He told us all Zethus was dead. When you two showed up, it was the first time I'd heard his given name since the boys were kids."

I gave Eadie a hug and thanked her profusely. The broach hadn't been what we'd come for, but it gave us some measure of safety, and I was humbled by her gift. I was excited to have met Zethus, and it was good to learn I wasn't the only one who wanted nothing to do with Zandra. Eadie had one of her sons give us a ride back to our rental car.

As for Crazy Horse's Mountain, I wondered how we would find a person with a magical arrow, with nothing to go on. Once we found him, would he be willing to give it up? Zethus said it was a human. What would a human do with that kind of power?

CHAPTER 9

Camille – Dublin, Ireland

Drake and I waved at the co-pilot who had traded his Bermuda shorts for a navy blue wool coat and blue jeans.

"Good to see you two. We were starting to worry. Camille, your father wants you to call him as soon as we're airborne. So, are we on our way back to Charleston?"

I looked at Drake. I could feel the hideous spider in my pocket, my hands instinctively playing with it. My home was in Oceanside, and I liked the idea of hiding in plain sight, blending in with the millions of people. I worried that Zandra would eventually zero in on us, even though I had the awful-looking spider to protect Drake and me from her.

Eadie told us the locket wouldn't protect us from anyone she brought with her, but I was pretty sure we could hold our own with everyone else. I thought of Will and Gretchen. I hadn't had much time to get to know them; I wanted more time with them. Going back to their house, there would be strength in numbers, and I doubted Zandra could do much against all of us, but I wasn't willing to put all of my family in her path on a hunch.

I took a deep breath, reached down, grabbed Drake's hand and told the co-pilot, "No. We're going to Rapid City, South Dakota." Drake gave me a reassuring squeeze back. It made me feel good knowing he would have been willing to go anywhere I chose, but I wanted to end this with Zandra. If we were going to have a chance together, we couldn't keep looking over our shoulders.

Somewhere over the Atlantic the excitement began to ebb. I thought about everything Drake and I had been through. It was good he had magic in him because a regular guy would have tucked tail and run by now. He had dozed off; it was one of my few chances to really look at him. I had already memorized his face. When I shut my eyes, I could picture every line, the symmetry of his face, all of his facial expressions, I could even hear his laugh echo in my thoughts. When I'd first met him, his hair was impossibly short, but in the last several weeks, it had grown out and was a little bit curly. I hoped he'd keep it this length.

Why had I fought so hard against marrying him? Maybe because my mom never had anyone, I had never been in a hurry to fill a void that I didn't know was there. When I graduated from high school, all my girlfriends grew one track minds. Either they wanted to go to college, get a career and settle down, or they wanted to find a man, settle down and start a family. I never understood the draw. I guess I secretly idolized my mom for being the only woman I knew who didn't need a man in her life to be happy. A different thought occurred to me: maybe I had it wrong, and she did want a man but couldn't have the one she wanted so chose to make a life by herself.

I was attracted to Drake. I loved him – but was it enough? Even if I were sure I wanted to get married, would he still want me? He was so set on all the Centaur rules, when I filled him in on certain aspects of my human life, he might change his mind about me. Those few weeks when

I thought he was dead, it was like losing my mother all over again – I wasn't sure I could take the pain if he couldn't accept me.

I smelled my mother's perfume, which startled me at first. On sheer instinct I looked at the vacant seats around us. Just to my right was her faint outline. I didn't want to wake up Drake, but I'd been trying to see her for so long, I couldn't help but blurt out, "Where have you been? How am I supposed to learn things from you when I can't hear you!"

For the first time since being in the garden with Phineas at Zandra's house, I heard her voice, "*Camille, I'm so proud of you, and you're as brave now as you were when you learned to ride a bike.*"

It wasn't my imagination: she was talking to me. The image of my mom's spirit came into sharp focus for the first time, "I didn't do anything differently. How come I can see and hear you now?"

"*You're finally ready to hear me. You've accepted who you are and all that goes with it. You are leading and making decisions for yourself. Our race is full of warriors who will fight to the death for whatever cause is thrown at them. It is the women Centaurs, the Centaurides, who lead. Up until now you let others decide your fate; you hadn't embraced the Centaur way, so you could not claim all that was yours to take.*"

"So, you're here, for good. You'll stay with me?"

"*Soon, very soon, I must go to the pasture. You have a family who loves you and your own Centaur to protect you. I can leave you in good hands and go take my place with the others.*"

I hated that I sounded like a child, but the words flowed out of me before I could stop them. "But, I don't want you to go. I want you to stay."

"*I'll stay as long as I can, but you are stronger than you know. You don't need me as much as you think you do.*"

A thought occurred to me, "Will said I need to ask you something about when you two met. What was so important for me to know?"

"*You do not remember your dream? I thought you were able to hear me in your dream.*"

I did remember the dream. It was on this plane during the flight to Ireland. The dream was so vivid I actually looked for her after I woke up. "The other night, in the dream, you said the Lost Herd found you anyway. You didn't seem that worried about your mom finding us, but you said the Lost Herd was after me."

"*I wish your father would have talked to you. William is a member of the Lost Herd, the Tak bloodline. He tried to make me believe that our meeting was merely a coincidence, but it was an impossible coincidence. The Lost Herd is from the original pasture, but they were cast out by Zeus. They have different abilities than we do.*"

"Different abilities, like what?"

"*There were so many rumors, but the Tak Centaurs are supposed to be wild and unstable. When I met William I knew he was a Centaur, but I never dreamed he traced his bloodline to the Lost Herd. I knew Centaurs were looking for me, but it was easy enough to evade them whenever they got close. Kyle gave up much of himself to protect me. His protection allowed me to make a life for myself and eventually for both you and me. With the one exception of your father, no one ever found me, or those who did were unable to bring attention to my whereabouts.*"

Her smile had returned, "*But those who are tied closely to Rupert, the original sire cast out of the pasture, are able to mask their bloodline. Your father is Rupert's direct descendent and can be a chameleon. He told me his last name was Strayer, and I recognized it from the pasture. He did not tell me and I did not realize what his real bloodline was.*"

"So you did know he was married?"

"*No. I believed him to be a lonely Centaur who had passed his age of selection. Once a Centaur is thirty, he is no longer eligible to marry a Centauride. Many become bitter – William was not. He was carefree and fun and completely charming. I had vowed never to marry, as I loved Kyle and knew I would never meet another like him. Your father was charming, and I was lonely. When he was preparing to return to South Carolina, he told me of his lineage and his wife."*

"He told you he was in the Lost Herd?"

"He did. He had been ordered to seduce me, to father a child who would unite the herds. When he left, he told me of his orders but said he would go back to his father and tell him that I was not Angela Chiron, that someone had gotten it wrong."

"But he knew he'd fathered a child?"

"No. He called me weeks later and even tried to see me in the subsequent months. I lied. I told him that the Chiron line was too strong to allow for a set of twins mixed with Tak blood. Zeus himself decreed the end of the Tak bloodline. I didn't know what to do. I told him his attempt had been a wasted effort, and he had betrayed his wife for nothing. I'm sure I said a lot of other things, as well. He swore he would keep my identity a secret. To his credit, your father kept his word."

"What about Kyle Richardson?"

"You know all about him. He hid me from everyone."

"Why did he hate me so badly the night I met him?"

"He didn't hate you. He was unaware that you existed. He was furious with William and me and he couldn't comprehend how William could be your father. I tried very hard for you to hear me that night to tell you what had happened."

"Why does everyone keep telling me that I have to unite the herds. Even Zandra wanted that."

"My mother isn't interested in uniting the herds; she merely wanted our blood tied to Winfield and Unice. There is much dissention among the Centaur herds and no clear line of leadership. Most believe Chiron to be the rightful ruler, but the Lost Herd, the Tak, were the true warriors of our race. You or Cameron would be the rightful Centaur leaders."

"Wait, Cameron? Is that my twin brother?"

"I gave birth to you and your brother. I worried that Kyle's magic couldn't protect all three of us, so I placed Cameron with a human for

safekeeping. He's protected, but is also unaware of his lineage."

"Does Zandra know where he is?"

"*Not yet, but after she found you, she began looking for him.*"

"Is he in South Dakota? I saw your old plane ticket in your closet. I saw the picture of the two of us."

"*He is protected by the same thing you seek. I'm merely a spirit now. I cannot see the future anymore. He was still in South Dakota when I died.*"

"Wait, the man with the arrow? No wonder Zethus gave it up to a stranger. I thought he was crazy when he said he'd given it to some guy he didn't know, but that makes sense. So, how do we find a man we don't know, who we don't have a description of, we don't know where he lives, who happened to have the arrow twenty years ago, and oh, by the way, is the guardian to my twin brother?"

"*I'm running out of time and the strength. Beware of Phineas. You are the rightful leader of the Centaurs: Daughter of Chiron and Daughter of Rupert of the Lost Herd.*"

"Wait, Phineas? Like from Zandra's house?"

"*Yes.* Phineas *is part of the Lost Herd. You feel a kinship to him, but do not turn your back on him. Know that he is seeking you now. Zeus isn't yet aware that there are Tak survivors, so for now, Phineas is your biggest concern.*"

"But he helped me find Drake. He helped me escape."

"*For his plans to work, you needed to be free of Zandra. I overheard him on the telephone after you were free. He didn't expect your father to arrange for your departure so quickly.*"

I needed her to tell me we were doing the right thing. "Finding Hercules' arrow seems like a long shot. Is this what we should be looking for?"

"*Follow your instincts. If that's where your instincts tell you to go, then you're on the right path.*"

"Can't you just tell me what the right path is?"

"*All the skills I possessed while alive and a Centauride did not follow me to the spirit world. I no longer see the future. I trust you. You need to trust in yourself, as well."*

A feeling of déjà vu crept up on me, and I remembered something else she said in her dream. "Mom, you told me if I loved Drake, I needed to let him go, the same way you stayed away from Kyle Richardson."

"*Yes.*"

"I can't do that. If he'll have me, I'm going to marry him."

She smiled at me, and it filled me with a warmth I hadn't felt in months. "*He's already made it very clear to you that he wants you as his wife; why do you think he would change his mind?*"

Wow, a conversation I never wanted to have with my mom when she was alive, I certainly didn't want this one now. I didn't have much of a choice. I needed to know. "Okay, from everything I've gathered, when Centaurs marry, they're um. . . each other's firsts." She nodded at me affirming what I already believed. I took a deep breath, "Drake wouldn't be my first."

"*I see. Have you told him?*"

"No. So, am I right? He won't marry me, will he?"

"*I don't know. That's up to him. I wouldn't keep it from him. It's a part of your past. He's in love with you now. Your past experiences are what make you who you are now.*"

"So you're saying it isn't that big of a deal?"

"*I'm saying you need to trust Drake enough to tell him the truth. Never be ashamed of who you are.*"

Another question had been burning inside me. "Why didn't you tell me any of this, Mom? All those months you knew you were sick. We were at the apartment together watching stupid re-runs on television. There's so much I should have learned from you."

She looked sad; her voice was a little lower when she said, "*I didn't want this for you. I didn't want any of it. I always hoped you and Daniel would grow beyond friends and none of this would matter. Before I died, he promised me he'd always be there for you. I believed any hole you felt when*

I was gone would be filled in, in a different way. I also hoped that Aphrodite's magic would still cloak you after I died."

"But you gave me William's name. You told me where he lived. You didn't think I'd contact him?"

"*It was a possibility. By the time I had decided to give you the one thing I had always denied you, I was too weak to look into the future, to see what would happen. I trusted that whatever happened, you would draw from your inner strength. You would make the life that you chose your own, whether that life be as a human or a Centauride.*"

"So you wanted Daniel and me to hook up? Ewww, Mom, he's like my brother."

"*Yet you keep secrets from Drake that I'm sure you willingly shared with Daniel. Do you question your decision to marry Drake?*"

"No. Drake is different." I tried to think of a way to put my feelings for Drake into words; the rush I get from him when I catch him watching me, or the tingles that rip through my body when he holds my hand. "He's so serious all the time, you know? I've never met anyone more conservative in my life. He has a way of pushing these images in my head that are – I don't know. . . lifelike. Like whatever he's showing me is reality if we just make it that way. I know what you said, but I won't leave him. I can't."

"*Are you convincing me or yourself?*"

I smiled at her. This was one of her favorite questions when she was alive, and I'd heard the same question at least once a week my whole life, and I couldn't help but let the smile loose. "Both. I'm convincing us both, Mom.

I saw her image begin to fade. I wanted to reach out and hold onto her. I couldn't. Despite what she said about growing weaker, I hoped this wasn't the last time I'd see her. When the last of her had faded away, I looked at Drake still asleep in the recliner next to me. My instincts told me we were doing the right thing. I wasn't convinced the arrow was the prize we needed, but we were definitely going in the right direction. I reclined my seat, closed my eyes, and snuggled in close to him.

Just as I was about to doze off, I remembered the co-pilot told me to call Will. As I reached for the phone, there was someone I needed to talk to more. I dialed Daniel.

He picked up on the second ring, "Oceanside morgue. You bag 'em, we'll tag 'em, now offering late night pickup service."

I rolled my eyes, "Some things never change."

"Cami?! Cami, is that you?"

"I think I'm partial to 'Hot Lips,' but yeah." It had been months since I'd spoken with Daniel. In our last conversation before I was kidnapped – he'd called me "Hot Lips."

"Where the *hell* have you been?"

"Oh, you know, touring the countryside, circumnavigating the world."

"I thought you were dead." His voice was. . . I don't know, serious. I couldn't remember ever having a serious conversation with Daniel.

"Hopefully you didn't file a life insurance claim. I'm still breathing."

"Don't be a smart ass. Where've you been?"

"It's a long story."

"Do you know I flew to Charleston two times looking for you? By the way, your father's a real piece of work. Why wouldn't you see me when you were at your grandmother's place?"

"You flew to Charleston? You were at Zandra's? In Florida?"

"What did you expect me to do? You didn't return my calls, emails, texts – I filed a missing person's report. Your dad didn't tell you?"

"I haven't talked to him much the last couple months. What do you mean he's a real piece of work? And when were you in Florida?"

"He wouldn't tell me where you were. He acted like it was this ginormous secret. He's a prick. Beau told me where your grandmother lived, but she wouldn't let me see you, either." I could hear the hurt in Daniel's voice.

My mind remembered Zandra coming into my room and speaking when I was still numb from losing Drake and Bianca and so starved I couldn't understand a word she said. I didn't want for Daniel to know what I'd been through. "I was pretty sick for a few weeks. I must have been out of it the day you stopped by."

His voice was guarded when he asked, "When are you coming home?"

"I'm not sure. Things are pretty complicated, but I'm okay."

"Where are you? Right now, where are you physically at this very second?"

I chuckled, "About 40,000 feet above the Atlantic Ocean, I think. I could ask the pilot if you want coordinates."

"Stop being a smart ass. I want answers, and I want them now." His tone had changed from serious to borderline angry, not at all the best friend I'd had since elementary school.

Drake stirred next to me. He was awake, but he didn't ask me who I was talking to. He reached up and gently stroked my hair. "It turns out that guy I told you I didn't like? I decided I liked him. We took a trip to Ireland, and we're headed to South Dakota for a while. If things go well, maybe back to Oceanside. We haven't made any long term plans yet."

There was no more borderline: Daniel was angry. "You couldn't pick up a phone?"

Trying to keep the conversation steered clear of rage, I answered, "I'm sorry, this plastic device with numbers on it that I'm holding in my hand looks suspiciously like a phone."

"So that's it, you're flying around the world with Bianca's fiancé?"

"His name's Drake. You'll meet him soon. They broke it off." It would be impossible to tell Daniel everything I'd been through, and I wasn't sure I wanted to share any of it with him. He'd always been a little hotheaded, and finding out I'd been held against my will, led to believe my actions caused the murder of two people I cared about, and finding that my mother had had roughly the same fate – it was just too much to burden him with.

"I can hardly wait. I guess my dad was right all along."

"Your dad? Right about what?"

"He told me you wouldn't be back. He told me that we were over."

"What do you mean *over*? Daniel, you're my best friend."

"Sounds like you've got a new best friend."

"It isn't the same."

"Yeah, I know. He's a pure-blood." The call disconnected. I looked at the receiver; I wasn't sure what I expected to see. I dialed Daniel's number again, but it just went to voice mail. Daniel knew about Centaurs? But how could he?

CHAPTER 10

Camille – On an airplane en route to Rapid City, SD

Drake pulled me from my seat onto his lap with about as much effort as lifting a pillow, "Who was that?"

"My friend, Daniel. He was pretty worried."

"It was a short call."

I did my best to mask the hurt in my voice. After everything that had happened, I really wanted to catch up and hear what I'd missed. "Yeah, I must've caught him at a bad time."

Drake lifted my hair away from my neck and pressed his lips to the now fully healed skin near my collarbone. "Good news for me. I've got plans for your lips that don't include talking." He slowly made his way up to my mouth as the embers inside me raged into an inferno.

As I sat on Drake's lap with his arms wound around me, questions started to churn through my thoughts. I had a twin who was being protected by a magical arrow – it really did exist. How had my mother been able to give him up and never check on him again? My father was a descendant of a lost Centaur herd, and I was somehow supposed to be poised to reunite herds, maybe with the arrow? I could finally communicate with my mom – but she couldn't help me with the future. Hopefully she'd be able to help me locate Cameron. Daniel knew about Centaurs – how long had he known that I was a Centauride?

When we both pulled back for air, Drake's eyes looked heavy. I asked, "Are you tired?"

He took both my hands and put them on either side of his face, the same as he had done three months ago on Will's yacht. An image of the two of us lying on a beach in the sun next to crystal blue Caribbean water played through my mind. The vision showed Drake lying beside me: his abs glistened in the sun and the smell of coconut oil filled the air. The vision was vivid, so vivid I could feel his hands rubbing the coconut-scented oil on me. The warm ocean breeze blew across my skin, and the heat from the sun burned down on us.

I moved my hands from his face and lost the vision. Drake was smiling when I asked, "So was that a fantasy or the future?"

"Both, Love. It was both."

"Tell me again – why are we going to South Dakota and not Grand Cayman?"

"It's your choice, Camille. I'll follow you anywhere." Drake pulled me in tighter to him. I thought back to our conversation the other day. As perfect as it felt in his arms, I knew we needed to talk. No matter the outcome, I couldn't let him believe I was something I wasn't.

I didn't look at him; instead, I found his hands absolutely intriguing and kept all my attention focused on them. "So, I've been thinking. There's this thing about me that I've never told you. I didn't think it was important before, but now I'm not so sure. So I'm just going to put it out there."

I was seated on his lap but craned my neck to glance up at his face. He was curious, but his expression wasn't registering any kind of alarm.

I took a deep breath and added, "And if you want to rescind your offer to marry me, I'll understand." I could feel his body go rigid beneath me. "I won't like it, but I'll understand."

I had his attention. He didn't interrupt, and I didn't dare look in his eyes for fear of losing my nerve. He said nothing, so I continued. "So, I dated a guy for a couple years, and I really thought he was the one, you know?"

Drake's quiet voice asked, "Daniel?"

"What? No! I've already told you I never dated Daniel. The guy's name was Ronnie, and incidentally, Daniel hated Ronnie. Every chance he got, Daniel told me how much he hated him." I realized I was stalling, took another deep breath and continued, "Okay, so, when humans date for that long, sometimes they do more than kiss."

Drake's muscles tensed further as I sat motionless on his lap. All I heard was, "Go on."

"So, we did, you know. . . with each other." Drake didn't ask for more information, and I was sure he got my meaning without me having to spell it out for him. When the silence became unbearable, I added, "At the time, I didn't know anything about Centaurs. But the other night, when we were in the hotel, you said you didn't want to be responsible for stealing my virtue before we were married. It hadn't occurred to me until you said it, but. . . that's when I realized that maybe you wouldn't want me anymore if you knew this."

Drake didn't say anything. His heart was still beating fast, and his muscles were still taut. "I really cared about Ronnie. I mean, we dated for more than two years."

Drake remained still. I was terrified he was going to end it with me right here. What would his mother say? Would she already know? Drake said his father was very anti-human; is this something that would blackball me from his family? From Centaur society? I'd been holding all these questions in for more than two days, and each one threatened to drive me insane. Finally Drake broke the silence. In a calm voice, he asked, "Is Ronnie still in your life?"

I shook my head that he wasn't. I was normally so good at reading Drake, but his face held no expression at all. This was just as difficult as I had envisioned. Luckily we were in the air, so it's not like he could take off running miles away where I couldn't catch him.

Drake's hand began to lightly caress the top of my arm. It felt like he was trying to soften his blow, and I braced myself for whatever he'd say next. "You said you cared about him. Did you love him?"

Wow, not what I expected. Guys usually hated to hear about other guys. "I thought I did, at the time."

"And now?"

"Now that I know what real love feels like, I know I wasn't in love with him." Drake seemed to be lost in thought for a moment. I didn't want to lose him over this. Unless Centaurs could somehow time travel, I wasn't going to be able to undo a bad decision.

Without letting the emotion overtake my voice, I added, "I didn't think I would risk losing the love of my life because I made a stupid decision and liked the wrong guy when I was nineteen."

Drake's hand squeezed my shoulder. His voice sounded hollow when he asked, "That's what you believe I am to you? The love of your life?"

This question forced me to look at him. Of all the things he could ask me, this was what he wanted clarification on? I didn't look away, wanting him to see my answer at the same time he heard it. "Yes. I know you are."

Drake cleared his throat, looked directly in my eyes and said, "Thank-you for telling me. I'm glad I know." It looked like he wanted to say something else, but he stopped talking and concentrated on the darkened television on the wall.

"Drake, I'm sorry. I didn't know that it was a big deal. I swear he doesn't mean anything to me, now. I haven't seen him or talked to him in over a year. I understand if you can't marry me, or if you don't want to, or if it's enough of a shock that you need some space."

It would kill me if this ended us before we ever had a real chance. The memory from Zandra's house, where she had lied and told me that Drake and Bianca were dead, washed over me. That pain was indescribable, but sitting here in the silence waiting for Drake to break it off with me was almost as bad.

His eyes sliced through whatever defenses I had, as I braced for what I felt was coming and looked away. I didn't want to see his eyes, but he held my chin so I was forced to look into his. Drake's voice was as tender as I had ever heard it, "So, if I don't want to rescind my offer, where would that leave us?"

I felt my blood pumping harder. Did I hear him right? "That would leave me begging you to make me your wife."

Drake's smile was the one that I had seen so many times, not forced, and still full of love. "Cami, relax. I'm not thrilled, but your relationship with this Ronnie has no bearings on my feelings for you – now or ever."

I hadn't realized that I'd been holding my breath, until he said it, and I was able to take in air again. I wrapped both my arms around him tightly, "So, you still love me?"

"Since the first moment I held you, Cami. And for the record, my love for you won't end even after my body stops breathing."

My heart leaped. The fire was again spreading through me. All the reservations I'd had about marriage and Centaurs disappeared in that instant. I wanted it. I wanted it all, and I wanted to be tied to Drake for all eternity. My mind drifted back to the dream on our way to Ireland when my mom had said if I loved Drake I'd have to let him go like she had done with Kyle – there was no way she could have felt the same kind of love I felt for Drake. If she had, she would have been willing to risk anything for Kyle. In that moment, I knew she was wrong.

I eased my body away from Drake's embrace and asked, "If a captain of a ship can marry a couple at sea, can a captain of a plane do it in the air?"

Drake's smile stretched wide, his arms mashed my body into his when he answered, "I don't think so, but I'm glad you won't be fighting me about it anymore. Since you're in an agreeable mood, I do have one small request."

"Anything."

"Until we make it official, I'd like for you to wear sweat pants and baggy t-shirts to bed." He smiled and then added, "Socks, too." I thought back to the night at the hotel when I'd emerged from the bathroom wearing the peach-colored nightgown. I smiled at the memory of his inability to look anywhere but at me. I loved that look. It was familiar to me. It was the same look I had for him right now.

"Sweat pants? I don't know. I hear South Dakota can be pretty hot in the winter time." Laughing at my own joke, I knew full well it could easily be minus twenty when we landed.

"It's hot no matter the location or the season where you're involved. Wear the sweatpants, or better yet, a snowmobile suit."

With the weight lifted off my chest, and with the knowledge that Drake was in it for the long haul, I told him everything Mom had shared: why I didn't have my powers until just today; I had a twin brother, Cameron; Jeb, a.k.a Zethus, had given Cameron's guardian the arrow. I didn't even hide that my mom expected me to go to Daniel rather than to embrace a Centaur. No secrets.

After I had relayed the whole conversation, Drake looked worried. "Your father is of the Tak bloodline?"

"Yeah. Will's Dad told him to seduce Mom, gross right?"

The color on Drake's face drained. His voice was hollow, "Yeah, gross." I got the feeling there was something Drake wasn't telling me, but his arms wrapped more tightly around me, and I didn't want to ask why.

CHAPTER 11

Beau Strayer – Camille's older brother, San Diego, CA

I got why Daniel was such a draw for Camille. The guy never ran out of energy. He'd be on the waves before the sun broke over the horizon in the east; by the time the rest of Oceanside was waking up, he'd already had two hours in the surf and was laying out his plans for the day.

Having grown up in my family, my brothers were fun to be around, but each day was meticulously planned, and our lives felt carefully scripted. Hanging out with Daniel felt like I was trying to keep pace with the Energizer Bunny. I'd never allowed myself to be around women. Daniel surrounded himself with them, from the beach, to the park, to the mall; he even had a flock around him when he went to pay his utility bill. I'd never seen anything like it.

He was three-quarters Centaur. His mother had been a half-blood, the daughter of a human mother and a Centaur father. Daniel's father was a full-blooded Centaur. I hated to admit it, but it never occurred to me that there would be different percentages. You were either Centaur or you weren't, and to be Centaur, you had to have pure blood.

I couldn't argue that there was definitely something more than human about him. He was charismatic, athletic and fearless. I'd always heard that Centaurs who settled into human lives didn't share their lineage with their children, but Daniel knew all about it. It wasn't a big source of mystery for him: if anything, he despised it.

I began to wonder how bad it would be to have a life like Daniel's father. I hated the fact that if I waited another year and wasn't chosen by a Centauride, I would essentially be cast out from the family. If I just stayed here, I would never have to see their disappointment in me. I could meet a girl and be like all those sappy movies I'd always seen. Something inside me was convinced this was where I was supposed to be.

"Hello, earth to Beau." Daniel's hand was waving in front of my face. "You ready, bra?"

I was still getting used to Daniel's slang: "Bra" was short for brother. I would have preferred "Bro," instead of a lady's undergarment, but that was Daniel. It wasn't a Centaur thing; it was what he called every person willing to catch waves with him. "Sure, where to next?"

He dangled a set of keys in front of me. "I have to work today, so you're on your own. Here's the keys to Cami's place." He motioned to his car, "Get in, I'll drop you there."

Mom and Dad had planned to have the apartment packed up and moved to our house in Charleston, but after Zandra kidnapped Cami, they wanted for her to have a home to go home to if she needed it.

There had always been rumors of what happened to Cami's mom, rumors as to why she may have run away and other rumors that she had been murdered. Dad wanted Cami to have a place that was all hers if she needed it, away from everything and everyone. Her apartment had been idle for the last three months. I didn't want to stay in a hotel and figured if I was going to learn how to be a human, her place might be a good start.

We were driving up the Pacific Coast Highway toward Cami's apartment. I wasn't paying attention to the road until I heard the echo of a blown out tire, the squealing of tires in all directions, and the metal bending crashes of a little white car flipping end over end up the highway.

Daniel slammed on the brakes. The seatbelt held me tight while we came a breath away from slamming into the car in front of us. When we stopped, I freed myself from the seatbelt, opened the door, and sprinted to the crumpled up white car. I wasn't worried that I'd used my Centaur speed to get there: so many people were desperately trying to avoid the cars in front of them that they wouldn't even notice my blur run past them.

When the white car stopped its cartwheels, I felt their magic. These weren't frail humans; there were three Centaurs inside. I saw gas leaking out of the car. Pulling them out was risky: always leave crash victims in the car until the emergency responders arrive. But smoke was rolling out from under the hood – where there was smoke, there would be fire.

I reached through the shattered passenger window to pull out the female sitting in the passenger seat. Her knee was wedged against the dashboard. I was pretty sure her leg was broken from the angle it was laying.

I pushed as hard as I could against the dashboard. It complained against my strength but moved the half inch I needed to ease her out of the front seat through the passenger side window, without doing further damage to her leg. I had taken four strides away from the car with the woman in my arms when I heard it.

The explosion engulfed the car and blew me forward. Her body was sheltered from the blast by me. I felt the back of my shirt catch fire, but I held onto her. I got five or six more steps, laid her down on the highway's shoulder as I felt someone extinguishing the fire on my back with a blanket. I could hear sirens in the distance.

I'd been burned badly, but I couldn't lay her head on the asphalt. Daniel came rushing up to me, "Are you nuts? You could have gotten yourself killed."

I nearly growled, "Give me your shirt, now!"

He didn't argue: he pulled it over his head and handed it to me. It looked like he was going to be ill. I think he thought I needed it for me; instead, I folded it up with my free hand and placed it under the woman's head. She had a shallow cut over her eye, a deep gash on her leg, and she was unconscious.

I looked back at the little white car; it was fully engulfed by flames. If the other two had survived the crash, there was no way they would live through the fire. I pulled what was left of my shirt off, wadded it up so the charred sides were wrapped up inside it, and applied pressure to the deep gash on her leg in an effort to convince the blood to stop flowing from her.

I heard what sounded like the echo of hooves on asphalt and knew the two who didn't survive the crash were on their way to the pasture. I couldn't see them, but I felt them leave. I held the woman's hand with my free hand and continued applying pressure to the gash on her leg. Daniel's voice was shaking behind me, "Is she going to make it?"

I didn't answer him. She was so young. Her dark blonde hair fell just past her shoulders; she wore a pair of gold earrings shaped like Centaurs and a bottle cap necklace. I lifted her eyelids to see if her pupils were dilated: her eyes were light green with brown halos around the iris. I squeezed her hand, trying to reassure her, "Stay with us. It's not your time to go. Hang on."

I could hear courage in my voice that I didn't feel. I, too, wondered if she could hold on. We didn't have to wait long. The first two emergency responders put a brace on her neck, lifted her onto a stretcher, checked her leg, her pupils, and were lifting her into the ambulance while a second team had brought a stretcher for me.

Through clenched teeth I motioned toward the young Centauride. "I'm fine. Take care of the girl."

The EMT did nothing more than glance at her over his shoulder. She was already inside the ambulance. "Hi, I'm Carl. What's your name?"

"I'm Beau, and I'm fine." I had stayed hunched over the ground where I had knelt by the wounded Centauride. I stood up awkwardly to walk away when the paramedic held my arm.

"You've got third degree burns on your back; we need to get you to the burn unit." I didn't feel any pain but felt like I was a little disconnected from my body. Begrudgingly, I lay down face first on the gurney in the back of the ambulance as I saw the first ambulance pulling away.

I hadn't been paying attention before, but a fire truck was on site spraying down the car, a tow truck was ready to haul the car away as soon as they got the all clear, and traffic was moving again on the far left lane. Another thirty minutes and the only proof that would remain of the two Centaurs whose lives ended here would be the scorched pavement from where the fire burned out of control.

Life was too short. We all could live for decades or days, and none of it was within our control. I made the decision, lying face down on the gurney inside the ambulance – I was done waiting. When I'd come to San Diego, it was to test the waters, to see if I could give up my Centaur life and make a life as a human. After watching what had happened on the highway, my mind was made up. I'd live my life as if every day were my last, starting today. I'd find a woman who would love me for who I am, not for my bloodline.

Daniel followed the ambulance to the hospital. After we'd been at the hospital for half an hour, he offered to call my family for me. I shook my head, "No, this is a call I need to make. Where's my phone?"

He reached into the drawer with my personal effects and handed it to me. Mom answered. She recognized my number, "Beau, how's your trip? Dad and the boys are missing you at the office."

"It's going great, actually." If she didn't know I was sitting in a hospital, I didn't want to send her into orbit by telling her.

"You sound different. Is everything okay?"

"Never better, Mom. So great, in fact, I'm thinking I'm going to stay a little longer." I saw Daniel's expression change. What would he think of me abandoning my family back east?

"Oh, okay. When should I tell your father to expect you back?"

"I'm not sure. I'll call in a few weeks." I couldn't see my mother's expression through the phone, but Daniel cocked his head to the side as if trying to understand what he'd just heard.

"Honey, you don't have much time. You should be. . ."

I didn't let her finish. She was going to remind me that I should be courting all the available Centaurides. "Yeah, I think I'm going to hang it up, Mom. I'm already twenty-nine. I'm done waiting. I'm going to start living."

Her voice cracked, "Your father is negotiating with another father now. Beau, you need to come home."

I knew it. I'd heard a rumor that Hannah's dad walked away with a pretty hefty payment when she and Bruce got married, but I didn't want to believe it. Hannah was great, she and Bruce would be happy, but I didn't want to be chosen that way. He'd tried the same thing for me before, and I'd stopped it. I couldn't stand the thought of a Centauride choosing me for financial gain for her family; selfishly, I wanted something more.

I'd heard humans were exactly the opposite; it was okay for a man to approach a woman, to ask her out on a date, to call her on the phone and talk. "Tell him not to do it for me. I'm not carrying the bloodline. I love you, Mom."

I disconnected quickly, not wanting to drag the discussion on. They'd come to accept my decision, or they wouldn't. I'd made up my mind, and for the first time – I felt free. The doctor checked me out shortly after I hung up the phone, "Must have had a rookie admitting you. Your chart says you have third degree burns on sixty percent of your back. I see one blister in the center of your back that is worrisome at a second degree, but the rest are just mild first degree burns. Looks to me like you got pretty lucky today, son."

"You're right, Doc. This was my lucky day. So, can I go?"

He seemed pleased to be delivering such a simple diagnosis, "A nurse will be in to go over discharge instructions with you. You should be fine in a week." The doctor scribbled something on a chart and left Daniel and me in the room.

Daniel walked over to my bed and looked at my back. He hadn't believed the doctor's words until he saw it for himself. "Beau, he's right. Your back's almost completely healed."

"Figured it would be. You ready?"

"He said you should wait for the nurse."

I took a look at myself; I couldn't leave the hospital like this. "All right. Hey, can you run down to the gift shop and get me a t-shirt?"

"What kind?"

"Anything loose. The last of the burn should be healed in the next hour or so, but I don't want the nurse to be suspicious if she comes in and I'm completely healed before she gets around to discharging me."

"What are you, genetically engineered?"

"No, a warrior, same as you." Daniel stopped and looked at me like he was going to argue. Three-quarters Centaur, I was sure he could heal almost as fast as I could, and when he turned away without arguing with me, I knew I was right.

CHAPTER 12

Beau Strayer – San Diego, CA

Daniel must have sprinted down and back up, because he was gone less than ten minutes. A very attractive, very bleached-blonde, very petite nurse wearing pink scrubs came through the door the same time Daniel did. "Hi, Mr. Strayer, I'm here to go over your discharge instructions with you." Daniel tossed me the t-shirt, and I slipped it on quickly before she could get a good look.

As I listened to her telling me how to treat my back, I realized this was it. I was free: for the first time in my life, I was *seriously free*. She sat down next to me on the bed and was going through a rather long checklist of how to care for the burns on my back. I did my best to pretend to listen to her, but her voice sounded like music to my ears. I looked into her eyes: were they blue or gray? Definitely blue.

I took my hand and pointed at something on the page, and as I withdrew my hand, I allowed my arm to graze the top of hers. Her skin felt soft, inviting. She didn't react the way I expected. She didn't lurch away from me; she didn't even seem to notice that I had touched her. I did it a second time, this time pressing my forearm a little heavier against hers as I pulled it across: still no reaction from her at my touch.

I tried to remember if I'd ever had casual contact with a woman before. Maybe in high school during gym, but touching her skin without her reacting to me felt liberating. I thought of going on a date with a human, all the movie scenes where the couple held hands or had a kiss good night. I felt a warm glow inside. I'd made the right decision.

The nurse finished my discharge instructions with the same bubbly voice she had begun with and asked, "So, do you have any questions, Mr. Strayer?" She stood up from where she'd been seated.

I was scared, but decided there was no time like the present. "Just one. Any chance you'd want to go to the cafeteria and get some coffee?"

Her brows furrowed and her voice lost some of its vibrancy. "Mr. Strayer. . . do you have any questions on your *discharge instructions*?"

"No. They seem pretty straight forward."

"Okay, sign here." She was all business, not even acknowledging that I had extended an invitation.

I handed her the pen back, took a deep breath to steady myself, "Now that that's out of the way, how about some coffee?" She looked annoyed, so I threw in, "Maybe tea?"

In a tone I guessed she saved for people she really didn't care for, she said, "This isn't speed dating, Mr. Strayer. Take care of your injuries. I don't want to see you back here."

Daniel was laughing in the corner, not even trying to maintain any amount of decorum. "Crash an' burn, Beau! I guess she told you. You catch on fire again, you better find another hospital." Initially his sarcasm reminded me of Cami, and I thought it was a charming trait. Now it was seriously pissing me off.

I caught the nurse's elbow just before she stepped through the doorway. "Hey, I'm sorry if I've offended you. I'm new in town, and I don't know anybody. I thought you might like just to talk for a minute."

"Nice line. Has that ever worked?"

"Line? It's not a line. I just wanted to get to know you."

"Sorry, I don't mix with patients."

"Well, that works great. You just discharged me. I'm not a patient anymore."

Her smile warmed, marginally, "Have a good day, Mr. Strayer. You can get your prescription filled at the pharmacy downstairs." She put her back to me and began walking down the hallway.

I sprinted the few steps to get in front of her in the hallway, "Will you be there?"

"In the pharmacy? Mr. Strayer, you seem like a nice enough man. I'm not meeting you for coffee, or tea, or down in the pharmacy." Her voice was stern. I shouldn't have pressed her, but I did anyway.

"Would you believe me if I told you I've never been on a date in my whole life? Today I caught fire trying to help someone in a car accident, and my life flashed before my eyes. I don't want to die not knowing what it's like to sit across the table from a beautiful woman and to have a normal conversation. C'mon, say yes."

Her voice suddenly took on the attributes of a drill sergeant when she said, "Mr. Strayer, for the last time, no. If you ask me one more time, I'll call security."

Daniel had caught up to me in the hallway, and this latest exchange made him double over with laughter, "Daaaaaamn, Beau, you need to quit while you're ahead. She's going to have your ass in jail." I decided that I was glad she didn't try to look under my new t-shirt. I was sure the burns had completely healed by now, and given this exchange, the nurse would probably turn me in for insurance fraud if she saw that I was completely healed.

Daniel was still laughing at the elevator, "What would have possessed you to try to pick up a nurse, while she was working?"

"Why not?"

"Chicks don't like it when they're working, Bra. At least not the ones I know. They think it's demeaning."

"Really? That's stupid. She was pretty. I just wanted to get to know her. I thought that humans didn't have dating rules?"

"This is California, Beau. All the girls are pretty here. You want a babe to hang out with, look for the one wearing the smallest bikini on the beach – there's someone who wants to be picked up. Not here."

"Thanks for the tip."

The last several hours had blurred together, but it occurred to me that Daniel had been driving me to Cami's apartment because he had to get to work. "Hey, man, are you late for work?"

Daniel looked at his watch, "If I left right now, I'd only make it in for three hours. It'd be better not to go in at this point. I already called my boss."

I nodded. I felt uncomfortable bringing it up, but I asked anyway, "Daniel, do you think it would be okay if I met your dad?"

"My dad? Why would you want to meet him?" Daniel eyed me suspiciously.

From things Daniel had told me, their relationship had been past strained since he returned from Florida. I didn't want to strain their relationship further, but his father might be the only person on the planet who I could talk to about my decision right now. "I've kind of decided I want to stay here. I'm ready to, you know, to be normal. . . if that's possible."

"What about Cami?"

Daniel's question threw me for a loop. "What do you mean? I'll move out of her apartment if she comes back."

"I mean, I don't trust any Centaur but you. If you aren't looking out for her, what's going to happen to her?"

"I already told you, she's got a Centaur who she's either already chosen or is going to choose soon. She's safe."

Daniel wasn't happy when he accused, "So, you're just turning your back on her?"

I couldn't understand Daniel's anger. Why did he think something bad was going to happen to Cami? I had to admit that when she was at her grandmother's house, I'd been worried, but she was okay now. Dad was hiding her, and she had Drake with her. "No, Daniel. Cami is. . . well, she's fine."

Daniel and I didn't know each other very well, so confessing my plan to him felt awkward. Unfortunately, unless he understood, my refusal to return to South Carolina would look like a betrayal of some kind. I didn't know if he thought I was betraying him or Cami. "Look, I'm twenty-nine. You know at thirty I'm no longer eligible to be chosen by a Centauride. I've seen guys like me my whole life – we're pathetic. You don't know what it's like to see the disappointment in your own father's eyes. I just don't want to do it anymore. I figure if I make the decision, maybe it won't eat at me so badly. I'm okay if I don't carry on my family's bloodline. I'm willing to give up my place in my family, not because I don't care about them, but because I wouldn't be able to survive their rejection a year from now."

Daniel didn't say anything. It felt good to finally say it out loud, so I just kept talking. "You wanna' know what scares the shit out of me? I don't know how to start a new life. We both just saw me strike out with a girl when all I wanted was a cup of coffee and conversation. I don't know how to be a human. I can't even pretend. You're the only human I know, and you're three-quarters Centaur."

"That's funny, Beau. Here I'm hangin' out with you, hoping you'll magically show me how to be a Centaur, and you're with me thinking I'll somehow turn you human. We're a couple of losers." Daniel cocked his head, then added, "But one of us is bound to come out happy."

"And the other is going to fail miserably."

"No offense, Bra, but I hope you fail."

"Me too, Daniel. Me too."

"I guess we could go see Pops. He's a little easier to get along with than your father."

I laughed at Daniel, "Dad's not so bad, unless you come unannounced at 1 a.m. after he's had the most stressful day of his life, then punch him in the face for good measure."

"What kind of an idiot would do that?"

I couldn't contain the laughter and neither could Daniel. I nearly buckled over remembering the night Daniel flew to our house looking for Cami. He didn't get the answers he wanted from my dad, so he hauled off and punched him. Mom and I watched the whole thing from the living room window. It was like watching a car accident – you know you shouldn't watch, but you can't turn your attention away from it.

Daniel led the way to the exit when a nurse in green scrubs caught us in the hallway and said, "Excuse me."

We both looked at her, a little confused because she wasn't familiar. She asked, "Are you the two who helped with the car accident on PCH?" I nodded; the road we'd been on was called the Pacific Coast Highway, but everyone shortened the name to PCH. "Lacey Perish was the girl you pulled from the car. She asked if she could speak with you. I went up to the burn unit, but they said you weren't admitted."

"Uh, yeah. They checked me out. I've already been discharged."

"If you have a minute to say hello, she's in room two twenty-nine. She'd like to say thank-you."

I looked at Daniel, and he shrugged his shoulders. She was a Centauride, so neither of us should be in her room without an escort. I started to decline when Daniel said, "C'mon, Beau."

I shook my head, "Naw, you go ahead, Daniel. I'll meet you outside."

The nurse gave me a strange look, "Mr. Strayer, it'll only take a second. She just lost her brother and her fiancé. She's very upset. Allowing her to thank you will help her grieving process."

I didn't want to be a jerk. I'd been so wrapped up in my own drama, I had nearly forgotten that I'd heard the two Centaurs ascend to the pasture after the explosion.

We followed the nurse into her room. "Lacey, I found a couple visitors for you."

Lacey was younger than I: she was really young. She looked like a sweet kid, probably no older than twenty. She'd been crying: her face was red and her eyes still shiny with tears. I saw her trying to sit up a little straighter and adjust her blanket to better cover herself.

Daniel was the first to speak, "Hi, Lacey, I'm Daniel." He motioned to me, "This is Beau."

She pursed her lips together. I recognized the look. She was trying to hold in a fresh wave of tears. After everything she'd gone through today, you'd think she'd know it was fine to be a little vulnerable. Her voice was strong when she cleared her throat and said, "I just wanted to say thank-you."

Daniel looked at me. I nodded in response to her. When Daniel concluded that I wasn't going to say anything, he answered, "It was all Beau. He's the one who pulled you out."

She nodded. I felt worse than I had five minutes before. If I'd just been a few seconds faster, I might have been able to save her fiancé, as well. She wouldn't recover from the loss any time soon. He had had a life to look forward to. I felt a loss for the Centaur I'd never known. Would his bloodline carry on? Did he have brothers or did my delay cause his bloodline to cease? "I'm sorry I couldn't do more." I hoped she had heard the words, but my voice was barely over a whisper.

Her voice was much stronger than mine, "You did more than most could have, Beau. Thank you."

I nodded, desperately wanting out of the room. I felt like the walls were closing in on me, and I needed air. Why would I be permitted to live when I had nothing to live for? I didn't have a life waiting for me. I would have to make my own, and it wasn't even a life I'd fought for. Why would their lives not be spared?

I couldn't take the feeling anymore, so I gave Lacey a half wave and walked toward the door, "I'm glad you're going to be okay."

When I hit the door's threshold, her raised voice found me, "Beau, be careful."

I stopped in the doorway, angled my body slightly, "I will."

"I mean on your trip. She needs you."

I'd already decided I wasn't going back to South Carolina. What was she talking about? "What? What trip?"

"To South Dakota. She needs you. I can see it."

I took a step back inside the room. "Who needs me?"

Daniel had been standing just to the side of Lacey; he leaned into her. "What'd you say? South Dakota? Is it Cami?"

Lacey looked a little confused, "Yes, I think so." Her head did the smallest of a circle as her eyes lost focus on us; it looked like she was concentrating on something not in the room. "I'm sorry. I'm not feeling well. . ." Her voice cut off for a second, she took a heavy breath, and when she spoke again her voice was shaky, "I'm sorry. I woke up this morning and had a really bad feeling about Ted and Tom. Tom was my brother, Ted was my. . . betrothed. They were going to play golf, but I had this vision of a car crash and their burning bodies. I begged them not to go. I told them I'd do anything if they just wouldn't go. . ." Tears streamed down her face, and she took several ragged breaths. Lacey was a seer: she saw the future. She had known of the accident that was to take their lives and couldn't prevent it.

Neither Daniel nor I said a word. Her sobs were deafening, and Daniel reached down and instinctively held her hand trying to comfort her. She didn't shrug away from his touch as I would have expected, not because he wasn't a pure-blood but because he was a male. She continued, "I couldn't stop it. It happened anyway."

Daniel's voice was kind, "You can't stop fate, Lacey. I'm sorry for your loss, but there's nothing you could have done. I'm sure they are both looking down and happy that you're alive, wanting you to make the most of the rest of your life."

She nodded through the sobs. I didn't want to be insensitive, but I needed to know what she was talking about. I inched closer to her, and when I was close enough to keep my voice low, I asked, "You said Cami needs me? Are you sure?"

"Not yet, but she will."

"Where is she?"

"I don't know. It doesn't work like that. She's in South Dakota, and I can see her screaming for help. I can see someone trying to help her. I see you, Beau."

"What's happened to her?"

"I can't see that, either." She gave an exasperated expression, "I'm sorry, I wish I could control the visions better. When I see the future, it's always just glimpses, sometimes words. In this vision I could see cars with license plates, so I know what state. Otherwise, they're really just random."

Daniel's face had turned sheet white, his jaw hung open, and it looked like he'd seen a ghost. "We gotta' go, Beau."

I turned to Daniel and asked, "What's wrong. What do you know?"

"I got a call from Cami last night. She said she was going to South Dakota."

"Was she okay?"

"I don't. . . I'm not sure. She and I argued a little, and I didn't answer the phone when she called back. C'mon. We gotta' go, now!"

I nodded respectfully to Lacey as a good-bye and rushed out the door after Daniel.

CHAPTER 13

Beau Strayer – Daniel's House, San Diego, CA

Daniel drove us to his father's house. We knew taking his father's plane would be the fastest way to get to Cami, but for that he needed to tell him what we were up to. When I met Derrick, Daniel's father, I wasn't surprised at all. Daniel looked like a younger version of Derrick, but Derrick's demeanor reminded me of my father. There was no mistaking it: he was a Centaur.

"Daniel, I haven't seen you in a week, and now you're demanding the use of my plane. Why can't you fly commercial?"

"I already told you, Dad. We need to get there fast. Beau's got his pilot's license. He's okay to fly your jet." Daniel was stuffing clothes in a backpack standing in the doorway of the living room.

Derrick eyed me suspiciously. He knew what I was, as well. "We think my sister's in danger. I called my father, but his jet's in Charleston. It'd be faster for us to take a commercial flight than it would be to wait for his plane to arrive. Daniel mentioned we might be able to use yours."

He grimaced. "I've known your sister since she and Daniel were in the same third grade class, so I can empathize." His looked passed me to his son. "I've told Daniel, she isn't his concern."

Daniel interrupted, "Dammit, Dad! I never ask you for anything. I'm asking for this now."

Derrick looked at Daniel and said, "You know how I feel about you around her. You know why I feel the way I do. Why do you need to go?"

"You told me once that if a Centauride were ever in trouble, it was every Centaur's responsibility to come to her aid. Cami's in trouble."

"Daniel, you aren't a Centaur."

"Thanks for the reminder, Dad. I almost forgot." The fury subsided and his voice lowered when he continued, "I couldn't do anything for her when she was in trouble before. I'm going to do this now, with or without your help." Daniel bowed his head and left; I could hear his footsteps climbing the steps to his room.

"Sorry you had to see that, Beau. Cami has a way of bringing out the worst in him."

"It's okay. He and Cami are really close."

"Despite my best efforts to the contrary."

"Daniel told me you weren't in favor of their friendship. Did she do something that made you feel that way?"

Derrick snickered. "I'm not human. Just because I couldn't carry my bloodline doesn't mean that I don't honor the traditions Zeus set down for us. She didn't have any business befriending a male human."

"Did you know who her mother was?"

"Do I look like an imbecile? Of course, I knew she was Angela Chiron."

"But you never told anyone."

He shook his head. "I wanted to. I wanted to call Angela's mother a hundred times. When I met Angela, I couldn't believe she was a single parent working as a waitress. She was a Chiron. She was our generation's

Centauride. She had responsibilities to our society."

"But you never called?"

"No. She and I spoke one evening when the kids were young. Like everyone else I believed she had been murdered, so when I saw her I was elated. I assumed she had married a Centaur who died and chose not to return to our society because of her grief."

"Did she tell you that's what'd happened?"

"No." Derrick paused as if struggling to put his thoughts into words. "When I recognized her, she said she intended to raise Camille as a Chiron and would introduce her to her herd the next year – she just needed more time. The following year, Cami was still enrolled in the same school as Daniel. And the next and the next."

"So you only confronted Angela the one time?"

"When Cami turned eighteen, she had a human boyfriend, and I was furious. Daniel had told me about him. He was a mechanic. Can you imagine? It wouldn't have made a difference if he were a state senator; the fact was he was human. He had a blue collar job and he had no business being romantically involved with a descendant of Chiron." Derrick wasn't putting on a show for me. I could tell he was still angry about the whole situation. Cami was twenty-two now, so I can just imagine his reaction four years ago.

"From my own experience, I knew how hard it is for a Centaur to find a Centauride. I couldn't believe Angela allowed Camille to date a human. I confronted Angela and asked her if she planned to arrange a marriage or to allow Cami to choose. Angela said Cami would make choices her whole life; she would let Cami choose to be human or Centauride when the time was right."

"So, what'd you do?"

Derrick's voice trembled, "I told her I might have to make a call to Zandra."

"How did she react to that?"

He shook his head, "She said, 'Go ahead and try,' like it was a challenge or something."

I couldn't understand why if he felt so strongly, he never made good on his threat. "But you never called Zandra?"

"That's the strangest part. Every time I picked up the phone to do it, I got distracted. I wondered if there was some sort of enchantment that wouldn't let me divulge Angela's whereabouts. After several days of trying to call, unsuccessfully, I picked up a pen and paper and tried to write a letter – I couldn't do that, either."

"Angela was protected by Aphrodite's magic."

Derrick smiled, "I knew it! I knew there was a reason I couldn't make that call."

"So why were you opposed to Daniel being her friend? At least he could offer her some protection if she were ever in danger."

"I saw that look in his eyes when he was in the seventh grade. I didn't want him to get hurt. He didn't understand things. You and I knew what we were from an early age, but Daniel's different. He carries Centaur blood, but he isn't a pure-blood. There aren't enough Centaurides to go around for the pure-blooded Centaurs. I couldn't let him get involved with Cami, knowing her future would never allow the two of them to remain in contact."

"So, you didn't have a problem with Cami. You just assumed she'd eventually join her herd, and you thought Daniel would get hurt."

Derrick tipped his chin as his eyes fell to the floor. I didn't have much time, and this might be my only opportunity. "Derrick, I'm twenty-nine."

"I remember that age. Why are you here with Daniel? You've only got a year of eligibility left."

"I've pretty much decided to hang it up."

His bewildered eyes met mine as his voice echoed the same confusion. "Hang it up? You mean you're leaving your herd?"

I forced a smile on my face, "I don't want my father to bribe another father just so I can carry on the bloodline. I have a brother who's already married; our bloodline's secure. I'd rather start my life now, on my own terms."

His voice was powerful and his tone unashamed, "Beau, don't waste a day, let alone a year. You have a finite period of time, and you're letting it slip away."

"You regret your decision? Marrying a human?"

"It wasn't a decision. There were no other options for me. You still have options. If your father is able to arrange a marriage, let him arrange it."

I shook my head. "I've decided I'm not going back. I'll find a human, and I'll do it on my terms."

"Or maybe ten years from now, you'll look back on this day and be upset that you didn't do everything in your power to fulfill your destiny."

Daniel's voice echoed in the hallway. "This is what you wanted to talk to Pops about? Hell, I coulda' told you he regretted every day of his life for at least the last twenty-three years. I've been nothin' but a disappointment, and Mom's never been good enough for him, either." His spiteful words didn't even register with Derrick. Daniel turned to me, "We're taking the plane. Let's go."

I looked back at Derrick as he glared at his son. Derrick was nothing like my own father. I never wanted to be like Daniel's father. I'd always disliked the Centaur way. It felt mechanical, in some respects unfeeling.

I refused to father a son who would grow up to think he was inadequate or a disappointment. The more I thought about it, the more sure I was that I was making the right decision. I could marry for love, have a family that wouldn't be governed by the rules that had nearly suffocated me my whole life. This was the life I wanted, and it was mine to take.

Derrick still held onto a lot of emotional baggage from not being chosen. Daniel was a constant reminder to him. The bitterness that Derrick felt was his own choosing. I refused to share it.

CHAPTER 14

Camille – Rapid City, SD

I was still groggy from the flight. Mom's spirit had told me the only thing impeding my powers had been the fact that I didn't embrace them. She wasn't kidding.

When we stepped off the plane and onto the tarmac, I could see spirits all around me, human spirits walking aimlessly on the earth mingled in with everyone else. I could feel their loneliness, their confusion, in a few – their anger. Living people walked through these scattered spirits. A baggage-handling cart barreled past, paying no attention to the lights of energy haphazardly sprinkled everywhere.

Several of the spirits had climbed onto the wings of an airplane awaiting take-off. I silently wished them luck, although I thought if their idea was to somehow launch themselves into the heavens, it may be a waste of what little energy they still possessed.

I felt woozy as we walked into the terminal building, as if I were at a cocktail party with voices in all directions. The constant chatter all around me was deafening. As I looked at the thirty or so people waiting, few seemed to be speaking aloud. I realized it was their thoughts spilling in from all directions: some soft and thoughtful, others angry and loud, a few in different languages – it was overwhelming.

I tried to steady myself by putting a hand up against a wall for support. I changed my mind: it didn't sound like a cocktail party – that would have been some assembly of civility – these competing thoughts in all directions reminded me of being at a rock concert with hundreds of people while the warm-up band played. No one really listened to the music at first; they just shouted over the music playing in the background.

I heard Drake's voice, but I couldn't understand him.

Bracing both my hands on my temples, "I need to get out of here."

"Cami, Cami, look at me." I looked at him. I hated catching anyone's eyes because the moment I did, their future lay out in front of me, like a slinky with all the twists and turns that would befall them mapped out in front of me. Drake saw my expression and took my hand in his. His touch blocked out most of the sensory overload. He led me toward a wall away from all the people. I heard his thoughts, "*Are you okay*?"

"Oh, it's too loud."

"What's too loud?"

"People, their thoughts, it's too much."

"You can hear everyone's thoughts?"

"Their thoughts are loud, some are in different languages. I keep getting glimpses of people's futures. It's making me dizzy." I tried to speak over the competing thoughts, but I ended up shouting. "We need to get out of here. I can't think straight."

"Concentrate on my thoughts. *Listen to what I'm thinking, and it should keep the others at bay.*"

I did what he told me, and to my relief Drake was replaying our conversation on the plane in a constant loop in his head until after we had our bags and a rental car. Once inside the car and away from the others I said, "Thank you. I'm not sure how I'm going handle all of this."

"We'll steer clear of crowded places until after you're used to it."

I had heard about Mount Rushmore growing up as a kid, but South Dakota had never been on my "must visit" list. It turns out there was a whole lot more to see than some presidents' faces on a mountain. From the minute we drove away from the airport there were billboards every fifty feet, each advertising some place we weren't supposed to miss during our trip: Mount Rushmore, Rushmore Caves, Bear Country USA, Custer State Park, Sturgis Bike Rally, Deadwood, old trains, Reptile Gardens, and hundreds of other possibilities, but we were driving so fast, I didn't catch what they were promoting. Every store we passed had a similar sign, "Black Hills Gold 20% off." Some said thirty percent, a few said sixty percent – I'd never even heard of Black Hills gold.

Thick lush forests hugged the outskirts of Rapid City and escorted us all the way to the hotel. Temperatures were frigid, and we knew we weren't ready for this type of weather, any more than we had been prepared for Dublin's when we arrived. After my quick experience around people when we entered the airport, I dreaded the idea of finding a mall to pick up winter attire.

Drake found a hotel that was ten miles from the Crazy Horse Mountain. As we drove, we could see the mountain from the road. Snow covered the top of the mountain, but the face of Crazy Horse somehow eerily peeked through the snow to the winding road below.

The hotel had a small gift shop inside proudly displaying what all the fuss was about from the signs we had passed: Black Hills gold. I was surprised to see pink and green leaf and flower patterns inlaid over the top of the traditional yellow gold I'd always seen. Not only had I never seen it before, I had no idea gold came in any color beyond white or yellow. I made a mental note to get a souvenir before we left this place, but not today. The clerk in the gift shop was obsessing about some loser guy, and her thoughts made me want to grab her by the shoulders and shake some sense into her.

We checked in and went to the room; for some reason, I wasn't surprised when I saw a taxidermied bison standing outside the hotel's bar. The room was spacious, with a king-sized bed, Jacuzzi bathtub, and a sitting area in front of a large window. The room was western themed with the feel of a hunting lodge with modern amenities.

Fluffy white towels hung at attention in the bathroom; granite countertops surrounded the sink. The shower had two shower heads and a lever for a steam room, but the furniture and bedding looked like replicas from a hundred years ago. This was a homey place to combat the jet lag I knew would quickly set in.

The airport had been sensory overload for me, so when we arrived at the hotel, I did as Drake had instructed and held his hand throughout the check-in process. It seemed to work; I only heard others' thoughts when I allowed myself to pay attention to them. Something about Drake's touch drowned them out, so they became background noise. I knew I wouldn't be able to stay at the quiet hotel and still hope to accomplish what we had set out to do. My voice sounded more defeated than I wanted it to when I asked, "How are we going to find Cameron if I can't be around people?"

Drake's hand squeezed mine, "As long as we're touching, you should get a stronger signal from me than you do any others. If you start to feel overwhelmed, just hold my hand. We'll figure out how to find Cameron. Give yourself some time to adjust; we just got here."

I smiled when I thought how Centaurs normally interacted with one another so formally. I looked down at Drake's fingers intertwined with mine, "I bet your father would have heart failure if he saw us now, huh?"

Drake nodded. He stood in front of the enormous bed in our room and let out a quick smirk, "About Dad, he's a good Centaur and has been a great father to me, but he isn't pleased that I've been gone for so long." Drake had been at Zandra's house for a month and with me for almost a week. "I spoke to him before we left for Ireland. I need to call him to let him know we've returned."

I could hear it in his voice: I wasn't going to like what he was about to say. Without cringing I asked, "And?"

Drake avoided my eyes, "I told him about my broken engagement with Bianca right before we left your father's house."

I could feel my eyebrows raise, "How'd he take it?"

Drake answered flatly, "He wasn't thrilled."

Still on a high from our conversation on the plane, feeling playful I asked, "Did you tell him you'd found another Centauride to fall madly in love with you, so he shouldn't worry?"

Drake looked at me and his easy smile warmed me, "No, I didn't." He didn't hold my gaze. His eyes dropped to the floor when he said, "Before we left for Ireland, I wasn't sure how you felt about me." I rolled my eyes because Gretchen herself had told him I was going to choose him the night we escaped from Zandra's. He looked back at me and added, "After our conversation last night, you seemed to be on board with getting married."

It would be bad form to say, "Duh," so I answered, "Very on board."

Drake's tone was flat, more matter-of-fact than the loving soon-to-be husband from the plane. I got a nervous pang in my stomach, wondering if he'd had time to reconsider. If he had, wouldn't he have gotten two rooms?

I stood staring at him when he continued, "If you're sure, I'd like for my parents to get the call from your father. I'm sure our customs sound stupid to you. . . they sound juvenile to me when I think about them. But it would lessen his frustration with me if he knew I had been chosen and the Nash bloodline will continue. Well, maybe not in name."

I was confused, "What do you mean: 'maybe not in name'?"

Drake's smile was warm. "I'll keep the Nash name, but our kids will take on yours, since you're a Chiron."

I'd gone from Benning, to Strayer, now Chiron – did it really matter? "What if I want to be Camille Nash?"

His smile grew, "Let's cross that bridge when it comes. Can you call him?"

I shook my head, still not understanding the change in him, "This doesn't sound like a big deal, Drake. I can call Will now if you want." After three days of agonizing over whether Drake would still want me, the fact that he did wasn't something I had intended to keep a secret.

"I was hoping you'd say that. Dad's set in his ways. When we last spoke, he wanted me to seek a blood debt from Bianca." My eyes grew to the size of quarters, but Drake held out a hand in a gesture to keep me from jumping to the wrong conclusion. "When I told him I broke the engagement, he told me to get it fixed or don't bother coming home."

My mind jumped to the worst possible conclusion as I took a step away from him. I thought back to our conversation on the plane. A hurt welled up within me, "So, that's why you're willing to stay with me: being stuck with me is better than being cut off from your family?"

No wonder he'd made it seem like it was the most normal thing ever while we were on the plane. Every other Centauride was a virgin; they weren't allowed to date and most got married in their late teens. He only said it was okay that I wasn't because it was either choose me or be cut off from his family. What choice did he have?

"What? No! Why would you think that?!"

"You just said you were going to be disowned if you didn't carry on your bloodline. So, what you're saying is you're settling for me. I'm the best you can do, is that it?"

Drake closed the gap between us. I expected him to shout at me again. He pulled me close as his lips found the nape of my neck and kissed me softly. His lips caressed my collarbone all the way to my earlobe when he answered, "You *are* the best I can do. Don't you see it? I love you. Do you understand what a gift it is for me to be loved in return?"

I didn't answer him. He grabbed both of my hands, his eyes locked on mine. "Few, if any, Centaurs have any choice in who they marry. They're just happy to be doing their duty for our race and their family. When Bianca chose me, I felt awful. I had always hoped the Centauride who chose me would choose me because she wanted me. With Bianca, it would be a loveless marriage – just like my father's and his father's before him." His blue eyes never let mine go, and I didn't know what to say.

"Then, you came into my world, breaking every tradition I'd ever known. You were so beautiful I was scared to look at you because I worried I'd never be able to look away. The more time I spent with you, I learned that your beauty wasn't your best attribute." Drake took his index finger and touched my chest, his touch sending tingles all over my body. "It was your heart. You opened it to me, and my whole world changed. Last night when you finally agreed to marry me, I felt. . . no, I knew, I was the luckiest Centaur to walk this planet."

I believed him, but a small part of me still needed to hear it. "Even though I'm not as good as all the other Centaurides?"

His voice morphed, his frustration loud and clear. "Why do you do that to yourself? Why do you sell yourself short? You're perfect. You're everything I've ever wanted, before I even knew that it was safe to want it."

"But your parents wouldn't be happy to know that I'd been with a human."

"Cami, I'll let you in on a little secret. I know you think that your relationship with that human before me somehow diminishes your worth in my eyes – you're wrong. Of everything you told me, the only part that bothered me was when you told me you thought you loved him. If another took up residence in even the smallest part of your heart, it would destroy me. You said you're sure you don't love him. That means your heart belongs to me. That's all I ever wanted."

Drake's hands pulled my face to his, our lips a whisper apart. I didn't need to say it, but I did anyway, "I'm yours, Drake." My lips closed the distance between us. One of his hands dropped, sliding under the back of my shirt; sparks rained as I felt his hand on the small of my back.

His mouth moved to my ear: I felt his breath, warm and heavy against me. It was more than his words, his love enveloped me. With both my hands, I grabbed the material of his shirt and lifted it over his head.

I traced the contours of his chest with my hands. He stood motionless in front of me: the longing in his eyes sent shivers through my body.

Drake closed his eyes, the corners of his lips turned up in a content grin as I watched goose bumps appear while I traced the lines of his chest. I wanted more than just to caress his skin; I wanted to feel his skin against mine. I couldn't be sure if it was his idea or if he was responding to what I wanted, but he slid his hands to my sides and pulled my t-shirt over my head. It dropped to the floor as I saw his eyes take in every inch of me.

I stood in front of him half-dressed. Both his hands wrapped gently around my shoulders. His hands began to tremble, and I worried that a rejection was coming. Turmoil shone through his eyes. He tried to look away from me, but I wouldn't let him. I reached my index finger to his chin and turned his eyes back to mine. His desire overrode his senses, and his hands shook as they began caressing me in a needy way. I stepped into him, molding my body to his, pressing hard against him. A moan escaped his lips.

I felt his fingers sliding just under the waistband of my jeans; I could feel the conflict in him. I didn't push harder. Drake's breathing was labored, his hands were taking in my exposed flesh, and the shivers I'd felt initially were replaced by waves of raw desire. His voice was barely more than a whisper, so low I wasn't sure if I'd heard him or if I had imagined the words, "I want you."

"Then take me."

His hands stopped the gentle caressing as his arms wrapped me in a steel grip. He was fighting the desire, as hard as I was hoping he'd lose the battle. He pulled me onto the bed with me on top of him – his decision finally made.

I heard Daniel's ringtone on my phone. I let it go to voicemail, too caught up in the moment to be interested in repairing the damage with Daniel from our earlier call. The phone rang again, and again, and again. After the fifth phone call in as many minutes, Drake whispered, "Go ahead and get it. It might be important."

I shook my head, "I'll call him back, later."

Drake reached up, grabbed the back of my neck and brought my ear to his lips. "I'm not going anywhere, Love."

A sixth call began ringing. I forced myself to get up, intending to silence the phone, but as I did, something told me I needed to take the call. Drake was right. If Daniel was making this many calls, something *was* wrong.

CHAPTER 15

Camille – Hotel near Crazy Horse Mountain, SD

"Hello, Daniel?"

"Cami, are you okay?" Daniel's voice was urgent, borderline panicked.

Telling him "yes" would be a gross understatement. "I'm fine. I tried calling you back last night, but I kept getting your voice mail."

"Never mind about that. Beau and I are at my dad's hangar. We'll be in South Dakota in five hours. Don't go anywhere, okay?"

"Why are you coming to South Dakota?" Drake could only hear my half of the conversation, so he gave me a questioning look.

"Just stay put, okay? We're leaving now. We'll be there soon."

"Daniel, what's going on? Why's Beau with you?" I missed them both so much, but I couldn't understand why they'd be coming here. Had Zandra found Daniel?

"We met this lady; she was a Centauride. She said you were in danger, and Beau needed to get to you. We're on our way. Whatever you do, just stay put until we get there. Is that Drake guy with you right now?"

"He's right here."

"Put him on."

"I'm going to put you on speaker, okay?"

"Whatever, just make sure the schmuck can hear me." I cringed at Daniel's "pet name" for Drake, but did as he instructed.

"Go ahead, Daniel. We can both hear you."

"Drake, I'm a friend of Cami's. She's in danger. Don't let her out of your sight. Her brother Beau and I'll be in at 3 p.m. Don't go anywhere, find a hotel and wait for us. Understand?"

Drake's voice was different, protective and nearly hostile when he answered, "Daniel, she has chosen me. Her life is my responsibility. She will be safe as long as I breathe."

Okay, that was weird. It didn't even sound like Drake's voice coming from him

"Yeah, whatever. Don't go anywhere, don't do anything. You feel me? We're on our way."

A soft knock sounded at the door. I motioned for Drake to answer it as I slipped my shirt back on. I took Daniel off of speaker while Drake put his back on, too. "Daniel, what're you talking about?"

"I wish I knew, Cami. Just don't go anywhere. Wait for us."

"Okay, we'll stay at the hotel. See you in a few hours." Daniel hung up as Drake opened the door and Phineas stood in the hallway, all smiles. "You two look much better than you did last week." It had only been a week since Phineas had helped us escape from Zandra's house on Friday. We were in Ireland Sunday morning, and now five days later we were in South Dakota.

It seemed so long ago and so much had changed that I had a hard time wrapping my mind around it. I was thrilled to see him even as my mother's warning from the plane replayed in my mind. The echo of her warning not to trust him was loud and clear.

I walked slowly to the door. A part of me was excited to see Phineas's warm eyes and happy face, but a part of me wondered why he would be here. Could my mother have been wrong about him, too? As a ghost of her previous self, maybe she was confused.

I shut off the silent argument in my head: I didn't understand Centaur politics, and I didn't care what herd Phineas was from. He was my friend. He was the reason I was still alive. Just as I was ready to embrace him, Drake held up an arm, blocking me from him, and asked, "Phineas, how did you find us?"

"William told me you were on your way back from Ireland."

I gave Drake an angry look as his arm was still held up as a barricade between Phineas and me.

Drake's voice remained protective when he answered, "Mr. Strayer did not know what hotel we were staying in. How did you find us, Phineas?"

Phineas returned Drake's angry stare. "I called hotels looking for reservations."

Drake nodded, then added suspiciously, "We aren't staying here under our real names. I'm going to ask one more time: how did you find us?"

Phineas stammered for a second, "I wanted to know. . . I was worried that. . . I just needed to know that Camille was safe."

"She is. She has chosen me. Cami is under my protection. You will not touch my Centauride." Phineas's eyes went wide. His expression turned angry as he looked from Drake to me, then back to Drake.

That was two times in less than a few minutes that Drake had told someone that I'd chosen him. I'd never heard him say those words when he was betrothed to Bianca. Why would he keep telling everyone that I'd chosen him? I was sure it was a Centaur thing that I'd have to get used to, but it still felt odd to hear, and I didn't understand what was so significant that he had to tell both Daniel and Phineas.

Drake heard my thoughts and answered me back before I understood I was hearing his answer resonate in my head. "*Anyone who I perceive to be a threat is given a warning, Camille. I am your Centaur.*"

I could feel the confused look on my face. How had Drake just heard my thoughts? I was still formulating my question to Drake when Phineas held out a hand to Drake.

Phineas acted as if he were happy for us, but something in his tone gave me goose bumps – and *not* in a good way. "Congratulations, young Nash. That is quite an accomplishment: coming back from the dead and being betrothed a second time, all in less than a week. This information was not shared with me by Mr. Strayer. Is her family aware of her choice?"

The tension between the two was difficult to watch. I hated that they were talking about me as if I weren't right there. I cut in and asked, "Phineas, won't you come in?"

He ignored me, still pressing further with his interrogation from the hallway. "If you are betrothed, your families are unaware." His tone was accusatory as he looked between the two of us. "You seem to be staying in the same room without an escort."

Phineas turned his attention from both of us to just me, "If I did not know better, Camille, I would think this Centaur had taken advantage of your weakened state following your imprisonment at your grandmother's estate."

I smiled, "No, Phineas. Drake has been a perfect gentleman. Thank you for your concern."

"Have you notified your parents of your choice?"

I looked at Drake. He'd wanted me to do that just minutes ago, but I hadn't. We had both gotten distracted. "I was just getting ready to make the call."

"Then I've made it just in time." Phineas looked to his left as four large Centaurs filed through the door. I could hear their attack on Drake before my eyes processed what they were seeing.

Drake yelled, "Run, Cami! Run now!" I stood in shock as the scene unfolded in front of me. Two of the four men were holding Drake down, a third was landing well-placed kicks and punches, and a fourth was standing to the side of the commotion with a large syringe.

I saw Phineas's face. He seemed to be enjoying himself. I screamed, "Phineas, stop this! Stop it now!"

Phineas's amused look smoldered in his eyes, "We'll do just that, my queen. This will only take a minute." Phineas reached down to pick me up; his arms wrapped around me in a vise, compressing my lungs and immobilizing my arms.

I wasn't able to resist even a fraction of an inch. My vision focused on Drake taking a worse beating than I'd seen in any heavyweight title fight. The image of his body slumping to the floor permanently etched itself in my memory. Tears rolled down my cheeks as I screamed for them to stop.

I watched in horror, unable to aid Drake. A conversation I'd had with Bianca came to me – she had told me as a Chiron I would be able to move objects with my mind. I concentrated with everything in me on a wooden desk off in the corner. I visualized the desk floating through the air and crashing into the Centaur who was still kicking Drake's body on the floor.

The table rose a few inches into the air, suspended, as if asking for the kill command. I concentrated hard, my sole focus on bringing the table down on the Centaur who was inflicting the pain on Drake. I closed my eyes to heighten my focus, and I heard a loud thump. When I opened my eyes, I was shocked to see one of the legs of the desk had impaled the attacking Centaur.

The man lay on the floor with blood oozing around the table leg stuck through his chest. Phineas shouted, "Camille! We're here for your protection! Sebastian, get over here with the needle, now!"

I didn't want to believe that Phineas could hurt me. I had thought of him as my own personal bodyguard and trusted friend while at Zandra's. I felt the prick of the needle in my skin. I watched Drake's lifeless body sprawled out on the floor next to the Centaur with the table leg stuck in his chest. I didn't recognize my own voice when it screamed, "Drake! Drake, wake up! Drake. . . help. . ." The room went completely dark.

CHAPTER 16

Drake – Hotel near Crazy Horse Mountain, SD

Camille's phone lay on the floor; the ringing wouldn't stop. I tried to open my eyes but could only see slits of light through my swelled-shut eyelids. The ache in my body was indescribable. When I tried to stand, I couldn't. I rolled onto my stomach and started crawling toward the ringing noise. I had moved several feet in the right direction when the ringing stopped. I put my head down, lying in the prone position, my body threatening to lose consciousness again.

The ringing began again. I still couldn't see the phone, but I could hear that I was close. I fanned my arms out, reaching in all directions, trying to get to it while my legs pushed my body further in the right direction. I had it in my hand, pressed the speaker button, and tried to say, "Hello."

"Cami? Cami, we're here. Where are you guys?" It was Daniel. Had it been five hours? She could be anywhere by now. Daniel's voice sounded frantic, "Cami? Hello?"

I tried to say, "It's Drake," but it came out a garbled mess.

"Drake? Is that you? Where's Cami?"

I took a breath. They were here to help. They knew she was in danger. I could taste the rusty flavor of blood in my mouth and tried to open my eyes again. "They. . . took. . . her."

"Who got her? Where is she!?

I felt my body trying to succumb to the dark again and fought with everything that I had. "Phineas took her."

"Who's Phineas?" Daniel was screaming into the phone. They'd been too late. I thought back to what had happened. I sensed the warriors in the hallway before Phineas told them to come in. I knew it was an ambush. I should have slammed the door and gotten Cami out the window. I should have attacked them instead of simply claiming her as mine. Phineas was right: without her telling her family, I had no claim to her.

Why hadn't I made her make that call? None of this would have happened if I hadn't let my desire for her overcome me. This was my fault. I could have prevented the whole thing.

Daniel's voice was screaming at me over the phone, but I only heard about every third word. I could feel my vision clouding, dizziness and nausea wrapped together threatening to knock me unconscious again. When Daniel paused after a string of questions I couldn't understand, I answered, "At Crazy Horse Lodge." The phone dropped back to the floor, and I surrendered to the darkness.

I heard Daniel's voice absent of any real concern, "Is he dead?"

Beau's voice answered him, "No, he's alive, but not by much. His shoulder's dislocated, his jaw's broken, and I don't know how many broken ribs, maybe internal bleeding, too." I didn't know if it had been five minutes or five more hours since Daniel's call. The two were talking to each other, unaware that I was regaining consciousness.

"Who did this?"

"I don't know. I've known Drake Nash since he was a little kid. He doesn't have an enemy in the world."

"There's a big bloodstain over here. That couldn't have come from him. You think it was Cami?"

"No. That much blood, they would have left her. Whoever did this to him wanted him dead, probably thought he was dead."

I tried to take a deep breath, but it hurt too badly. I managed to get out, "Not dead. They took Cami."

Beau's voice was loud and close to my face, "Drake? Drake, you can hear us? Drake, what happened?!"

"Phineas took her."

"Who's Phineas?"

"Friend of your dad."

This time Daniel screeched, "I told you your dad was a piece of shit! I hate that guy. Call your dad and ask him where Cami is!"

Beau didn't hesitate. I heard the phone dialing. I needed to stay conscious. My left eye could open further than my right. I winced from the light in the room but stared through the pain, so I could look at the two standing to my side. "Dad, it's Beau. Cami's in trouble." Why wouldn't he put it on speaker? "South Dakota. Daniel and I just flew in. We came to Cami and Drake's hotel, and it looks like an earthquake hit their room. Someone beat up Drake pretty badly. He says it was Phineas." More silence, then, "I'll ask. Drake, you're sure it was Phineas?"

I nodded, making eye contact with Beau with my one almost good eye. "He's sure, Dad." I heard Beau take in a breath, "Sometime in the last seven hours. We called them from San Diego before we took off and everything was fine. When we got here, Cami was gone and Drake was bloody and passed out." More of a pause, then I heard, "I'll put it to his ear."

I heard Will's voice when Beau put the phone up to my ear, "Drake, it's Will. Can you tell me what happened?"

It took all the strength I had, but if I didn't use it on this conversation, I might never get Cami back. "Phineas came to the hotel with four other Centaurs. I didn't recognize the other four. She told Phineas that she chose me." I needed to get that information out there. According to our traditions, he had to hear it from Cami, but with the circumstances, he would take my word for it. A Centauride's choice trumps everything, and Will would be forced to devote all his resources to help me find her instead of conducting his own search and possibly leaving me out of it. "He stopped her from calling you and then knocked her out with a drug."

"Where did he take her?"

"If I knew that I'd already be there."

"Drake, did you two get what you were after in Ireland?"

"No, but I don't think Zandra is our biggest problem right now."

"You're right. I just. . . don't worry, Drake, we'll find her. Phineas is an old friend. If he did this, he'd never hurt her."

"Not *if*. He took her." I thought back to my last few minutes of consciousness, "She killed one of the Centaurs before they got her."

"She killed one? How?"

"She has her powers, Will. She got them when we left Ireland. She made a table fly across the room and staked one of them through the chest."

"You three, stay put. The boys and I will be on the plane tonight."

I needed for Beau to take the phone. Something bothered me. Why would Phineas have done this? What was in it for him? If he wanted to take Cami, he had every opportunity at Zandra's house. He'd helped us escape and delivered us to Will. What would have changed? Why now?

My body repaired itself faster than I would have dreamed possible, maybe out of sheer will. Broken bones took longer than tissue to heal, so my ribs and jaw would be a day or two before they'd fully mend, but after just a few hours, my eyes opened and the bruising all over me was a greenish-yellow rather than the purple and blue colors that Daniel and Beau had found me wearing.

I knew Cami had all of her powers. I kept hoping to hear a telepathic thought from her. Telepathy didn't work over great distances for most, but as *her* Centaur, she should be able to speak to me from any distance, even if we hadn't yet united. I called out to her in my mind but heard nothing in return. Either she was still sedated, or. . . I wouldn't think about the other possibility.

Once I'd had a shower and put on some clothes that weren't crusted with blood, my mind seemed to be more alert, as well. I emerged from the bathroom and saw a note from Beau to come to his room. The door was ajar, and I heard Daniel and Beau planning their strategy quietly. I'd known Beau most of my life, but this was the first time I'd seen Daniel. He was more than a half-blood, but not a pure-blood. He was Cami's close friend; I never would have guessed that he was a partial Centaur.

I stuck out my hand, "Hi, Daniel, I'm Drake."

He looked at my outstretched hand. He took it, but not because he wanted to make my acquaintance. Daniel used it as a handle to draw me closer to him – so I could feel his rage. "You were supposed to protect her. All that bullshit on the phone: that she was under your protection. When I find her, I'm going to kick your ass all over again."

Beau shook his head, "Daniel, take it easy. It's not like he handed her over. You saw him when we got here."

"Yeah, I saw him. I heard him say Cami killed one of 'em, too. How many did pretty boy take down?"

It didn't matter that I agreed with Daniel, Beau was quick to defend me. "He was outnumbered, Daniel. If he weren't a Centaur, he wouldn't be alive right now."

Daniel mumbled, "It's not like he's doing us much good anyway." Daniel refused to speak to me directly, in favor of bashing me to Beau. "I had a better chance of protecting her from three states away than this douche." His tone was bitter. He was right – things never should have happened the way that they did. She was taken, and it was my fault.

Daniel was definitely more Centaur than human. We all tried to pretend to be civilized, to mask the fact that we were born of beasts, but when angry, our civility nearly evaporated. He was a hundred and eighty pounds of rage, and even as a pure-blood, I wouldn't provoke him. Daniel would be an asset despite the human blood that ran through him. Trying to get involved with the plan, I asked, "Has anyone called Zandra?"

Both sets of eyes shot daggers at me as if I had suggested summoning Lucifer. "Look, I don't like her any more than either of you, but she's the most powerful Centauride on the planet. She could be an asset."

Beau answered, "No, and we aren't going to call her, either."

I didn't think they were looking at the bigger picture, "Beau, whoever took Cami had it planned out. She could be anywhere by now. Zandra is not my favorite Centauride, either, but she could help."

Daniel stood up; he was eye-to-eye with me. I wasn't sure if he planned to take a swing at me or not. He was furious when he answered, "Zandra took her away from us all. She's not going to do it again. Don't call her."

Daniel was right. Defeated, I left Beau's room and went back into the room I should have been sharing with Cami right now. The ache I felt was overwhelming. I'd lost her again, this time maybe for good.

I remembered my mom and dad when I was a kid. They'd carry on whole conversations without ever saying anything out loud. I hadn't heard any of Cami's thoughts since I came to, but maybe she could hear mine.

With all my concentration, I thought, "*Cami, if you can hear me, tell me where you are.*" I waited, hoping to hear something. I turned off the lights in the room and took a seat in the chair. "*Cami, I can't lose you. Help me find you, Love.*" I could hear a train through the window, I could hear my heart beating wildly in my chest, but I couldn't hear Cami.

I remembered back to the day at Zandra's estate when my so-called death took place. I was still on a high from having spent the night with Cami. Gage set it up so that Cami and I could have some alone time. Gage told me to stagger our appearances at breakfast, so Zandra wouldn't grow suspicious. While I was back in my room getting dressed, I was thinking about how I was going to corner Gage to see if he had come up with a plan yet on how we were going to bust out Cami.

While I was lost in that thought, Bianca and Zandra walked into my room. Bianca couldn't meet my eyes, so I knew something was wrong, but I didn't know what. Zandra summoned one of Cami's guards; he bound our wrists, gagged us, and then put a blindfold over me. I overheard her whispering to the guard to take us to the guest quarters. She told him to be careful to avoid the gardens. I didn't know why at the time but found out later it was because Gage and Cami were waiting for her there.

Just before we were taken down the hallway, I heard Bianca whimper from behind me. The guard held me tight in position. I heard a louder, muffled scream from Bianca. I didn't know what Zandra was doing to her, and I couldn't see through the blindfold to help her. After a third scream through Bianca's gag, Zandra's venomous voice answered, "It was only a scratch, you nag. You're lucky I don't strike you down where you stand."

I felt the slice of the knife across my forearm, then a second and a third. I didn't know at the time what she had been up to, but I learned later that to make our murder scene more realistic, she splattered our blood on the walls.

Bianca told me after we were at the guest quarters that she'd been caught leaving Gage's room that morning. I was guilty by association because Bianca and I were betrothed.

Technically, I was guilty, too, for having spent the night in Cami's room – Zandra just didn't know it. We weren't mistreated during our imprisonment, but neither of us was allowed to leave the guest house or to interact with anyone besides the guards. We didn't find out until Cami rescued us that everyone, including our parents, had been told we were dead.

I secretly wondered if that was the event that drove Cami into my arms. Until our rescue, I knew Cami had feelings for me, but she refused to make any plans for the future. Even though I brought it up at Zandra's estate, Cami wouldn't entertain even the idea of marriage. During those three weeks when she believed I was dead, something had changed in her. I was worried that it was just the shock of finding us alive, that maybe she'd wake up one morning and decide she didn't feel for me the way I felt for her.

I started broadcasting thoughts to Cami again, hoping she could hear me. "*You know, I wanted you to be mine from the first second I saw you. On our trip to Ireland when you told me you chose me, my heart ballooned. You are everything I've ever wanted and then some. I was worried that you only chose me because you were shocked to see me alive. That's why I didn't push you to call Will. I'm a frickin' idiot, okay? I should have had you call Will before we ever got off the plane. None of this would have happened if I'd have just made you call.*" I wiped the stupid tears away hard, glad that I was alone in the dark where no one could see me.

"*I never would have guilted you into choosing me. I was willing to wait decades for you if you needed them. I told you I'd wait as long as it took. I'll still wait as long as it takes; I'm not going anywhere.*" My eyes were pouring and the ache in my chest refused to subside. "*The last six days have been more than I could have ever hoped for. More than I'd ever allowed myself to dream of. You chose me, Cami. You chose me.*"

The savages who stole her would know my wrath soon. I would use every weapon in my arsenal. As I felt my fury for her kidnappers, I realized one of the weapons in my arsenal, whether or not Beau and Daniel approved, was Zandra.

Throughout the last week, I saw a whole different side of Cami. She was no longer the Centauride who didn't know her way around her new world. She was confident, smart, and decisive – I didn't think it was possible to want her more than I did at Zandra's house, but she'd proved me wrong on that front, too.

Centaurs don't date the way humans do. Physical contact of any kind is frowned on. If my family had seen us and how familiar we were with one another in Ireland, I could be in some serious trouble. I knew William was putting Cami's safety over customs, but I don't imagine he would have been thrilled, either.

Yet, even knowing the repercussions for our actions, I wouldn't have changed a single second in the time that we had together. Every time we were alone, we crossed the line a little bit further than we had the time before.

I wanted her so badly that my body ached for her. She always seemed so oblivious to it, too. I wasn't sure why I needed to tell her these things, especially when I was pretty sure she couldn't hear me. "*When you came out of the bathroom at the hotel, the night we'd found the pasture of Thessaly, wearing the nightgown: Wow.*" A smile I wasn't expecting stretched wide across my face at the memory. "*Frickin' wow, Cami.*"

My mind wandered to our short time at this hotel this morning. Had Daniel not called when he did, or if Phineas hadn't decided to make his appearance exactly when he did, I couldn't be sure what would have happened between us. I'd like to think that we would have put the brakes on, but I loved her, and more than that – I wanted her.

She believed that because she had been intimate with a human before she met me it would somehow make her less desirable. I'm sure I would never admit it to anyone except Cami, but it just made me want her more. She wasn't a pristine flower to be worshiped from afar. She didn't fit into the cookie-cutter image of what I'd grown to believe Centaurides to be. She was real. She had passion, desires, and this sexiness about her I'd never seen in another – Centauride or human. Who wants pristine when you can have perfection?

"*Cami, if you can hear me, I love you. I love everything about you. The Ronnie guy you told me about, I don't care. Just tell me where you are. You're mine. You belong to me.*"

CHAPTER 17

Zandra Chiron – Camille's Grandmother, San Diego, CA

I'd been searching for Camille and Drake for a week. William Strayer was more cunning than I had given him credit for being. I found the passenger manifest of his sons taking a vacation to San Diego. It didn't make sense that two of his sons would take a vacation to the very place Camille felt most at home. I was sure he had smuggled the couple here under the guise of his sons' names.

After four days the only thing I had turned up was William's son, Beau, and that vile half-breed, Daniel, who had come to my estate. It was time to go back to Charleston and retrace their steps. They couldn't stay hidden from me forever, and I couldn't afford to waste anymore time.

I was the leader of the Centaur Council. I didn't understand how Camille and Drake had successfully evaded me. I needed them apart before the Centaur society found out about Camille.

Seeing the future brings grave responsibility. The very night I brought Camille to my estate, I saw one horrific possibility play out in front of me.

I couldn't let that be her destiny.

At first, simply educating Camille seemed enough. She was as intelligent as her mother, and given the right information, she would choose the wise path. But as the days passed, the horrific possibility I'd seen began to solidify more rapidly.

She would live out her days as a Centauride, eventually taking my place as the leader of the Centaur Council, so long as she did not choose Drake Nash.

Choosing Drake would set a chain of events in motion that even my authority couldn't save her from. I'd made mistakes with her mother. I'd vowed not to make the same mistakes with Camille. History repeated itself right before my eyes, as if I were powerless to stop my own actions.

I had carried so much resentment for Angela over the years, there were days I thought it would swallow me whole. Camille looked exactly like her. When she spoke, her voice was Angela's. Her mannerisms, body language, even humor – it was so disturbing, but I could never bring myself to tell her how much I missed Angela.

The night of her arrival, I couldn't speak to her. It was as though I were looking in my daughter's eyes, the eyes I had forced into hiding with a heavy hand and a short temper. Instead of the contempt I remembered staring back at me from Angela's, Camille's harbored only fear. When I was finally able to speak to her, I had to keep reminding myself I was talking to my granddaughter, not Angela.

Fear was an improvement from contempt. Once Camille understood our past and her importance to our society, she would be able to embrace her role as a Centauride, she would gain her Chiron powers. She could be groomed to take my place in our society.

The only thing in the way was Drake Nash. If she chose him, nothing would be able to stop the repercussions. Both would share a dismal life together, they'd be on the run, and. . . I couldn't bear to think what would happen if they had the arrow. I'd known Drake's mother for years.

If Camille chose him, his bloodline would cease to exist – I couldn't allow that to happen, either. I had to find them, do whatever I could to keep the two of them apart.

My phone vibrated, quickly returning me to the present. I looked at my phone but did not recognize the number. I started to send it to voicemail when my inner voice told me to answer it.

I answered the cell phone, "Hello?"

"Zandra, it's Drake."

"Ahhh, back from the dead I see. And how is my granddaughter? Has she come to her senses yet?"

"They've taken her." Drake's words were hollow.

My mind screeched to life, "What?! Who's taken her?"

"Phineas. He's part of the Lost Herd. He took her about eight hours ago. Do you know where he would have taken her?"

"The Lost Herd?" It was coming true. . . all of it. . . right before my eyes. I took a breath, found my best condescending voice and said, "They are no more than a fable now, Drake. Zeus, himself, cast them out long ago."

"You're wrong. Phineas has her, and I need your help."

"What makes you think I would help you or that I even care for the whereabouts of Camille? You left my estate. You left my protection."

"Protection? Look, I'm not going to argue with you. You had the leader of the Lost Herd right under your nose and you suspected nothing. Now he's got Cami, and. . ." Drake paused as if the words burned his tongue, "I need your help."

Now may be my best opportunity, "I'll not help you unless. . ."

The boy cut me off, "I'll do anything. I just need you to help us find her."

"Agree to stay out of her life. Let her lead the life she is destined for. If you are no longer in the way, I'll find her."

"No! You will help me find her. You owe her that. I am her Centaur. You will help me." His voice was angry, demanding, the voice of a true warrior, not the sniveling I had expected of a love-struck boy.

I tapped my fingers on my purse. Their destiny was in motion. At this point I might be powerless to stop anything. Hercules' arrow was my last hope. "Or what?"

Drake's tone raged on, "She. . .chose. . . me. I am her Centaur. I will find her with or without your help. After everything you've done to her, you owe this to her. Do what you want, but you'll be judged by Zeus when you arrive at the pasture. The Chiron may become the next Lost Herd, and it will be at your hands."

He hung up. If only he knew what awaited him if he found the arrow before I did. The fool hadn't even told me where Phineas had taken her from. Up until now I'd been looking for Camille and I couldn't find her, so she was nowhere near San Diego. If she were in danger and anywhere near me, I would have felt it. No, she was not in California. I hadn't felt her presence in South Carolina before my departure, either. Would she have left the country?

I scrolled through the contacts on my phone and selected William's number. He picked up on the second ring, "Zandra, now is not a good time."

I'd never been one for pleasantries, so I simply asked, "Did you have a hand in it, William?" Silence echoed back at me over the phone. "Do you know where she's been taken?"

"Of course, I don't. I'm on my way to look for her now."

I needed to bluff enough to make him show me his cards, "Phineas has her." Drake would not have accused a Centaur of such a heinous crime unless he knew it to be true.

William sighed, "That's the assumption we're under, yes."

"Where are you searching?"

"Zandra, you've done enough damage. Stay away from my family."

"Are you aware that she has chosen Drake Nash?" More silence. It seems Drake had been telling me the truth on both counts. If she had not made her choice known, William would have denied it. "Have you located her brother?"

"What brother? No. Angela only had a daughter."

"You know better than that, don't you, William? You fathered the most powerful Centaur warrior the world has ever seen. Do not try to tell me you haven't looked for him."

"Do you hear yourself? Camille was kidnapped hours ago, we don't know where she is or what they're doing to her, and you're what? Chalking her safe return up as a lost cause and looking for her twin?"

"Phineas is very cunning. If he was in my employ and I did not detect his motives, you will not be able to find him unless he wants you to find him. Our best bet is to find her twin. They will have a connection like no other, and it's possibly our only hope for finding Camille."

"How would you know about their connection? They've never met."

"You forget, William. I, too, have a twin. Until we severed our connection to one another, we could locate each other anywhere."

"We're already in Rapid City; the trail's still hot. We'll find her." His voice sounded as though it had lost some of its strength. He had given me the information I needed; Rapid City, South Dakota. There was not a large Centaur population there; the winters were too cold. Angela had done well hiding him.

"I'm leaving San Diego now. I'll call when I arrive."

CHAPTER 18

Lacey's Father – Rapid City, SD

My son's body had not yet been laid to rest when Lacey insisted she was needed in South Dakota. Her injuries were already on the mend from the car crash this morning. She'd need a few days for the bone to repair itself in her leg, but otherwise she was okay. Luckily, I'd been able to contact Dr. Olreck. He was one of the few Centaurs in San Diego who was also a licensed physician. He signed her release paperwork from the hospital without anyone noticing her injuries were almost healed.

Lacey demanded I escort her to South Dakota to help a Centaur I didn't know. She hadn't even begun to grieve the loss of her brother or her betrothed yet. I worried that her emotions would get the better of her on the flight, but I'd been wrong.

She'd always been a tough kid. Centaurides are known for their skills, sought out for their special talents, but there was more to Lacey. If I had to give it a name, I could only describe it as an unwavering force of will.

Lacey had always been strong, never satisfied to sit idly by while her premonitions unfolded. She always wanted to get involved with them, to manipulate them. She refused to accept a premonition as anything more than a possibility.

Lacey had a premonition of Ted and Tom's death this morning before they had left the house; she was adamant that the two stay home. I only found out about her premonition after the car accident happened and both had left for the pasture.

Both boys were headstrong and refused to take orders from her. If I had known of her warning, I would have ordered them to stay home, but some things must just be fate. Sometimes no matter how badly you wish for an outcome, destiny has a different plan.

I wasn't blessed with an abundance of children, just two. Most Centaurs had four, some even ten, but my wife died when Lacey was two. When she left for the pasture, I didn't believe I would have the strength to raise Tom and Lacey on my own; little did I know that they would be the source of my strength and had been for the last two decades.

I wish she knew why she needed to be in South Dakota. I'm sure when she knows, I'll know. As we walked into the terminal from the frigid temperatures outside, a young human behind the counter commented, "It's another one. Hey, Spence, did ya see that jet? I've never seen so many private jets in my whole life."

"Oh, shore did. Fred's gonna' run outta' parkin' places soon."

The human named Spence looked closer at Lacey and me, and asked, "Hey, Mister, what's goin' on? What's with all the private planes?"

It was a sleepy little airport. Snow dusted the runway, and over a foot had been shoveled into piles on either side of the taxiway. He was right; all the planes stuck out like a sore thumb. Centaur family planes all carried the required FAA markings, but they were obvious. Each family plane was painted maroon with a yellow Centaur on the tail. Seeing one occasionally was normal, but as a rule, all families kept their planes in hangars. Very few were kept at public airports: most families maintained private runways in secluded areas near their homes. Once we found out what was going on, I'd mention to whoever was in charge that we may need to relocate a few of the planes to surrounding airports before the locals got more suspicious. I answered, "Family reunion," as we walked past him.

Spence called after me, "What family? The Trumps?"

Lacey smiled up at me, her voice soft, "Thanks for doing this, Dad." There wasn't anything in the world I wouldn't do for her, and she knew it, even if it meant delaying Tom's funeral. She'd already told me he was in the pasture with their mother, so at least I didn't worry about her being alone anymore.

I didn't want to pressure her, but it had been hours since she decided we needed to go. "Lacey, I'm still not sure why we're here."

"A friend's in trouble, Dad."

"What kind of trouble?"

She furrowed her eyebrows and shook her head. "I'm not sure. I've been getting these strange visions all day. Something important has happened."

"Where are we going?"

"I'm not sure."

I stopped just in front of the doors that led to the rental cars. For the first time in recent memory, I had a sliver of doubt. I motioned to the chairs just inside the door, and we sat down. "I've been accommodating, given the circumstances, but those are all Centaur planes out there. Is there some sort of battle being fought?"

"I think. . . more like a coup. I'm not sure. I just know someone needs me."

"Who?"

"I already told you, Beau Strayer."

"Sweetheart, I don't know Beau Strayer."

"You'll meet him," she smiled before she added, "and you'd better be on your best behavior."

It felt as though Lacey were hiding something from me. I was doing everything in my power to mask my frustration, but she had to sense that I wasn't happy about being kept in the dark. "Why is my behavior of any relevance?"

"Because he's the reason you didn't lose Tom and me both this morning in the crash. He's the Centaur who pulled me from the car and took care of me until the ambulance arrived. I thanked him at the hospital, but when I did, I realized a Centauride was going to be in trouble and she needed him."

"His wife?"

"I don't think so."

"His betrothed?"

"Dad, I don't know. All I know is it's someone important to him."

"Why you?"

She looked back through the windows at all of the family planes; we could see all the jets racked and stacked on the tarmac. "I don't know, Dad. Something's going on. All those planes are here for a reason."

She was right. The only time I had seen this many Centaur planes gathered at one airport was when there was a dispute between herds or at the meetings at Centauride in South Africa. If a Centauride was in trouble, it was common for families to band together, but never this many.

Something important was going on. Before we moved from our airport seats, I called my brother. "Norman, it's me. Lacey and I just landed in Rapid City, South Dakota. It's a long story and not one to share over the phone. There are at least twenty *family* planes at the airport, and from the looks of it, at least that many chartered planes, as well. Do you know what's going on here?"

Norman and I spoke almost every day. He had always had a knack for knowing when something important was going on. I was disappointed when he answered, "In South Dakota? No, I haven't heard a word. Do you want me there?"

"No. We've only just arrived. I need you to find out what's going on. Call me back."

I flipped the phone shut. Lacey looked at me, questioning without words. "Sweetheart, we don't know what we're walking into. I don't want to sound callous, but as of this morning you are no longer betrothed. Promise me you'll take precautions. Stay with me at all times."

Her green eyes looked up into mine. She knew my meaning without me having to say it. From the time she was sixteen, I'd had fathers applying pressure to me for a betrothal. I wanted to give her as much time as I could, but sadly I had only been able to buy her two years.

When she turned eighteen, I told her she needed to choose a Centaur or I would select one for her. Centaur fathers could be ruthless: I'd had my job threatened, envelopes stuffed with cash nearly forced on me, and one that made me laugh – season tickets to the Chargers. Lucky for Lacey they hadn't had a winning season! Thankfully, Lacey made her own decision. She'd selected Ted on her eighteenth birthday. He had been close to her age, headstrong and willful, but he had been her choice. I breathed a sigh of relief after making the phone call to Ted's parents.

A sadness that only a father could understand washed over me. She wouldn't be given long to grieve before Centaurs would again be bombarding her. I sympathized with their desperation. I felt for the Centaurs, but few, if any, knew of the emotional toll on the Centaurides.

Lacey knew which hotel the others were gathering in. We drove to the hotel with little conversation. I was too lost in thought, dreading the coming months. All Centaurides were prized, but Lacey's bloodline was predominantly from the Barber herd. As a result, she could see the future, sometimes just glimpses, other times with uncanny accuracy. When word spread of her abilities at sixteen, I was overwhelmed by the number of Centaurs who came to introduce themselves. I dreaded that the same process would start all over again, too soon.

Lacey stayed close to me while I checked us in. She was careful not to make contact with anyone, preferring instead to stay close to my side with her eyes pointed toward the floor.

"Lacey? Lacey is that you?"

She cautiously looked at the young Centaur who had approached. I heard her let out a breath as if pleased to see him. "Daniel, oh, I was worried we wouldn't be able to find you."

He asked, "What're you doing here?" I looked at the Centaur standing in front of Lacey. No, he wasn't a Centaur – he was human. I instinctively took a step in front of her.

Lacey pushed my arm to shove me to the side. "Get a grip, Dad. This is Daniel Ward. He's a friend of Beau Strayer."

I was confused: Centaurs and humans didn't mix. They were beneath us. The last thing I needed was a half-breed in the mix now that she was available. Instead of forcing myself between them, I waved the little plastic cards and said, "Lacey, I've got our key cards. Let's go."

She glared at me. I hadn't seen her do that in years, and I took a step away as if her stare could produce a laser beam. I doubted a laser could inflict much more damage than she could. She turned her attention back to the half-breed. "So, you didn't get here in time?"

The half-breed's face was laced with pain. His voice lowered when he answered, "No. We were too late." He reached out and put a hand on Lacey's shoulder. I felt a guttural growl release from me on pure reflex. Lacey shot me a second glare. He ignored my warning and added, "But, hey, thanks for your help earlier. We wouldn't have even known if you hadn't told us. They got her a few hours before we got here."

"I'm so sorry." Lacey hated it when she couldn't stop the bad premonitions. I was silently kicking myself for not asking more questions during the flight. This had to have been a tough day for her: two premonitions in the same day and both had come true.

The half-breed asked, "So, what are you doing here?"

She chewed her lower lip. Lacey only did that when she was nervous about something. "I thought maybe I could help. I mean, I've been having weird visions all day. I don't know who she is, but I think I was connected to her for a while. Not long after you left the hospital, I tried to connect with her. I tried to warn her, but I couldn't make the connection. I could see things through her eyes, at least for a little while, then everything went black. I didn't know what happened, but I thought you might need me."

A Centaur walked past and Lacey began shouting. "You, hey! Hey, you. Yes!" Lacey had gotten the Centaur's attention and motioned him over. Without any of the manners she seemed to come by naturally, she blurted out, "Who are you?"

The Centaur didn't take offense, but he responded, "Excuse me?"

"My name's Lacey; I'm a seer." A look without any sort of recognition spread on his eyes as she continued, "I saw you a few hours ago in a vision. The girl, you were with the girl!"

The Centaur's expression soured. He nodded respectfully, "Yes. I was. I'm Drake Nash. I was with her. . . I was there. . . when they took her." His voice cracked. I wasn't sure how all the pieces were fitting together. Lacey had come to help the Centaur who pulled her from the car accident, Beau Strayer, who we had yet to meet. A Centauride important to him was in danger, but it was not his wife or his betrothed. Judging from the reaction of this Drake Nash in front of us, Drake had been the Centauride's betrothed.

I grew tired of trying to assemble the jigsaw puzzle while I was still missing pieces. I stepped forward and asked, "I'm Lacey's father. Who was taken?"

The Centaur who stood before me was broken. Not the physical injuries, although he must have been in a tough battle and fought hard. There was no swelling in his face, but the remnants of bruises that were only hours old still shadowed his face. He answered, "It was Camille

Strayer."

"Who is Camille Strayer?" Hmmm, Beau Strayer, the Centauride had to have been a sister or a cousin. That explained his connection. I didn't know the name Camille Strayer as anyone of importance, certainly not enough to warrant this much attention.

Drake's answer was absent any emotion when he answered, "Her mother was Angela Chiron."

I felt my heart skip. It couldn't be. Angela was dead, or so I and every other Centaur believed. She was the closest thing to nobility any of us had ever known. Angela had been of betrothal age when I was. Every Centaur on the planet knew of Angela: she was the last female Chiron; then she disappeared. She had been betrothed to Winfield and Unice's descendant, Kyle Richardson.

We all believed she'd backed out of the marriage, so he had killed her. Her body was never found, and he had never been held accountable for the crime. It couldn't be. I wanted to make sure I had heard him correctly, "I'm sorry, you said this Camille, *she* was the daughter of Angela Chiron?"

He nodded. "She was kidnapped late this morning."

Rage grew within me. How could this have happened? It was every Centaur's duty to defend the Chiron family. Why was her safety in the hands of one Centaur? "Has the Centaur Council been notified?"

Drake shook his head, "I don't know. Her father is over there." Drake pointed to a Centaur surrounded by young Centaurs. He was not someone I'd seen before. I'd never claimed to be very political, but having a Centauride of age forced me to get to know the influential families. I had never heard of William Strayer.

My curiosity had definitely been piqued. I didn't like the idea of leaving Lacey alone, but she seemed to feel comfortable with them. I would only be a few feet away. "Lacey, excuse me. Remember what I told you."

"I remember, Dad. I'll be okay."

So many thoughts were racing in my mind, I had trouble keeping up. When I was mere feet away, I held out my hand to the distraught father, "Mr. Strayer, my daughter, Lacey, and I are at your service. She is a seer; how can we help?"

He held out his hand, "Hello, brother. I'm William Strayer. These are my sons. We are mounting a search now."

"Did I hear it correctly? Your daughter is the daughter of Angela Chiron?"

A stoic expression looked back at me. "Yes. Yes, she is."

"Has the Centaur Council been notified?"

William flinched, "Not yet. We didn't want to draw more attention to ourselves than we already have. Right now we've taken over this entire hotel. There are no humans other than the hotel staff."

"You are mistaken," I angled around and turned to the half-breed Lacey spoke to. "There is one over there talking to my daughter."

"Ah, yes. That's Daniel. Although his blood isn't pure, his Centaur lineage is strong. He's a close friend of Camille, so he has been permitted to stay."

"Your daughter has a half-breed friend? As a pet?"

William laughed heartily, and I could tell from his reaction that he did not approve of this friendship. I was pleased that Lacey had never befriended one. "No, Camille was raised as human. She's a recent addition to the Centaur society."

I started assembling what he had said in my mind. Camille was the daughter of Angela Chiron and William Strayer. William had four sons flanking him, but they could not be Angela's. Chiron Centaurides only gave birth to a single set of fraternal twins: always a son and a daughter. How was this possible? He could not be the father of Angela Chiron's daughter unless his sons were adopted. But the resemblance between William and his sons was uncanny. They were not adopted.

To make sure I wasn't missing something, I asked for clarification. "But these Centaurs are your sons?"

"Yes, Brent, Ben, Bart, and Bruce," each nodded a silent greeting as William pointed to them. His eyes darted around the room, as he added, "Beau is around here somewhere."

Still not understanding, "You have five sons *and* you fathered twins with Angela?"

William lowered his voice, "I do not have time to share the details with you. As you can imagine, in this instance, notifying the Centaur Council would not be in Camille's best interest. I appreciate your offer to assist, but understand if you lack conviction."

Lack conviction? William Strayer broke the first of Zeus's seven tenets. Those were the rules set down by Zeus himself: they were the laws all Centaurs followed. How could he have taken two wives? It wasn't possible. "William, it is not my conviction in question, it is your integrity. Camille cannot be the daughter of Angela Chiron."

He didn't answer me. I saw a petite older woman with long flowing silver hair step through the hotel entrance. All the Centaurs in the lobby backed away to allow her passage. She was walking directly toward William. I would recognize her anywhere. It was Angela's mother, Zandra Chiron.

The woman didn't acknowledge my presence. Instead she asked, "William, have you located Camille?"

"Zandra, I'm so glad you could join us." From William's tone, nothing could have been further from the truth. "I trust you had a pleasant trip?"

"No small talk, William. Do you know how much attention you're drawing to us? You booked an entire hotel, kicked out the humans, and the airport looks like O'Hare. Are you an idiot?"

His answer was respectful. "I believed it better to relocate the humans to avoid the risk of their overhearing what we are or what we're doing here. The hotel staff believes we are here for a family reunion. They've been told we require no support, so what little staff is on hand is simply handing out room keys and conducting parameter surveillance. I called the airport. All available pilots are shuttling aircraft to Omaha, Sioux City and Denver to private hangars; only five private jets and five charters will remain in Rapid City."

Zandra nodded. I shouldn't be party to this conversation. My curiosity, rather than having been satisfied, grew by leaps and bounds. I needed to call my brother, Norman, and fill him in. I backed away a few steps, allowing the two to strategize as I walked back over to the area of the lobby where Lacey stood.

She was very animated when I returned. "Dad, *this* is Beau."

I sized him up. He looked very much like his father, which worried me. His father had children with two different Centaurides; he had broken the first of the seven tenets. He couldn't keep this a secret. His actions will bring the wrath of the Centaur Council down on his family. Putting on my best poker face, I held out my hand to Beau and said, "I understand I owe you a thank-you for your actions this morning."

"I wish I could have done more."

His answer was genuine. It hit me that if he chose, he could enact the third Centaur tenet. A pit began to form in my stomach. I needed to get Lacey back on a plane to San Diego. I didn't want to let on that my worst nightmare could come true. "Lacey tells me you pulled her out just before the explosion."

"I did. I heard the two warriors galloping to the pasture immediately after. They didn't suffer."

It struck me that he mourned their loss, although he had never met Tom or Ted. Strange. Not at all the response I would have expected. "Thank you, for that; and for giving me Lacey back. She's all I have left." I quickly changed the subject to try to shift the focus off of Lacey, "So, your father tells me Camille is your sister?"

"Yes." Beau's gaze moved to the distraught Drake, "Drake is her betrothed."

Finally the pieces were fitting together. I was sure when they were all assembled it would still look like a Picasso, but at least I understood why Lacey felt the need to help. She owed her life to Beau. He looked much older than she, but if he were still within eligibility age, it would be within his rights to claim her as his own.

Camille Strayer was, in fact, the last Chiron Centauride and had been kidnapped. The fact that her father had broken one of Zeus's tenets to the Centaur was dangerous, and I worried what it would mean if Beau claimed Lacey as his. A debt would be paid for breaking the tenet, and the payment would not be isolated to William. His whole line would pay the price when word of his actions became known.

CHAPTER 19

Phineas – Leader of the Lost Herd, at his home, FL

"I said, give her another shot!"

Sebastian cringed but held his ground, "Phin, she doesn't need it. She's still out cold."

Sebastian rarely disregarded an order, and I couldn't think of a time when he had stood up to me for anything of consequence. He was my nephew, was fiercely loyal, and could be trusted to do what he was told. I reminded him, "If she gains consciousness, we'll have a hundred Centaurs on us in a matter of hours. Keep her out until we get things in order."

"If we keep sedating her, we're going to need to give her an IV or something. It's been over twelve hours since we got here." Although loyal, he didn't want his hands dirty, or at least not dirtier than they already were. He had been an active participant in the kidnapping, but he wasn't happy about it.

My frustration wasn't with him. I purposely calmed myself down and answered, "Then give her an IV, but make sure she stays out."

"We're going to have to get a doctor here."

"Fine, get a doctor, get a nurse, for all I care you can assign a candy-striper, but do not let her wake up."

Sebastian left the room, and I was alone with my thoughts. Drake Nash was alive. I told them to check before we left. Idiots. She'd already chosen him. As long as he lives, he will have a hold on her. Unless she rejects Drake's betrothal pledge, she may not be able to unite with my son.

Camille could bring legitimacy to the Lost Herd. The Centaur Council wouldn't be able to destroy a precious Chiron. They would have to accept us back into the Centaur Society. All the careful planning my father had done twenty-three years ago could be lost because these idiots didn't bother to check for a pulse.

Zandra had the right idea. She could step down as the Chairman of the Council and pass the torch to Camille rather than to Angela's brother, Angelo. The thought of Angelo made my skin crawl. How he bore the Chiron name baffled us all. I'd always heard when twins were involved that one was as evil as the other was good. Angela had been known for her kindness, her beauty, and her grace. Her twin, Angelo, was well known, but not in a good way.

Most of his life Zandra had tucked Angelo away in South America, in remote villages where his exploits would not catch the attention of Centaurs or humans. No way would she turn over the Centaur Council to him; I was convinced she had long ago decided to outlive her son. Camille was the best choice to replace Zandra as the Chairman. I wasn't sure how Zandra would explain Camille's other bloodline if anyone were to become aware. Camille was a Chiron and a Tak, but Zandra had always had a way of spinning things in her favor. Now was the time for action.

William Strayer was a Tak, and if Camille were to rise as the Chairman of the Centaur Council, word of her lineage would spread quickly. The Centaur Council would have no choice but to accept her and, by extension, accept the Lost Herd. For added measure, having

Camille betrothed to my son would solidify the safety of all remaining Tak Centaurs. My teeth grinded as the thought of Drake Nash came to the surface. I needed to get him out of the way. A second team had already been dispatched to tie up that loose end.

Drake Nash would no longer be a concern, and when Camille becomes betrothed to my son, LeRoy, I will carry significant influence. The Lost Herd will no longer have to hide in the shadows, denying our legacy.

Sebastian returned. When the door swung open on me and my thoughts, I immediately crouched into a defensive posture. "Easy, Uncle Phin. It's just me." A thin grin appeared on his lips, and if it had been anyone but me, I'm sure he would have poked fun at my response.

He already knew the severity of the action we had taken. I thought it only fitting he understand why. "Sebastian, do you know why we're doing what we're doing?"

"It's not for me to question your methods, Uncle Phin. You can trust me."

"Indeed I can." I answered honestly. Sebastian was, in fact, more trustworthy than my own sons. I hadn't included them on the mission as they were headstrong, willful, and would not have followed my instructions. "Did your father ever tell you why Zeus cast our family out from the other Centaurs?"

Sebastian cocked his head to the side. This subject was never spoken of. To our young Centaurs, it was taboo. His eyes were curious, but he didn't press for information; his quiet respect told me he could be trusted with our secrets. "Our family successfully deceived the gods. Doing so proved that our family was a threat. The skill our bloodline has which the other Centaur bloodlines do not possess is to plant memories in others' minds. It seemed a harmless skill, barely more than a parlor trick, until the Centauride Phyllis used her skill against the gods."

I watched Sebastian's reaction. His expression remained unchanged. "What I am about to tell you is only for the tight-lipped. You are not permitted to share this story with anyone outside the Lost Herd, and only those in the Lost Herd who you believe would sacrifice their lives before revealing it. Do you understand?"

"I do, Uncle." Sebastian made a fist and crossed his right arm diagonally over his chest. It was a symbol among our herd, a silent gesture that we could bestow on one another. I'd seen it many times from strangers in strange cities. The gesture meant many things: sometimes it was simply "hello," other times it meant "I have your back," but this time it meant, "your secret is safe with me."

Centaurs of the Lost Herd were different than other Centaurs. We could not only feel the presence of another Centaur, but distinguish our own bloodline from the others, too. It wouldn't be safe to speak openly to a Centaur in front of others, so this gesture was adopted as a way to acknowledge our shared lineage with a stranger, without putting the other at risk.

I doubled up my fist and stretched it across my heart, as well. "Phyllis met Sisyphus, the King of Ancient Corinth. King Sisyphus was a mortal who had been known for his desire to cheat death. Phyllis thought it would be entertaining to plant the idea in the mind of King Sisyphus that Charos, the ferryman who carried souls across the River Styx, could be captured.

She inserted the thought that if Charos were chained to the gates on the underworld side of the river with the three-headed dog Cerberus, the ferry would no longer traverse the river and mortals would no longer die. King Sisyphus took this vision and did exactly as his memory instructed him, chaining Charos to the gates on the other side of the River Styx in Hades. Phyllis had been right, and no more humans died – even the old and feeble lived."

Sebastian rarely asked questions, but I was giving him information about our family that had been withheld from him. He shook his head slightly, "But how could King Sisyphus have traveled on the ferry if he were still alive and in his body? Only souls are permitted on the ferry."

"How he was able to accomplish it was never part of the story that my father shared with me. I just know that the actions of King Sisyphus' were the result. Regardless of her intentions, the memory was inserted in his mind by the Centauride Phyllis."

"I still don't know how that was such a horrible crime? As you said, it was akin to a parlor trick."

The gods were furious with King Sisyphus. After investigating, they realized that it was a Centauride from the Tak family that had planted the idea in his head. As punishment, the Tak family was shunned by all other Centaurs, forbidden ever to return to the pasture of Thessaly. Phyllis' actions condemned us to becoming the Lost Herd."

"So, for simply inserting a thought in a human's head, our whole bloodline was cut off from the other Centaurs?"

"The gods believed that the humans would begin to worship King Sisyphus, and in doing so, it would reduce their power over the humans. The gods felt that we were a risk that had to be isolated before word could spread of what Phyllis had done."

"So the gods kicked us out of Thessaly? Why did the other bloodlines not come to our aid?"

"We were not gods, Sebastian. The Tak family was Centaur, and playing a trick on the gods, regardless of intentions, is never looked upon favorably. The other bloodlines were not willing to anger the gods."

"But our ancestors didn't kidnap or chain up Charos."

"No."

"Why did the Centaurs from the other bloodlines hunt our ancestors? Are those stories true?"

"Yes, they're true. Most believe our family has long since died out; the overt hunting of our bloodline stopped over a millennia ago. When Phyllis first played the trick on King Sisyphus, the gods did not tell the other families what had happened, only that Zeus himself cast us out from the pasture. Word also spread that Zeus wanted vengeance on the

Tak family.

Any time Centaurs from the remaining six bloodlines encountered a Centaur from our bloodline, they attacked without mercy, even killing our wives and our children. The remnants of the Tak family banded together and sought a pasture where we could be protected from the gods and the other Centaurs, to live out the rest of our existence in peace. We were protected so well that centuries passed, and they believed we had perished."

"I don't understand. Did we kidnap this Centauride," pointing to Camille's unconscious body, "to seek revenge on Zeus?"

"No, we kidnapped her to seek legitimacy."

Sebastian did not see the connection. "My daughter, Violet, is one of the few Centaurides from the Lost Herd. If we timed it perfectly, Violet would be able to plant the memory in Camille's head that she was already betrothed to my son, LeRoy. Violet could make Camille believe that Drake had abandoned her, better yet, Drake had handed her over to me for a price. She would believe that I bought her."

"How can tricking a single Centauride gain our legitimacy?"

Execution would have to be precise. If we woke her up and Violet couldn't get the ideas planted quickly enough, Camille might know we were manipulating her memories. "Camille will be the next chairman of the Centaur Council. She is the last Centauride heir of Chiron. If she openly accepted our family, the remainder of the Council would follow suit. Zeus still holds the Chiron family in high esteem, but to ensure they do not become too powerful, he limited the number of direct descendants."

If we were successful, the Tak family would no longer be the source of whispers tantamount to the Boogie Man. My daughter, Violet, shared no other bloodline but the Tak and was one of the few Centaurides still able to plant memories in the minds of others. If she were unsuccessful, we would again be forced into hiding. The rewards outweighed the risks.

Sebastian must have sensed that I was lost in thought on how best to execute the plan. He interrupted my thought with, "Uncle Phin, I found a doctor who can be here in an hour. He's willing to work for cash, and he isn't interested in the patient's name."

"Good work. How soon will he be here?"

"He'll be here any minute."

I looked Sebastian in the eye to be sure he understood my meaning. "When we're done, you know the doctor's not going anywhere, right?"

Sebastian dropped his eyes to the floor. "Yeah, I assumed that. No loose strings, right Uncle Phin?"

"That's right, no loose strings."

"I think we should move her to a bedroom, get her away from all the racket."

"Fine, put her in the bedroom next to the den. She was like Houdini after she left Zandra's place. I want a watch on her the whole time, understand?"

"Yeah. Got it."

CHAPTER 20

Drake Nash – Hotel near Crazy Horse Mountain, SD

What was William waiting for? We had all been at the hotel for more than twenty-four hours. He said he was going to mount a search, but only a few Centaurs had been sent out, and they had come back hours ago – empty-handed. Zandra had arrived, and the two of them were huddled in a corner together. My patience was gone. If they wouldn't do anything to get her back, I'd do it on my own. I couldn't wait for Cami's dad any longer.

I was halfway to the elevator when Zandra's voice stopped me short. "Drake, would you come here, please?"

My pulse quickened. This was what I had waited for; this was why I had called her in the first place. I found myself standing in front of her with William looking nervously to the side. Her tone was pleasant, neither heated nor angry, "I need you to leave the search to William, Drake."

"What? No."

"I'm sure you find it hard to believe, but all my intervention has been for both your and Camille's protection. If you continue your search, neither of you will be happy with the outcome."

Nearly speechless, the only words I could find were, "She chose *me.* I am her Centaur."

Flatly, Zandra replied, "I am aware of her choice."

"So, you will ignore her wishes? Again?"

"I know if you don't leave now, I won't be held responsible for the outcome. Go to your family. I've known Hallenjah for many years; your mother misses you. Let us, Camille's family, work on her safe return."

"I won't abandon her, Mrs. Chiron."

"Aaaah, yes, Drake. If you could see through my eyes, you would leave now. Camille would want you to go."

William didn't make eye contact with me. I started to argue with her, but understood her mind was made up. I didn't regret asking her to help find Cami, but I had no intention of leaving. Phineas had her. I didn't know much else, but I knew that much.

I ran up to our room, taking steps two at a time. Our room had been cleaned, I didn't know by whom as the cleaning staff had been sent away. The blood that had soaked into the rug was nothing more than a memory now. My hand stretched out flat as I touched the area of the carpet where the Centaur had been killed with the table leg. Not only was the bloodstain gone, but the carpet was dry, too.

I found Camille's backpack tucked on the floor in the closet. I dug down to the very bottom, hoping it wouldn't be there, but it was. My hand emerged with the hideous spider that Eadie had given Cami in Ireland. I clasped the menacing charm in my hand, closed my eyes, and prayed, "*Athena, I don't need your protection from Zandra, but Phineas has taken Cami. She's not with me right now because I wasn't strong enough to defend her. I need your help to get Cami back. Please help me find her.*"

I didn't feel or hear anything. I tried again to see if I had some sort of connection to Cami. "*Cami? Cami, can you hear me? It's Drake. Where are you? Tell me where they took you."* My hands began to shake. I could feel the loneliness I had felt in Zandra's guest house creeping back to me. In the weeks that I spent in that guest house, not knowing what had happened to Cami tore me apart. I remembered staring at the walls, sure I wouldn't see her again until it was too late.

When I was given a second chance with Cami, I vowed I'd never let her out of my sight. A single tear formed in the corner of my eye. I felt it drip down my face. Why would Phineas do this? Why would he take her away from me?

They had drugged her before they took her away. I'd watched one of them plunge the syringe into her neck. Was she awake now? Was she hurt? What if they had poisoned her?

"Cami, if you can hear me, I love you. I've loved you from the very first second I saw you. You are mine. When the breeze blows across your face: that is my caress. When the blanket of fog rolls in so thick you cannot see: those are my arms covering you. When you look up into the heavens: the star winking at you is me. You aren't alone. I promise I'll never rest until I find you."

I didn't hear a voice. I didn't get any kind of sense for where Cami was. Somehow I knew what I needed to do. Reaching for the door, I hesitated a second. I had asked Athena to help me, but maybe that wasn't the right goddess. She was vengeful and jealous. Those weren't the feelings in my heart for Cami. I walked over to the dresser where an unopened bottle of wine stood next to a basket of fruit. I picked up the basket, examined the fruit, and removed a bruised apple from the basket.

I threw the bruised apple in the trash and laid the basket of fruit on the floor in front of me. I fell to my knees, and bowed so low that my nose was just above the carpet, and I prayed. "Blessings my Aphrodite. My love has been stolen. Protect her. Keep her safe. I belong to her and will not rest until I have found her. Please. . . please protect her until I am able to protect her myself."

I felt a twinge of warmth. I couldn't be sure if Aphrodite had heard my prayer or if my own heart had reacted to my pleas. I stood up, wrote a note on hotel stationery that read, "Do not move. This basket is an offering to Aphrodite."

I ran to the stairs and returned to the lobby. Nothing had changed. William and his sons were tucked away in a corner with Zandra. I felt a fire beginning to burn inside me; I'd called her and asked for her help, yet she stood across the room and did nothing but try to convince me to leave. Zandra wore a smug look before turning her attention back to William.

I caught Lacey's attention and motioned for her to come over. Lacey looked concerned, but I cut her off before she could ask me a question, "I need your help."

She reached out and touched my forearm. Her touch sent a strange sensation through my body: not the way it felt when Cami touched me, but the way it feels when your body is sunburned and an ice cube contacts your skin – a welcomed and comforting touch.

Without an explanation of what I needed, Lacey answered, "Drake, I see who you're looking for."

Lacey had been asked by nearly everyone where Cami was, but even Zandra couldn't give that answer. I think Lacey was pleased to be able to finally give someone an answer they needed. "Cameron lives on Warrior Way in an old farmhouse. Look for an old blue pickup truck in front and a henhouse just to the side."

I was pleased that I didn't need to explain myself. She was a talented Centauride. Lacey knew instinctively what I was after. I wondered silently how Lacey could know exactly where Cami's twin brother was while Zandra and the others were clueless.

Still maintaining her hold on my forearm, she answered my silent question quietly, so no other ears would hear. "You are her Centaur. She is connected to you. Cameron is her twin. Whether you know it or not, you share a similar connection to him, too."

I didn't even try to mask my appreciation. "Thank you, I don't want anyone to know where I'm going. It's my only chance to save Cami. Will you keep my secret?"

She looked down. Lacey wasn't comfortable with deception, even if it was for a good reason. I didn't want to put her in an awkward position, so I offered, "Would you be willing to give me a fifteen minute head start? They're going to ask you where I went. If you could just hold them off long enough for me to get to Cameron's and talk to him, I might have a chance to find Cami."

She eagerly agreed. Her smile was so bright I worried it might draw attention as every other face in the lobby looked sullen. "Any more time would be great, but if I can get there before everyone else, I can tell Cameron's guardian what's going on and get him to safety. With any luck, I'll get what I need to save her."

Lacey nodded her understanding. I could only hope she could make a wish reality when she answered, "Be safe, Drake."

CHAPTER 21

Drake Nash – Camille's twin brother's house, SD

I had asked for a fifteen minute head start, but I hoped she'd reconsidered and given me thirty. I used the rental car's GPS, but it didn't have any better idea where Warrior Way was than I did. After having driven past the same unmarked, snow-covered dirt road several times, I noticed a small faded sign nailed to a tree. It read "Cameron's Collectables," with an arrow pointing down the road. Crazy Horse's mountain was directly in front of the little dirt road. The mountain was easily seven miles from this road, but as I turned down the lane I could feel the mountain's eyes staring at me through the barren winter trees.

I stopped long enough to look at the mountain through the rear view mirror. All I could make out was the enormous head peeking over the top of the mountain, as if the mountain itself were watching the little road I was parked on.

My heart skipped then began racing, the same way it did when I was near Cami. He was here. I eased down the dirt road, my heart still throttling wide open in my chest. The steering wheel felt wet under my hands as my nerves took control of my body.

I pulled up in front of a house that had a 1970's Ford pickup; at some point in the last forty years it had been blue. To the right of the house was a small empty chicken coop, both just as Lacey had described. I didn't waste any time, preferring to sprint to the house's front door.

The man who answered the door was unmistakably Cami's brother. He had the same symmetrical face, the same brown hair, and the same milk-chocolate colored eyes. He was absent her charismatic demeanor, instead adopting a curt, "Sorry partner, closed 'til 10 a.m. tomorrow." He moved to close the door on me. I wasn't sure how many after-store-hour visitors he would have had; judging from the signage on the main road, only locals would know this store's location.

"Wait, I'm not here to shop. I'm Drake, Drake Nash. I'm here about your sister."

He shook his head. "I think you've got the wrong guy. I don't have a sister." He moved to close the door a second time.

I jammed my foot in the door to prop it open. "Yes, you do, and she's in trouble. I need your help."

He gave me a semi-hostile look. I began to question whether I had gone about this the wrong way. It may have been a better idea to do this with William. "Look, you don't know me, but I know about you. You were raised by a guardian. Could I talk to him? I can get this cleared up right away."

"A guardian? My dad doesn't live here. Now move your foot."

"I know a lot about you, Cameron. Your father is William Strayer, your mother was Angela Chiron. Your grandmother is Zandra Chiron, and I met your Great-Uncle Zethus in Ireland just last week. Look, I really need your help."

"My dad's Roger Brown. My mom ran off when I was a baby. You got the wrong guy. Now go on!" Outwardly he seemed frustrated, but my connection with Cami allowed me to sense things with her. This was her twin; I could feel it. I could feel Cami through him and the worry he tried to mask behind the frustration.

I started searching my mind for a shred of evidence that would make him believe me. I had my phone with me and had taken pictures of Cami while we were in Ireland. "Hold on, let me show you a picture of your sister."

"I already told you, I don't have a sister. Get off my property a'fore I git you off."

I fumbled with the pictures until I found one of her standing in front of a moss-covered rock. The flowing green hills were behind her, fog settled low to the ground. It wasn't a close-up of her face, but the resemblance to Cameron was uncanny. Even he had to see it. "Here," I held the phone up to him, "this is Cami. Tell me she doesn't look just like you?"

"Yeah, she's real pretty. Now git."

"Look, I don't care if you believe me. She's in danger and I need something from you."

"The only thing you're going to get from me is buckshot square in your ass if you don't git back in that car."

I glanced at my watch. They'd be here any minute. "An arrow. A very special arrow."

"I got lots of arrows, arrowheads, tomahawks in the store, and I'll be happy to show 'em to you, *tomorrow.*" Cameron kicked my foot and tried to close the door.

I wedged my shoulder in the door jam. I was too close. Cami needed me to make him understand. "I'm sorry I don't have time for that. Your family is probably already on their way here." Cameron's eyes grew large, and I recognized the look staring back at me – panic. Cameron knew more than he was letting on.

"Roger told you, didn't he? He said never to look for your family, am I right? Do you know why he told you that? Because your mother was hiding you. She died a few months ago, and they found your sister. I need that arrow so I can get her back." I hated to need something so badly, "Please."

The brief glimpse of panic I'd seen in his eyes was covered up by the slow country bumpkin impersonation he was so adept at making, "Afraid I don't know what you're talking about."

Cami's fate was in my hands. I didn't know what Will or Zandra would do if they got their hands on Cameron or the arrow. "You have a twin sister. She's in real trouble. I wouldn't be here if it weren't life and death."

Cameron stopped trying to push me away from the door. "Where's she now?"

"A man named Phineas kidnapped her. That arrow you have is very powerful. I need it, or I'll never get her back."

"How do I know you're on the level?" Cameron didn't deny he had it.

I shook my head, "You don't." Cameron was a Centaur. He was built like Cami, but there was no doubt he was deceptively strong. "You are a warrior. You should be able to sense another warrior. Do you feel anything strange near me?"

Reluctantly he answered, "I do."

"Using that same sense, do you feel as though you are in danger from me?"

"No."

"It's because I am to be your sister's husband. I am no threat to you because you are a part of her." I begged, "Help me."

Cameron stared at me for what felt like minutes. He must have decided that I wasn't lying. Cameron opened the door to let me walk past.

He had lost the hick accent that he was obviously used to using, when he asked, "So this family I was being hidden from, what do they want from me?"

"I don't think Angela meant for you to stay hidden forever. I think she wanted you to stay hidden long enough for you to grow and to make your own choices about your future." Did I really have time to get into the details? I chastised myself for not bringing Lacey with me; at least I would have had a warning if the others were getting close. I looked at my watch. I'd been gone from the hotel for forty-five minutes. There'd be a knock on the door any time, and my time would be up.

"Listen to me. This will be hard to accept, but it's the truth. You are a Centaur warrior, a very special warrior. Trust whomever you believe is trustworthy, but be wary of anyone you believe is deceitful. Your sister and I went all the way to Ireland to try to find a way to keep your grandmother from finding us. Unfortunately, I think she's on her way here now, and it turns out she wasn't the one we should have been worried about."

He didn't flinch at this revelation. He definitely knew more than he was letting on. Would his guardian have told him? I couldn't tell if it was genuine interest or if he was playing along when he asked, "My grandmother? Why would you be hiding from a grandmother?"

"Zandra is the most powerful Centauride in the world. She is the chairman of the Centaur Council and wanted to force Camille to marry a different Centaur."

"Sounds a little like Romeo and Juliet action, then huh?" As stressed out as I was feeling, he made me smile. Cameron was like a chameleon, switching quickly between a backwoods and an educated accent in the blink of an eye. He had probably been hiding most of his life, better aware of his surroundings and the company he kept than most.

"No, not at all like that, but a tragedy all the same. Cami and I escaped from Zandra's house a week ago. We found your Great-Uncle Zethus in Ireland, and he told us to look for you here."

"You two were looking for me?"

"You and the arrow."

His eyes narrowed. I'd said something wrong. Cameron was suddenly on the defense and was viewing me as a threat. His tone was icy when he answered, "I think I'll stay put and see who knocks on the door next. You can take a seat and wait with me." He motioned toward the sofa.

I heard car doors outside. I was too late. They were here. I'd never find her now. My heart was breaking as the reality took hold – I could lose her, really lose her. I saw Cameron walk over toward the fireplace mantle when we heard the knocking on the door. His expression gave him away. He didn't want to leave me alone in this room. He struggled with what to do. His eyes kept looking at a bookshelf in the corner.

A second knock, louder than the first sounded on the door, and Cameron found his hick accent again. "Looks like we've got some more guests. Best go welcome them to my humble abode."

As soon as he had cleared the threshold of the door, I was off the couch and searching the shelves. One very large, hardcover book stood out on the top shelf. The title was *Crazy Horse – a Photographic Chronology*. The book was an oversized picture book, one someone might keep on a coffee table. It set on the top shelf, by itself – centered with not a speck of dust around it.

I took a deep breath and one quick glimpse over my shoulder. I reached up to the top shelf, removed the book, and flipped it open. Pages had been sliced out of the book to allow room for a very ancient, ornate-looking arrow. I could feel the arrow's power without touching it. The arrow's tip had been encased in a plastic covering. The plastic covering sheltered the blood of the hydra that still clung to it. This had been Hercules' arrow.

I could hear Cameron's voice speaking to whoever was at the door. "I don't take kindly to people showin' up unannounced, but you aren't the first ones tonight. Come on into the living room, so we can sort this out."

I had what I'd come for. The arrow's charms would do Cameron no good now that they knew who he was and where he lived. I wheeled around looking for an escape route and found a door that went through a laundry room and out a back door. I ran as fast as I could run; I didn't look over my shoulder, and I didn't stop running. I had the arrow. No one could keep Cami away from me, and no one would try to hide her from me now that I had it.

CHAPTER 22

Camille – Four days after being kidnapped, FL

Haziness enveloped me. Flashes of light nearly blinded me while glimpses of conversation lay scattered. I tried to make sense of them. Drake's voice, "I can't sacrifice my bloodline. . . she'll be better off with you. . ." the image of Phineas shaking Drake's hand.

I screamed, "Nooooo!" Silence was the only thing that escaped me.

More flashes of light, a tunnel of haze, then Phineas's voice, "I accept your choice to marry my son. You will lead us out of the Dark Ages. . ." More silent screams from me.

I clung to the happiest memory I had. It was Drake's betrothal pledge. I tried to replay it in my mind, but the words were all garbled.

More flashes of light. A man I'd never seen before was giving me his betrothal pledge with Phineas watching. It didn't feel right.

None of it made sense. Where was I? What was the last thing I could remember? Drake. Drake in the hotel. Daniel called on the phone and warned us we were in danger. Phineas at the door. . . the blood. . . Drake was on the floor . . . then darkness.

Bright lights flashed in my mind. More images that didn't belong there. Something was wrong . . . seriously wrong. It felt like someone was *in* my head, a stranger, manipulating memories, planting images.

It was a woman. I zeroed in on her thoughts and sifted through the jumbled mess in my head. The memories she was trying to put into me were wrong, all wrong. Memories at the surface of my consciousness were in high definition, then static-filled images intermixed. The static-filled images weren't mine.

I began pushing against her. A new memory, not fuzzy like the others, shone through my mind.

I concentrated, willing all the strength left in my body to force her out of my head . . . to weed through the images that didn't belong there. My muscles ached and I felt numb, but I continued to push. I uprooted anything that wasn't clear, yanking out memories that didn't belong.

Minutes passed. Exhaustion drained me of what little strength remained, but I couldn't let my guard down. Whatever was happening had been an assault. Someone had been in my head, not like when my first Centauride friend, Bianca, had read my thoughts. Someone was in my head, inserting memories that didn't fit – memories that weren't true.

When I was sure I had gotten all of the memory remnants out of me, I went on the offense. I zeroed in on the Centauride who had been in my head. Physically she was only a few feet away, but her mind was locked away, her thoughts hidden behind a steel door. I wanted to rest, give into the exhaustion, let my body float effortlessly back to my dreams of Drake.

Just as I was about to fold back in on myself, I heard my mother's voice echo in my mind, "*Your life is full of choices. Choose wisely.*"

In that moment, if I were to escape back into my dreams, I would lose everything. A new strength began growing in me, anticipating what I must do. I stood at the steel door that was protecting the Centauride's thoughts. I reached for the handle. It wouldn't budge. I pounded feebly against it. I saw myself standing tall in front of the door. I summoned every ounce of strength I had, put my hand on the handle, and turned.

Someone was on the other side holding the handle in place with every ounce of her strength. I could hear her grunts behind the door, desperately trying to keep me out. I didn't relent. I let go of the notion that I could fail and kept turning. Sweat peppered my brow, veins stuck out on my hands, muscles throbbed in my arm, and finally . . . the door gave way. I was in the Centauride's head, behind her protective door and able to rummage around her thoughts.

Her mind replayed a conversation with Phineas speaking to William on the phone. William had called Phineas, threatening to publicly renounce the Lost Herd if I wasn't returned.

The Lost Herd had been hiding from the rest of the Centaurs for millennia. Phineas had a plan to try to convince me I was betrothed to his son.

He had set up a meeting with my father where Will thought I would be handed over. It was a ruse: I wouldn't be there, and they planned to slaughter my family. My mother's final gift to me was a family so I wouldn't be alone; Phineas wouldn't take her gift away from me.

I rummaged through all of the Centauride's memories, forcing her to hide in her own mind. She was defeated.

I felt my Chiron blood pumping through my veins. It was stronger than the Tak blood. I finally understood why people treated me differently. When Zandra said we had been touched by Zeus, it was all I could do not to roll my eyes at her. But with my rage toward Phineas, I could feel Zeus's rage, as well. If I were in different circumstances, the power would have been frightening.

The Centauride whose mind I had rummaged through had hidden herself away. I willed myself to fight off the drug in my veins that kept me immobile. I forced the drug out through my pores and felt my consciousness slowly returning.

I awoke to darkness. My hands and feet were bound. I had a blindfold on my face. I was a little disoriented, and the strength I had used against the Centauride had drained me.

A Centaur stood guard over me in this room – I could feel him. Whoever he was, this Centaur hadn't been at the hotel, and he was not masking any of his thoughts from me. I couldn't detect the Lost Herd's blood in him. I couldn't distinguish anything beyond the two bloodlines in my own veins, but his didn't feel like either. I wondered to myself how a dominant bloodline was established? Considering how long Centaurs had roamed earth, we should all have fractions of all bloodlines running through us, but in myself I only detected two. I couldn't explain how, but I knew this Centaur's bloodline was neither. When I got myself out of here, I needed to ask Drake.

I cleared my throat, "Hello, who's there?" I almost didn't recognize my own voice. My throat was dry and my voice barely more than a whisper.

"It is Brutus, my lady. Can I get you some water?" His thoughts were pure. He was not okay with this kidnapping. He heard what had been done to Drake and was furious with Phineas. I didn't answer at first, trying to pinpoint how he belonged to the Lost Herd, then I realized his wife was a member. I saw an image of the team that took me, and the young Centaur who Phineas had called Sebastian was Brutus's son.

My scratchy answer, "Yes, water."

He put his hand behind my back and gently lifted me to a seated position. He left the blindfold I was wearing in place as he brought a glass of water to my mouth. I'd never had someone else give me a drink, and I expected to dribble all over myself, but Brutus was far too attentive. He brought the glass up only enough for me to drink. When I'd had enough, he was quick to notice and to put the glass back down.

The water made an immediate difference. After having been knocked out for I didn't know how long, my throat should have been completely raw.

Either Brutus had just given me magic water, or I had crazy healing powers.

"Thank you, Brutus." The water made my mouth come alive. "More water." By the time he'd helped me slowly drink two full glasses, I felt much better.

"Can I get you some food, my lady?"

"No, not right now. Call me, Cami, though."

He didn't respond. "Brutus, you're a good man. Am I right?"

"Not as good as I'd like to be, my. . . Miss Cami."

"Do you have a family, Brutus?" I knew that he did; I'd already seen them in his mind.

"Yes, yes I do."

"I suggest you leave this place now. Go be with your family."

"Miss Cami, some of these men are. . . savages. I cannot leave you alone here."

I smiled. I hoped Brutus could see, but I couldn't be sure if we were in a lighted room or a dark one. No light penetrated the blindfold I wore. I looked into Brutus's future. It was like looking at every kid's ideal father: the one who coaches little league and soccer, the one who takes friends camping with his family. I wouldn't be able to forgive myself if anything happened to him. "I'm leaving. Untie me and go home to your family. You have protected me while I was unable to protect myself, but you need to think of your family now. Go."

"Miss Cami, I can't leave you."

I smiled at Brutus, "Watch this. If you decide I still need your protection, I'll do my best not to hurt you."

With as much volume as I had ever produced, I yelled, "Phineas, I'm awake! I want to see you *now*!"

Fear shown on his face, "Shhh, Miss Cami, he's not here. Be quiet. The others will hear you."

"I want them to hear me."

"No, you don't." His hands worked feverishly unbinding my hands and my ankles. I took off my blindfold as he asked, "Can you walk?"

I could see Brutus's thoughts: he was scared of Phineas. He tried to shelter my body, standing in between me and the door. More quietly I said, "Brutus, move to the corner of the room."

He reluctantly took a few steps to the right, but he was definitely not out of the way. I felt a Centaur approaching. I heard the door squeak as it was opened. "My lady, I'm so glad you're awake. Phineas will be pleased." His voice was jovial, as if we had just come back from a baseball game and he was taking me back home, rather than having been a part of my abduction.

"I have a message I'd like you to carry to Phineas." My voice was strong and full of authority. I still had the bottled rage pumping through my arteries. I could feel him cringe at my demand.

I watched the jumbled thoughts in his head trying to come up with a plan. He noticed the Centauride on the chair next to me, looking as if she were dead. He saw Brutus standing to the side. Ignoring my "message" comment, the Centaur began reiterating the false memories I had already ripped out of my head. "He understands the importance of you leading the Lost Herd. Your father has given his blessing for you to marry Phineas's son. Once you two have gotten to know each other and produce an heir, Phineas intends to step down as the leader of the Tak family and pass it to you."

"I've already chosen Drake. Phineas knows that. Let me go, and I'll let you live. But know this: if Drake suffered any permanent damage, I'll be back. I'll not just extinguish you – I will take out everyone involved." I felt Brutus stepping further away from me like I had asked him to before this Centaur arrived.

"Camille, I don't want to, but if you force me, I'll go get you another shot." It was a hollow threat. They didn't have any more of the drug with them. His thoughts gave him away: he was scrambling. His fear was becoming more pronounced as my strength refused to waiver. I kept seeing flickers of a Centauride in his mind: her name was Violet, and she lay seemingly lifeless in the chair next to my bed.

"You've got to the count of three to move out of my way."

"My lady, in all due respect, you may be a Chiron, but you aren't in any position to be making demands."

"One."

"That's cute. You're counting just like my wife does with our youngest."

"Two."

"I'm not sure what you hope to accomplish. You are going to take your place in our herd. Fighting it will just make it worse."

"Three." I could feel the Centaur's nervousness. He didn't know what to expect. His mind raced to the way I had killed the Centaur who had attacked Drake in the hotel, the first time I had moved an object with my mind. The rage inside of me boiled, begging to be unleashed. I didn't think of an object to toss at him for fear that I would hurt Brutus in the process.

"That was pretty dramatic, my queen. Now if you'll just settle down for a minute, I'll see what I can do to make you more comfortable. Phineas and his son will be here shortly."

I was wholly focused on the Centaur's thoughts. I could hear them more clearly than I could hear the jumbled up mess coming from his voice. I concentrated on his thoughts, visualizing the blood vessels in his brain. I could feel the blood pumping. His blood called to me because I shared the same lineage: it was easy to hone in on it. I called to his veins, seeing them constrict, manipulating them to stop the blood flow. The Centaur didn't realize I was doing anything at first.

"Trust me when I tell you that it is your destiny to bring the Tak family back to the rest of the Centaur community. We don't want to hide in the shadows anymore. We've more than paid our debt to Zeus. It's time for us to emerge, and you will be our leader."

I heard his words but refused to stop my concentration. The Centaur brought both hands to his temples as if he had an excruciating headache. As he fell to his knees, both hands were on his head and his eyes were wide. I watched for another thirty seconds before I heard Brutus's voice, "You're not a murderer, Miss Cami. Spare him and you have my word, you'll go free."

I saw the memory of Drake being kicked and punched in the hotel room while Phineas watched. Phineas had held me immobile, so I was unable to help Drake. Phineas had enjoyed the pain being inflicted; he was sadistic and wanted Drake dead. This centaur kneeling before me on the floor had held Drake down. I wanted retribution.

I wanted this Centaur to feel the life being squeezed out of him. Brutus came to me and touched my shoulder, "Miss Cami, mercy. Show him mercy. This Centaur is not to blame. He was only following orders. Let him live."

Brutus's touch was kind. With it, the guilt of taking another's life reined me back. He was right. I wasn't a murderer, at least not a murderer by choice. I thought of the Centaur who had attacked Drake in the hotel. I'd killed him. It wasn't what I wanted; I just wanted him to stop hurting Drake. I nodded my answer and let go of the veins I had manipulated in the Centaur's head. I could feel the veins open wide, blood pumping back to his brain.

I turned in the direction of Brutus's voice. I looked at Brutus for the first time. His name could have been "brick wall," and it would have aptly described his physique.

I was in a bedroom, nicely decorated with antique lamps resting on doilies protecting an intricately carved wooden bedroom set. While I had been blindfolded, I smelled a mustiness in the air and had envisioned being captive in a room similar to the one at Zandra's house. This room wasn't nearly as large, the paint wasn't peeling, and there wasn't a thick layer of dust everywhere. I was in someone's home, but whose?

My hands gently massaged my wrists where I had been bound. I realized I was wearing a hospital gown and had a catheter and IV in me. I wasn't sure if I should be happy that they hadn't let me lie in my own urine or furious because someone had removed my clothes and hooked me to these devices.

I saw the Centaur writhing on the floor, no doubt still suffering from the pain in his head. I refused to feel bad about it. Brutus took a step away from me as he saw me taking in my surroundings. He was dressed in blue jeans, a black t-shirt and black motorcycle boots. If I had to guess at his age, I would say late-thirties, but Centaurs seemed to mask their age better than humans. In spite of witnessing what I was able to do, he didn't appear to be frightened of me.

"Where am I?"

Brutus didn't answer right away. He decided to conceal his thoughts from me. When he answered, his voice was quiet, "You are in Phineas's home."

"And where is his home?"

"Melbourne, Florida."

"Florida?" I need to get back to South Dakota. "How long have I been sedated?"

"Four days."

"Four days? What day is it?"

"It's Thursday."

"I need a phone. Now."

Brutus reached in his pocket, fished out a cell phone, and handed it to me.

I wanted to call Drake. I wanted to know that he was okay, but I didn't know his phone number. I dialed Daniel. It went to voicemail. That was just like him. I left a message: "Daniel, it's Cami. I'm okay. I'm going to give Will a call next."

When I dialed Will, he answered right away. "It's Cami."

"Camille, are you okay?"

"Yeah, no thanks to Phineas. How's Drake?" He didn't answer right away. “Will?”

“I’m here, Camille. We’re all in South Dakota right now. Where are you, sweetheart?”

“I’m in Melbourne, Florida. Is Drake okay?” I eyed the Centaur still on the floor. If Will told me that Drake was still hurt, murderer or not, I would finish him as a message to Phineas.

“I haven’t seen him since yesterday. I’m here with Zandra.” My veins iced over. Was he now her prisoner?

I was guarded as I asked, “Can you talk?”

“Yes. We were both worried about you. We found your brother.”

“Cameron? You found Cameron? Don’t let her get him!” How could they have found him so quickly? He was able to stay hidden for twenty-two years, and they found him in four days?

“Zandra feels bad about taking you before. She, Cameron and I are flying to Florida. Why don’t you stay there, and we’ll meet you at her estate.”

“Have you lost your mind? I’m not going anywhere near her place! Where’s Drake?”

“It’s a long story, and we can’t talk about it on the phone. Cameron wants to see you. He didn’t know he had a twin, either.”

“You’re not listening to me! Where’s Drake?”

“Cami, we’ll worry about Drake after we know you and Cameron are safe.”

“I don’t need your help. I’m going back to South Dakota to find Drake.”

“Cami, wait. Don’t hang up. Cameron says Drake has the arrow.”

“What?” Remembering how Zethus had protected the truth and hidden it for so long, I couldn’t believe Will was talking so openly about it and in front of Zandra. “I don’t know what you’re talking about.”

“Drake stole the arrow from Cameron. He’s pretty shaken up about it. Stay there. We’ll be back soon, and I’ll explain everything.”

My mind raced. Drake had the arrow? Why would he have taken the arrow and not protected my brother from Zandra? He knew what she was capable of. Something didn't feel right. More was going on than he was telling me. "Put Cameron on the line."

"Camille, we're taxiing down the runway now. We'll be there soon. We can talk about it when we get there."

My anger began rising a second time, "No. Put him on the line."

Will stopped arguing with me, and a voice that sounded remarkably similar to mine came on the line. "Hello?"

"Cameron, it's Cami. Tell me what happened."

"That Drake came to my house last night. He told me that I had a sister, you, and that you'd been kidnapped. He said he needed my arrow to get you back."

I breathed a sigh of relief. He was okay. But why would he have stolen the arrow and left Cameron? "You're sure it was Drake?"

"Yeah, that's what he said his name was. I didn't want to give it up because he was a little crazy. He was ranting and raving about Centaurs and all kinds of craziness. I'd had that arrow my whole life. When William and Zandra came to the door, Drake took it and ran out the back."

"Where did he go?"

"I don't know. He's nuts, though. As soon as he took it, he disappeared into the woods behind my house."

None of Cameron's explanation made sense. Why would Drake take it if he knew it was the only thing protecting Cameron from Zandra? "Yeah, I don't know what's going on. That doesn't sound like Drake."

"William, Beau, Lacey, Zandra and I went looking for him, but he was gone."

"Hey, I'm sorry. I was hoping to find you before they did. Can you get off the plane and stay there?"

"Cami, I want to go with them. I hate the cold and Florida's sounding pretty good right now. Can you stay there? I want to meet you."

"I need to find Drake and find out what happened. I'll be in touch, okay?"

"Hey, Cami? Is all this for real?"

What do you say to a question like that? "They're our family. Don't turn your back on either one of them. Something's going on that they aren't telling us. I need to find Drake. What's your address, and I'll see if I can pick up his tracks."

"What are you, part bloodhound? That was yesterday."

"I'm just tuned into him. Hey, Cameron, have Will and Zandra told you anything about our family?"

His voice was quiet, as if he were trying not to be overheard, "Not really. They're both doing a whole lot of whispering. Is it true that they just found you a few months ago in San Diego?"

Remembering back to the thrill of finding a family after being alone, I wanted to warn him to keep his guard up. We had both been protected by magic, sheltering us from all of this. "Yeah, it's been a crazy few months. Watch out for Zandra. I don't trust her."

"But you think Will's okay?"

Will and Phineas were tight. It didn't seem like Will was involved in my kidnapping, but I couldn't be sure. He'd been warm and welcoming since my first day and definitely helped Drake and me escape, but maybe he was just letting us do his dirty work for him. Maybe he wanted the arrow all along and knew Zethus would never give it to him. "Jury's still out. Just be careful, okay?" Cameron gave me his cell phone number and his address.

I needed for Drake to be okay. I handed the phone back to Brutus, "I'm going to need a shower, clothes, and a plane."

CHAPTER 23

Daniel – Hotel, SD

Cami's dad, her grandmother, and her twin brother left; her half-brothers, except for Beau, left too. Bastards. I heard them talking about going to Florida. No one was even looking for Cami anymore. I hate the whole lot of 'em. Four days, not a phone call, not an email, search parties in every direction, Drake disappeared, and all of a sudden nobody was even interested in where Cami was. It's not as if any of them kept me in the loop anyway. Good riddance. Beau was the only one I trusted. He was on the phone in his room calling the emergency rooms, again.

I picked up my phone. A lonely voice mail was staring back at me. I took a deep breath. It wasn't Cami's number, and I didn't recognize the area code. Phone coverage sucked here. Only about every other call I got rang through; all the others kept going to voicemail. I went to press the message when my phone began ringing.

It was Drake's number. Schmuck. I hated this guy. Maybe he'd decided to go to Florida, too. I hadn't seen him in two days. Or maybe he'd actually found her. "Holy shit, where've *you* been? You find her?"

"Daniel, it's Drake."

"I know that, Moron. I've got this newfangled gadget called 'caller ID.' Ever hear of it?"

He ignored my insult. What the heck did Cami see in him anyway? Instead of answering me, all he said was, "Hey, I need you to take care of Cami for me."

"Take care of her? What're you talking about? I'm still looking for her. Where've you been?"

"She's free. She's on her way back to South Dakota. You need to take her home, okay?"

"On her way back to South Dakota? Where is she?"

"I'm not sure. I think Florida. She's on her way here. You've got to protect her."

Florida? If she'd been in Florida, did the others not know she was on her way back? The hair on the back of my neck stood up when I realized he was asking me to *take care of her*. "You talked to her?"

"Not exactly."

"How do you know she's okay?"

"I just know. I need to know you'll take care of her."

Not only was he a jerk who let Cami get kidnapped and who knew what else, but now he "just knows" she's okay. It's probably a trick. "So, if you didn't exactly talk to her, how do you know where she is or that she's coming back here?"

I heard a frustrated sigh on the line, like I was wasting his time. "I'm her Centaur, Daniel. I have a connection to her. She was drugged, or something, but she's okay. She's coming back here. Will you take care of her or not?"

What was *he* doing? "I thought that was your job? You had pretty big words a few days ago."

"Look, I'm not calling to argue with you. I can't protect her. You can. I need you to convince her to go home with you."

"What? Home where?"

"Home where she belongs, San Diego, with you."

I couldn't believe my ears. This schmuck flew all over the world with her, didn't do anything to stop her from being kidnapped, then just decided he wasn't into her? He was a bigger loser than I thought. "So, what, you're turning your back on her? Cold feet, now you're kicking her to the curb? You're not even going to make sure she's okay?"

"It's not like that. Just promise me you'll protect her."

"I'm not promising you shit. What's she need protection from? Grandmommy Dearest just flew out."

Another loud sigh, "She's due to land at the airport in an hour. I want you there to meet her plane. Get on it and take the charter home."

"That's it? You're going to ride off into the sunset, and it's my job to pick up all of her pieces and try to put her back together. After you obliterate her?"

I'd been through this with Cami once before. That loser she dated for a couple years, out of nowhere he decided he'd outgrown her. She cried for two days solid. I wasn't sure if she'd ever come out of it.

Just as she was getting back to normal, Ronnie tried to worm his way back in. He called me giving me this sob story that he'd made a mistake. He wanted to try patching things up with her. He came to me asking if I could arrange a meeting for him with her. Yeah, a black eye, a busted lip and a smashed windshield, and he knew not to ask for my help. Once he got the bleeding under control, I told him if I found out he tried to contact her directly, I wouldn't be satisfied with a flesh wound next time. He was smart enough to stay away.

Drake's voice brought me back to the present. "I can't be with her. Tell her I'm sorry. Tell her to forget about me."

"I ain't a message service. How about I just tell her you're a slimy, lying bastard, and you left? How 'bout I tell her that?"

"Fine."

"I don't get you, Drake. You're an idiot. Just so you know, Cami isn't someone you get a second chance with. Don't try playing head games with her."

"I'm not playing games, and I won't be looking for a second chance. Everyone around you knows how you feel about her. I'm stepping out of your way. You got the girl."

"You're blowing the best opportunity you'll ever have."

"I don't have a choice."

"This is some more of that stupid Centaur shit, isn't it?"

"Daniel, just promise me you'll take care of her."

"Tell me the truth." Silence echoed. I could hear my own voice screaming in my head to stop antagonizing him. Let him go. If he was willing to give her up, it was his loss. He was just lucky he'd picked up the phone to call, because if he were here right now, I'd level him for leaving her.

I wonder what Beau will think of his great friend now? Beau told me he'd known Drake his whole life and trusted him. Wait 'til he hears about this stupid vanishing act. When he didn't answer, I told him, "You know what? I don't care. Have a nice life."

I hung up. My watch said 9:30. I dialed Beau, "Hey man, we're pulling chocks."

"We're what?"

"Pulling chocks. You know, the things in front of tires on planes, right before they taxi away. Cami's en route; we're going back to San Diego."

"En route? To San Diego?"

"She's flying into the airport here. We'll meet her here and head back."

"Uh, okay, that's great. Let me call my dad and let him know. She's okay, right?"

I thought about all of them heading to the airport without so much as a word to me. I should have known. "He must already know. He and your brothers took off thirty minutes ago."

"They what?"

"Saw the big happy family leaving, myself." It occurred to me that I'd just twisted the knife for Beau. If they left and hadn't told him, that wasn't a good sign. These freaking Centaurs were a bunch of odd ducks.

"But Cami's coming here? She wasn't with them?"

"No. They took off. She's supposed to land in an hour. Time to pack it up. I'll meet you downstairs in five minutes." There was no way I was going to try to explain the call I just got from Drake, so I hung up before he could ask any more questions.

Beau didn't say a word the whole way to the airport. We returned the rental car, grabbed a cup of coffee, and both stared at the floor. I could see it; he didn't need to say anything.

When he flew to San Diego, it was his choice on his terms. After Lacey's car accident, something changed in Beau: his resolve not to go home was solid. Finding out that his family returned home shouldn't have bothered him, but finding out they left and didn't bother to tell him they were leaving had to hurt. Maybe it was their way of acknowledging his choice; they were already treating him like a human.

We didn't have to wait long. I saw a jet just like Dad's pulling up to the terminal building; it was a family plane. I didn't recognize the tail number, but the plane's color and Centaur gave it away. Cami came through the doorway of the terminal and looked amazing. I hadn't seen her in a few months, and the transformation was remarkable. Her hair was longer, it was shiny and wavy. I guess because we'd been pals for so long, I was used to seeing it in pony tails or plopped on top of her head with a clip. Her complexion had always been great. I don't remember her ever having a blemish, but her skin looked like she was almost glowing.

Cami wasn't dressed in anything fancy, running pants and a t-shirt, but maybe it was the way she carried herself – she took my breath away.

I told myself not to be stupid; she probably only looked this way because it had been so long since I'd seen her.

Her face registered relief when she saw Beau and me standing together. She raised her arms just as she got to me and gripped me in a tight hug. I couldn't help it: I swung her around like a little kid. She felt incredible, her iron grip around me, clinging to me, and I could feel her warm breath on my neck. I heard her whisper, "I've missed you so much." It felt like my stomach took up break-dancing.

"You, too, Cami." I'd been holding onto her for too long, way too long, but my arms ignored my brain when it told them to let her go. I felt her grip on me ease, which was her cue for me to let her go. I didn't. I pulled her in closer, drinking in her scent, absorbing the heat she was giving me.

In a reassuring tone she said, "Daniel, I'm okay."

I heard Beau say, "We were worried about you. Are you okay? What'd they do to you?"

She shook her head in response to Beau, but must have realized my arms were unwilling to let her go. She whispered, "Daniel, I'm fine. People are going to get the wrong idea if you don't let go."

I didn't give a crap what anyone else saw or thought; I was just glad Cami was safe. My emotions were getting the better of me when I whispered, "I was scared, Cami." Embarrassed that I'd let it slip out, I let her go. Luckily, Beau was right there and grabbed her in a hug before the awkwardness of what I'd said or my astronomically long hug could make her any more uncomfortable.

Beau didn't hold on as long as I did, and when he let go, he was all smiles.

Cami looked around the room. I knew exactly who she was looking for. I didn't want to hear the question, so I answered before she could ask it. "He split, Cami."

"What? Who split?"

"Drake. He's not coming. I grabbed your stuff from the hotel. Let's go."

"What do you mean he *split*?"

"Just what I said. C'mon, I'll fill you in when we're on our way." Beau had been so lost in his own thoughts that he hadn't noticed that Drake hadn't shown his face. Instead of one questioning pair of eyes, I was looking at two. Great.

"I'm not going anywhere without Drake. Where is he?"

"Didn't say. He just told me to take you back to San Diego."

"You talked to him? Is he meeting us there?"

The best answer I could have given her was a lie. I knew if I told her, "yes," she'd get on the plane and not give it a second thought. I'd never lied to her, though, not about anything minor and nothing of this magnitude. I wouldn't start now, no matter how much better that little lie would make my life. "I don't think so."

"So where is he?"

"He didn't say." She shook her head like she was talking to an imbecile. Just because I didn't want to lie to her, I didn't want her turning the waterworks on, either.

"Well, what *did* he say?"

"He said you were en route to the airport. He told me to take you home." I knew if I threw in the part about protecting her, that'd just piss her off. Cami didn't like the idea of anyone "protecting" her. She never had.

"But he didn't say he'd meet us there?"

"It didn't come up."

She shook her head again, "Let me use your phone."

I handed it over and gave her his number. She didn't have it on speaker, but I could hear it ringing. I heard his stupid voice mail playing. "Drake, it's Cami. I'm fine. Where are you? I'm at the airport with Daniel and Beau. Call me back on Daniel's phone."

"Cami, he said for us to go back to San Diego."

"I'm not going anywhere without Drake."

It was dark outside. If we left now we wouldn't get into San Diego until the middle of the night. My dad had sent a pilot up to get his plane a couple days ago, so having Beau fly us back wasn't an option. I wasn't even sure the aircrew who just flew Cami in would be willing to fly again tonight.

We'd known each other forever, and if I forced her to dig her heels in, she'd get bullheaded and fight me on everything. I took a different approach, "Beau, can you talk to the pilot and see if he can be ready to leave by nine a.m.?"

"Sure." He zipped up his coat, flung his hood over his head, and walked through the doors toward the plane.

Cami hadn't given me my phone back, and she was gripping it like it was a lifeline. "He's okay, right? You saw him?"

"I saw him a couple days ago. He looked okay to me."

Her voice started getting shaky, "That morning at the hotel, four of them attacked him."

"He told me."

"What aren't you telling me?"

"There's nothing to tell. He called me and told me to get you back to San Diego. End of story."

"Does Zandra have him?"

"Nope. Your grandma, your dad, and all your brothers, except Beau, took off hours ago."

"I bet Drake's looking for Cameron."

"Nope. Cameron was on the plane with everyone else."

"I know, but maybe Drake doesn't know that."

"Possible. He didn't mention it."

"So tell me what he said. *Exactly* what he said."

"Geeze, Cami, I already did."

"I'm not leaving without Drake."

I shook my head, "Well then, you might be here a while."

"What's that supposed to mean?"

"It means. . . it means he isn't. . . he broke up, okay? He's a jerk, and he's probably the only person on the planet who I like less than your dad." My face was warm, my hands were shaking, and my nerves were shot. I reached over to pull Cami close. I had to do the same thing when her last boyfriend got a bad case of the "stupids."

She backed away from me, unwilling to accept any comfort I had to offer. Her voice was hallow, "I don't believe you." Her back was arched and fury shot through her eyes. She thought I was lying to her. Well, wasn't that a kick in the pants?

"Okay, don't believe me. Wait for the phone to ring. Wait all frickin' night if you want to. He's not calling you back."

Her eyes narrowed, her brows furrowed, and she leaned in toward me, accusing me as much with the sound of her voice as with her words, "What'd you do to him?"

I put my hands up like she had a gun, "Whoa, Cami. I didn't touch him. I've told you what he told me. If you want to hang out until the morning for him to prove that he really bailed, fine. But tomorrow morning, you're getting on that plane." As soon as the words were out, I knew I'd screwed up royally. I couldn't help it. She'd been pissed at me before, but she'd never accused me of something like that. What'd she expect?

"You can get on that plane tomorrow. But I'm not going anywhere. Not without him."

A million things shot through my mind. He doesn't deserve her. She's just going to get hurt. Centaurs are idiots. Her family turned their backs on her. None of those thoughts formed into words. As true as they were, I couldn't hurt her the way everybody else could.

Drake was right about one thing: I loved her. I had my whole life. I wish he would take her phone call. Even if he were a jackass to her, at least she'd know I was telling the truth and hadn't done anything to him. If she never heard from him, she'd always think in the back of her mind that I was somehow involved or was responsible for sabotaging their relationship.

CHAPTER 24

Camille – Two days later SD

I'd been searching for two days; several times I felt close but hadn't found Drake. I opened the door at Cameron's house. I expected the emptiness, the darkness of the room. He wasn't inside. I could feel it – Drake had been here. Even before I shouted, I knew I wouldn't get a response, "Drake!" I touched the doorknob, hoping to find some hint of where he might be. I spoke to him, willing him to hear me, "Drake, if you can hear me, I'm coming for you."

I had been concentrating so hard to find Drake, I was startled when a voice hissed from the hallway, "Well, isn't that sweet? My granddaughter, looking for her lover. Did you lose him?" She had plastered a sentimental look on her face that was a stark contrast to her acidic words.

I looked her square in the eye, the hatred I felt for her clear, "What are you doing here?"

"Cameron is all settled in at home. I flew back to this miserable place. I needed to see how your search was going."

"Where is he? What'd you do to him?" She should be down south, with all of the others. Why was she here? Zandra was manipulative and vindictive. I wouldn't allow her to gain any control over me a second time. I backed myself into a corner waiting for whatever onslaught she was planning.

"Did to him?"

"You're responsible. Where is he?"

"Am I? And how is that possible, my dear?"

"Drake would never abandon Cameron. If he were here, he never would have just left with the arrow. He would have stayed. He never would have left Cameron alone."

"Oh, wouldn't he now? Cameron told you what happened. You don't believe your twin? Did you ever ask yourself what Drake's motivation was? Why was he so willing to fly halfway around the world chasing an arrow? It couldn't be to take out a feeble old woman – you yourself know he had other motivations. His soul yearns for the same power that you already yield. You were his drug, Camille. I'm afraid he's found something new to tickle his fancy."

"Drake only wanted the arrow to stop you."

Her evil little grin morphed into a wide, condescending smile, "Yet, here I am. The arrow was in his possession. It is gone, and Drake is gone, too. If he was so worried about you, where is he now?"

This was her trickery; she was more cunning than I had given her credit for the last time we met. I wouldn't make the same error this time. "Say what you want, Zandra. Drake risked everything for me. I love him."

"There is a fine line between hate and love, Camille. The slightest action, with the best of intentions, can make that line blur." I wondered silently if this was how she viewed me, with a blurred line? Loving the idea of keeping a piece of my mom even after her death, but hating all but the sliver of my mother she saw in me.

He loves me. He wouldn't leave me. He was trying to protect me.

Whatever had happened, I wouldn't let her words make me believe otherwise. "What do you want?"

"What I've always wanted: To honor my family, the Chiron legacy. Your brother, Cameron, was alone. His guardian abandoned him when he turned eighteen." She looked around the ramshackle house. "He is part of my legacy. I've been looking for him ever since I felt you leave for Ireland." I froze. I didn't know how much she knew about my trip, and I wasn't about to give her any more information than she already had. Zandra asked sweetly, "You met my brother while you were in Ireland. How is he?"

Reiterating what Zethus, a.k.a. Jeb, had told me, "Your brother's dead."

"That is merely wishful thinking on my part, I assure you. Zethus is very much still in the land of the living, although each breath he takes becomes closer to his last. I'll let you in on a little secret: I do not fear death. When I leave this world it will be with a clean conscience. I may be a tough woman. Some have described me as ruthless and brutal, but I've never taken another's life."

"Doesn't killing your own parents constitute taking a life?"

"I didn't kill my parents. I assure you: they died of natural causes, despite what Zethus's twisted mind has led you to believe."

I didn't believe a word from Zandra. She was manipulative and had just admitted she was brutal. The pain she had inflicted on my mother and on me proved it. This was just her new way of achieving the same result. Rather than letting any doubt seep into my mind, I accused her again, "What did you do to Drake?"

"I did nothing to Drake, you stupid girl. He found the arrow, and he took it. I tried to protect you from him and the future I saw for both of you. You still found a way around me." A look of disbelief must have shone on my face because she continued, "With twenty-four hour guards, a betrothal to an exceptional Centaur – you still found a way. I don't know whether to be proud of your cunning or furious with your intellect."

"You tried to force me to marry a Centaur I didn't choose."

Zandra stepped closer to me and placed her hand on my shoulder. "I saw your future, Camille. I saw it the day you and Drake found one another, before you and I had even been introduced. I couldn't allow it to happen if it was within my power to stop it. Drake is not who you believe him to be, I can assure you. You do not want to find him."

Fury with her words erupted with no warning. "You are a manipulative, deceitful, evil. . . bitch. Think what you want, Drake saved me from you."

"Yet, you've not married him. Somewhere inside, you know the truth. Had you married him, you would have an unbreakable bond – you could find him anywhere. All you have now is the betrothal bond, which is not enough to locate him. You know he is not the right one for you. You've known it since the beginning."

"I don't believe that." I turned to storm away, hoping never again to see this woman.

Her voice caught me as my heavy steps walked to the door. "Cameron will be at my estate. I hope you'll join us soon. Go ahead and look for your Centaur. When you find him, retrieve my arrow. Zeus's curse is unforgiving of thieves, and he has stolen Chiron property."

"If you don't know where he is, then he and the arrow are both safe. He's hiding it from you."

"Safe? That is a matter of perspective. Let me share what I've pieced together. I knew Drake Nash's intentions toward you. I did everything in my power to stop the two of you, but he was able to escape and convince you it was your idea to go. You flew to Ireland. Why? To find an arrow that belongs to our bloodline. You located the arrow that should have been used against your enemy – me; but where did it go? I don't have it. You don't have it. Not only does Cameron not have it, he no longer has its protection. What is your priority now, my dear?"

"Once I've found Drake, I'll be there to collect my brother."

"I wish you the best of luck, Camille. Once you learn the truth about your Drake, you can rest assured no one else will have you. All the Centaurs will soon know of you and your ties to the Lost Herd, so finding a suitor now would prove difficult. I think you have earned the destiny I tried so hard to keep you from. Enjoy it."

As I stood holding the door, she walked past me. I remembered my time at her estate. She cut me off from everyone. She refused to allow anyone to talk to me. She led me to believe Drake and Bianca were dead, and she tried to force me to marry Gage. She was more manipulative than any person I'd ever known. She was more than capable of lying to me: this was just her latest lie. Of all the powers I possessed, being a lie detector wasn't one of them, but if I had to choose between Uncle Zethus and my grandmother – I would believe my great-uncle.

Last time she had pretended Drake was dead when he was safe. I wouldn't be manipulated by her; I wouldn't allow even a morsel of doubt to seep into my mind. I just needed to find him before she did.

CHAPTER 25

Camille – Looking for Drake, SD

I had walked seven miles past Cameron's house, following Drake. It wasn't his scent, or a path through the snow; it was as if I were following his energy. I couldn't count the number of times I'd called him on my cell or called out to him with my voice and through my mind. I was exhausted. He wasn't dead, and I was sure he was close.

I could feel his energy getting stronger, more pronounced the further I walked. At the end of the overgrown gravel driveway stood a long forgotten farmhouse. Paint chips peeled up toward the sun as if begging for a little more warmth to escape the frigid air. More fresh snow had fallen today, and no footprints had disturbed the snow but mine. It was early December. I'd gotten back from Florida a week ago and had searched for Drake every waking minute since my return.

I had felt this close before, but each time I felt he was around the next corner, I lost him again. Time alone was my enemy. Each night since my search began, Beau and Daniel were waiting for me at the hotel.

Each night I could count on one or both of them trying to talk me into returning to San Diego with them.

I didn't want Beau's comfort or Daniel's friendship; I was still blinded by the loss of Drake. Neither had returned to San Diego, but I wouldn't let either of them help me search for Drake, either. I'd watched Phineas's men beat Drake to within an inch of his life. I knew Daniel had told me the truth when he said Drake didn't want to see me again, but I couldn't let it go. I couldn't let my last memory of Drake be the terror I felt in that moment in our hotel room. If he had changed his mind and no longer wanted me, I could accept it, but I needed my last memory of him to be one where he was okay.

I could accept if he blamed me for what Phineas's men had done to him. I wouldn't deny that if I hadn't met Drake that day at Bruce's wedding, he would be way better off for never having met me. I would accept his hatred, or contempt, or whatever he was feeling, so long as I could see him one last time, even if it meant our last conversation would be a good-bye.

No matter how I tried explaining it to Beau or Daniel, neither understood why I had to find Drake. After I told Beau I had run into Zandra at Cameron's house, he and Lacey insisted on helping me search yesterday. This morning I got up and left the hotel before either woke up, so I could do this on my own.

Both Beau and Daniel believed that if we all went back to San Diego, eventually Drake would get over whatever was going on with him and maybe he'd come looking for us there. Something told me that would never happen, and I needed to find him now or know that I would lose him forever.

In my heart I knew Zandra was full of lies. I didn't want them to, but her words had made an impression on me. She had done everything in her power to keep us apart, but I thought it unlikely she did it for me.

My search continued. I'd felt his presence several times this last week, but I was never able to find him. It was as if he were just outside my reach. There was one person I could call on, the one person who'd been there for me my whole life. Our bond was so strong, I could even call on her in death. "Mom? Mom, are you there? Mom, I need you."

Her faint outline materialized in front of me. With the cold temperatures, my breath turned to vapor in front of me. As I exhaled, it went straight through her. Her response was audible, but barely. "*Camille, it's almost time.*"

Sadness pulled at my heart, and a tear threatened to streak down my cheek, "You have to help me find Drake."

"*I'm sorry, Camille. I'm just a spirit, and it is past my time. It's time for me to go to the pasture.*"

I begged her, "Tell me how to find him. Please. I just need to know he's okay." The hurt that I'd felt for days when Daniel told me that Drake had abandoned me threatened to swallow me whole. The vicious words from Zandra and the insane loneliness were almost too much to bear. "Please, Mom. Help me."

"*Your Centaur is alive. If he were not, I would have seen him on this side. I don't know where he is.*"

"Did Zandra do something to him?"

"*I don't know, Camille.*"

I saw her image fading. In my heart I knew this would be our last visit. She had grown weak. I wanted to say something profound, something that would let her know how much I knew she gave up for me. I came up empty; I was too broken, too alone, too cold and too exhausted to think straight. Instead I asked a question I already knew the answer to. "Wait. . . will I ever see you again?"

She smiled and the image of her took on a yellow, almost comforting glow. "*When your time is over, I will be waiting for you in the pasture. You were the only joy I ever had in my life. Thank you for making my life worth living.*"

Choking back the tears, "I wish I'd been a better daughter. I wish I'd known what you sacrificed for us."

She smiled, and the soft warm glow surrounding her brightened. "*There were no sacrifices, only choices. I chose my life, and I lived it without regrets. I'm proud of you, Camille. My only sadness is that I didn't have more time here, to see the choices you will make.*"

"How will I learn anything without you?"

"*It's in your blood, Camille. You don't need a teacher. Remember your life is a gift and choices you make are yours and nobody else's.*"

I was running out of time: her glow began to diminish. "Do I have any special powers I can use to find Drake?"

"*Yes. You have your love for him. Love is the most powerful magic in the universe. Listen to your heart: it will lead you to him. Trust in yourself and believe in the love in your heart.*"

Her spirit faded away completely. There had been a pressure on my chest that I didn't know I'd been carrying. I felt her spirit leave, and she took with her the pain I'd carried with me all these months. I had been holding her here. I was so scared of really losing her that I couldn't let her rest. I took a deep breath, held it in, and then slowly let it release.

I didn't want to be alone, but as my mother's spirit crossed over to the pasture, I no longer feared the loneliness. I could leave the Centaur world behind just as she had. I wouldn't need magic to hide me – I could just leave. I would always have my family if I needed them, even if I chose to live as a human rather than as a Centauride.

Mom's final gift to me was the knowledge that I would only be alone if I chose it. I stood at the end of that gravel driveway for a long time, not in terms of minutes or hours, but a long time, finally saying my good-bye.

When my numbed mind returned to reality, the crisp air against my face, the chill of the wind, and the deafening silence reminded me of why I was here. Drake. Dusk was over, and the moon was rising. I should have returned to town, but something prevented me from leaving. The temperature had dropped, and the snow crunched under my feet as I made my way up to the abandoned farmhouse in front of me.

I climbed the step to the rickety old porch, silently praying the wood was strong enough to support another step without buckling under my weight. It didn't appear that there was any electricity to the dilapidated house. I pressed the chime on the door, knowing that no noise would sound inside. Even if it did make a sound, I could feel that there were no living souls to hear it.

Refusing to accept what I already knew, I raised my fist and pounded hard on the door. Nothing. I was so sure Drake would be here. Gingerly, I stepped off the porch, trying to put my weight only on the boards that looked like they could support me.

As I looked in the backyard, tall grass stood wildly, covered under the blanket of snow. I could feel something about this place. This was where I was supposed to be. I felt eyes watching me. Both my hands rested on a fence post. I closed my eyes and let my mind wander, looking for the one watching me.

I felt the charge of unexpected electricity jolt me. Drake was here. I'd found him. I could hear my own heartbeat against the silent backdrop. I closed my eyes and began walking, letting his heartbeat serve as a beacon for me to find him. I thought of the day at our hotel before I had been kidnapped: the unfettered desire I felt for him and his willingness to finally quench my thirst. I let those images free in my thoughts, willing him to see them in my mind, too.

He didn't come closer. I couldn't see him, but I could feel he was just behind the abandoned barn. I couldn't understand why he didn't come to me. Couldn't he feel my approach? I walked slowly, trying to detect any traps that may have been set by whoever was holding him. I stepped behind the barn. A thick grove of trees all but blocked out light from piercing through the branches. Darkness had fallen. Drake stood in front of me; even twenty feet away in the near pitch black, pain shone clear through his eyes.

He was standing a few yards just inside the tree line. My voice shook, "Drake, it's me." He couldn't make eye contact, or at least he *wouldn't* make eye contact, and he didn't answer. "Drake, I was worried," my voice cracked, "I thought Zandra had gotten you. I thought I had lost you."

When his eyes finally met mine, a sorrow so powerful emanated from him, it nearly brought me to my knees. I took him in: he stood before me in the freezing temperatures with no coat or shirt, bare-chested in the moonlight. I froze. What had happened? Someone had kidnapped him and left him outside to freeze? I unzipped my parka and pulled it off to hand to him. Drake shook his head; my mind wasn't processing what was happening. I took another step in his direction, still holding the parka out for him. He shook his head a second time, his voice quiet, "I don't need it."

"Of course you need it! You're going to freeze to death!"

Drake didn't argue with me. Instead his eyes looked off behind me, over my shoulder. His voice sounded hollow, the only sound for miles in an ocean of silence, "There's nothing I wouldn't have given you."

The tears I held back clouded my vision, "Where have you been? I've looked everywhere."

"I had. . . I had to go away."

Something wasn't right. He couldn't have been held captive. He wasn't warning me to be careful; I didn't sense any danger at all. "Where's the arrow?"

"It's safe."

Forcing Zandra's voice not to echo in my mind, I asked, "Where's it at?"

"Never mind the arrow. You're safe from Zandra so long as you keep Zethus's locket with you." He tossed the hideous bug locket the few feet to me. I caught it while he warned, "Stay away from her."

"Did she do something to you?"

I took another step toward Drake. He held his hand out as if he were a traffic cop. "No! Don't come any closer."

I was confused by his reaction to me. It had been over a week since I had seen him. Why didn't he come to me? Why didn't he pull me to him and tell me he loved me? Did he blame me for Phineas's attack? Was he hurt? I could only choke out, "What's wrong?"

I took another step forward, ignoring his hand. His words were harsh, "Camille – STOP!"

He stood, his chest bare, the moonlight illuminating every ripple across his chest. He stood behind a thick evergreen bush and made no movement in my direction. I couldn't understand why he wasn't wearing a coat, a hoodie or at least a t-shirt. Seeing him standing as he was, I wondered if I were hallucinating.

I didn't care how much he protested; I wouldn't let him freeze to death. Still holding the parka, I closed the last few feet between us, stepped around the evergreen bush, and reached up to wrap it around him. When he tried to shrug the jacket away, I slid it over his shoulders and held it firmly around him. To make sure he didn't pull it off, I left my arms strung around his neck anchoring it to him.

I don't know how long I stood there, my hands involuntarily began rubbing his shoulders through the jacket. Drake closed his eyes as his arms glided gently to my waist. We stood there stiffly without words until he leaned over and rested his chin on my head. Drake looked exhausted, and he finally said, "You need the jacket more than I do."

His skin was warm, more than warm – it was hot. It felt like he had a fever. "Why are you out here without a coat?"

Instead of answering me, his arms that had been stiffly resting on my waist suddenly pulled me tight against him. I felt his breath against my neck as he spoke directly into my ear, "I didn't want you to see me."

I started to feel dizzy and knew if he hadn't have been holding onto me so tightly, my legs would have folded under me. My worst fear was actually happening. All his tender words, his promise of eternity, it was just gone. It was just like Ronnie all over again, but this time so much worse.

I wouldn't let him know what his words had just done to me. I'd always used humor as a defense – and sarcasm was far better than letting him know he'd just shattered me. "Running scared, huh? Second thoughts on that whole 'choose me' thing?" I'd hoped I'd masked the hurt in my voice.

He'd changed his mind. He didn't want me anymore. Daniel had told me the truth. I bit back the tears of rejection skimming the surface, not wanting for it to be true and not willing for him to see me cry.

Once I was sure I could keep tears from escaping, I opened my eyes and saw him looking back at me. The sorrow I'd seen in them just minutes before had morphed into pain. I had to let him go, but my arms refused to release him. My body revolted: my arms cinched tighter around his neck, and my face buried itself in his chest as his arms pulled me from the ground.

When I'd buried my face in his chest before, I was on my tippy toes, but today, no part of my feet even touched the ground. Had Drake grown taller? I went to look toward the ground to see if he was standing on a rock. As I looked down, his hand grabbed my face, forcing me to stare into his eyes.

His voice echoed the pain I'd just seen in his eyes. "Forget me, Camille."

None of this made sense. Why would he pull me into him then tell me to forget him? I could feel it; he was going to dump me; maybe in his mind, he already had. I felt like an addict trying to get a fix, drinking up his scent, absorbing the feel of his arm around me while his hand held my face taut. A single tear dripped down my cheek. Drake's eyes clouded, and he kissed the tear away before it could roll off my chin.

Until now I was sure someone or something had stolen him, had held him against his will – had kept him from me. That was the wrong conclusion. Drake had run away and hidden from me. Zandra told me as much and so had Daniel; I hadn't believed either of them. Whatever his reason, I didn't care. "Drake, whatever I did. . . I'm sorry."

Drake let go of my face and wrapped both arms around my waist, pulling me up so my chin rested on his shoulder. I had to convince him that whatever he was upset about, we could fix it. When I opened my eyes, the image didn't make any sense. I jerked away from him, on instinct, which surprised him enough that he let me drop to the ground.

I smoothed the bushes away from him and saw his legs. I was speechless, or dumbfounded. This had to be a dream. . . or a nightmare. Drake's gaze never wavered. He simply said, "Just forget me, Camille. Just go." Drake started to back away from me. I heard his heavy steps on the earth and felt my heart breaking.

Still in shock, I could only ask, "Wait! How did this happen?"

He shook his head, still holding my gaze, "The arrow did it."

No lesson I had learned from Zandra or Gretchen had prepared me for this. I said it out loud more for my benefit than for his, "The arrow? It turned you into a Centaur?"

"I've always been a Centaur, Camille. At least, I've always had Centaur blood. But touching the arrow that didn't belong to me. . . it had to have had some sort of a curse on it." Zandra's warning echoed in my mind: *Zeus's curse is unforgiving of thieves, and he has stolen Chiron property.*

"Did you try giving it back?"

"Back to whom?"

"To Cameron."

"He's gone. I've been outside his home for days, but he hasn't returned."

"Give it to me. I'm a Chiron."

"No!"

Zandra's words of doubt began playing in my head. Why did he refuse to return the arrow? "Drake, it could break the curse. You could go back to normal."

He shook his head, pulled my jacket off his bare shoulders and helped me into it. "I'm not taking a chance like that with you. You're not touching it."

"You can't stay like this. We have to do something with it to lift the curse."

Drake's voice was defeated when he put his head down and said flatly, "Go home, Camille."

"Home is wherever you are, Drake. I'm not going anywhere." My eyes took him in. Once I'd gotten over the initial shock of his transformation, I realized he was magnificent. From the waist up, Drake looked the same as he had, but at his waist, his body morphed into the body of a brown horse. He stood taller than he had, by at least six inches.

"Cami, just go. I'm going to try to contact your uncle Jeb."

A normal person might have run away, or maybe screamed, or I don't know. . .maybe curled up in a ball on the ground rocking themselves. I didn't do any of those. I stepped closer, my palms extended, placing them on either side of his face. His skin was smooth, not even a hint of stubble greeted my palms. I slid them down his shoulders; Drake's whole body was warm, even in the frigid temperature. My hands came together at his chest, his eyes fixed on me the whole time. As my touch slid down his ribs and onto his abdomen, a euphoric feeling took me. It was still Drake.

He stood in front of me, the island oasis I had escaped to when I was captive at Zandra's house. The man who had haunted all of my daydreams since our escape was right in front of me.

I was curious and let my hand trail down his waist onto the velvety hair of his new body. His right hoof stamped involuntarily when my hand traced his leg. His voice was soft, full of emotion when I heard him say, "Just go." I didn't listen to him. I stepped to his side and let both my hands feel the haunches that held his body.

He side-stepped and turned so that he was facing me again. There were so many things going through my mind, but only three words escaped my lips, "I've missed you."

"You've missed me? Can't you see what I am? I'm in front of you, Cami. I'm not a human."

The emotion of finding him was overwhelming. I murmured, "I

don't care."

"Are you blind?"

I could feel my head nod, "I love you, Drake. I don't care."

"I'm a freak, Cami! Open your eyes!"

"They are open." I shook my head and closed the distance to him again. When I did this before, when he was a human, I could bury my face into his chest: I loved that feeling. Drake was much taller now, and my face was just over his abdomen. He tried to back away from me, but I refused to let him go. I wrapped both my arms around him and held on. When I did, he hesitated for a few seconds then leaned down and wrapped his arms around me, as well. I don't know how long we stood there. The temperature was dropping fast, and I began to shiver even with his arms wrapped around me.

His voice was softer, "You should go. You're freezing."

"I'm not going anywhere."

He stood erect, towering over me again, his ice blue eyes staring down into mine, with sadness like before, but intensified. "Cami, you. . ." I put my finger to his lips to stop his protest. He gently took my hand in his, kissed the back of my hand, and said, "If you won't leave, let's at least get you out of the wind."

Drake led me to the abandoned barn. The door complained as the hinges creaked, but he led me into the massive structure. I looked around thinking one good solid gust of wind would bring the whole thing crashing down on us. There was no straw on the dirt floor. The only light was what was streaming in from the cracks in the wall of the barn from the moon. I could hear wings fluttering above us as we'd disturbed whatever fowl inhabited the rafters. A camping lantern hung just over the side of a stall. Drake lit it.

He reached over and grabbed a small backpack. As I looked around the dimly lit barn, my heart ached: this is where he had been staying. Drake withdrew a blanket from the backpack and laid it down on the ground. He eased himself down to the floor and motioned to the blanket in front of him.

I remembered the story of Winfield and Unice: the man who had fallen in love with a Centauride. At the time I thought it an impossible love story: in this moment – I understood. My heart went out to the couple all over again. I took my place in front of Drake on the floor, his arms tentatively reached out for me, and when I moved toward him, his strong arms encircled me.

Drake brought his hand to my cheek, caressing my face with the back of his hand. It was a tender touch and spoke volumes to my soul. I understood why I had searched so long without finding him. He had purposely evaded me. His voice told me what I already knew, "I never thought I'd feel your skin again."

My hands reached for him as I heard the longing in his voice and answered him with strength in mine. "No one can keep me from you. You're mine. I chose you."

He shook his head at me, "You don't know what you're saying."

My hand rested on his jaw as I said it again, "I chose you, Drake."

"You chose me before all of this." His hand swept out as he motioned to himself. "You need to choose someone else; there's no future with me."

"You don't believe that. You can't believe that. I just want to stay here, with you."

Drake's eyes closed as his lips softly met mine. He was tentative, as if he couldn't commit them to me. My hand instinctively went to the back of his head and pulled him in closer as I whispered, "Kiss me like you mean it."

Whatever doubt he was feeling evaporated as his kiss deepened. His hand went to the small of my back as shivers from his touch rocketed in all directions. Drake's lips moved to my clavicle as a soft moan escaped him. My mouth found his ear lobe as I whispered, "Better, I'm starting to believe you missed me, too."

"There are no words, Cami."

I breathed a sigh of relief. He was no longer telling me to leave. Whatever had happened, it had to be temporary. My mother had warned me in a dream, telling me I had to leave him to protect him. I began to wonder if this could have been prevented if I'd just followed her advice.

Zandra told me she'd looked into my future and decided to keep Drake and me apart. Could either or both of them have seen this coming? If I'd let them help, could I have kept Drake safe? If his transformation wasn't temporary, there were two truths I knew: one, I loved him with all of my heart, and two, I didn't care what shape he was in, I would never want anyone but Drake in my life.

Drake tossed the backpack behind me. He leaned me gently on the blanket, placing my head on the backpack as a pillow. It was awkward at first, but he'd somehow tucked his legs in under his body and found a way to curl up beside me. I stared straight into his beautiful blue eyes, losing myself. Drake's hand began to tremble. There was no reason for him to be apprehensive, but with each new movement, it felt like he had to convince himself that it was okay.

His hand reluctantly slid under my shirt and grazed the skin on my abdomen, sending goose bumps all over my body. He was waiting for me to tell him to stop. I closed my eyes and enjoyed his touch, savoring whatever we were afforded. I didn't care that he had been transformed. I didn't care about the arrow. I only cared that I'd found him and no one would ever take him away from me.

CHAPTER 26

Camille – Abandoned Barn, SD

I had dozed off, but Drake shifted, and when the warmth of his body moved away from mine, the frigid temperature attacked my skin, jolting me awake. My eyes popped open, and I saw that he was still beside me. I could feel his breath against my ear and my neck rested on his arm while his other lay over me. It wasn't a dream. I eased up into a sitting position to get a better look at what I'd been too nervous to see before. It was such a foreign sight that I wanted my senses to take him in. I reached toward his legs with my hand when I heard, "Cami, don't."

I felt my body go rigid. I'd thought he was sound asleep. When I looked up, his eyes were giving me a warning. I answered with a smile, "I just want to touch your legs."

He threw a weathered blanket over himself to hide them. He let out a deep sigh, "Cami, this won't work."

"It worked for Unice and Winfield."

"No, it didn't. Aphrodite felt sorry for them and made Unice human.

She did it because it couldn't work any other way."

"That's not true. She could have made Winfield a Centaur."

"Don't say that, Cami. Don't even think it."

"Why not?"

"Because that was thousands of years ago. There weren't that many people back then. Centaurs could live away from humans without being discovered. How long do you think I can stay hidden, looking like this? Wait until the Centaur Council finds out. They'll sign my death warrant just to make sure no one finds me."

"So, we'll stay hidden. Do you remember the promise you made me?" Drake's eyes narrowed, but he remained quiet. I asked again, "After I'd chosen you, do you remember your promise?"

"That was before I had hooves."

"So, you take it back?"

"Cami, we can't be betrothed. We can't be married. We don't have a future together anymore."

"We do if you want it. You want to make sure no one ever sees you, fine. I'll ask Will to buy us a thousand acres somewhere. We'll put up a huge fence so no one can get through. We'll shove a couple king-sized mattresses in a barn. You know why? Because you promised me I'd never be alone. You don't get to take that promise back. It's mine. You gave it to me!"

Drake's fingers weaved through my hair, his lips crushed hard against mine, and the hurt I'd felt turned to anger against him. I wanted to hear him say that things were going to be fine. I refused to listen to his crap about I needed to get on with my life. Drake was my life. Our kiss deepened, sending heat from my hair to my toes. I pressed myself fully against him, and I heard my favorite moan escape his lips.

As I pulled away from him, my stare wouldn't let him go. His voice was thoughtful, "Okay, I get it. You're not going anywhere."

"Don't sound so thrilled."

A gentle smile formed on his lips, "I'm not thrilled. How could I be? By staying with me, you'll never have a normal life, or any kind of life you deserve."

"It's temporary, Drake. And even if it were permanent, it wouldn't change a thing."

"Temporary? I don't think so."

"So did you get ovaries with those hooves?"

"What?!" Drake's eyes opened wide and he stood up from the floor.

"The last time I checked, *I* was the Centauride. *I* was the one who could see the future."

"No Centauride can see her own future."

"I'd buy that except Zandra can see the future. She knew about Zeus's curse and told me she wanted her arrow back. I think it's within her power to remove the curse."

"But the arrow has never belonged to her. And even if she could, you think she'd remove the curse, from me?"

"If she could remove the curse, so could I. It's got to be a Chiron thing."

"You aren't touching that arrow, and we can't let Zandra have it."

I agreed with his thoughts on Zandra. I'd do nearly anything to have Drake normal, but giving Zandra any more power than she already had wasn't something I could agree to. Then it occurred to me, "What about Zethus?"

Drake cocked his head to the side. "I've already tried to call him. He never gave us his last name. At least not the one he uses."

"We could be on a plane tomorrow."

Drake's eyes looked at his body in a silent answer.

"Right. So maybe flying you there isn't the best idea. Give me the arrow and I'll go."

"No. I don't want you touching it."

"Geeze, Drake, Cameron had it his whole life, and he was fine."

"You're not Cameron, and I'm not taking the chance that he was just lucky."

I heard footsteps crunching in the snow, off in the distance, walking toward us. Drake heard them at the same time and trotted over to a gap in the planks of the barn to see who the intruder was. His voice was quiet as he reached up to turn off the lantern, "They're here for you." I was standing beside him and wrapped my fingers around his. Drake leaned down and gently kissed my cheek. "You can't stay here, Cami. It's ten degrees out. Let them take you back to the hotel."

I tried to look through a smaller gap in the boards, but I couldn't make out who the figures were. "I'm not leaving you."

"I don't want you to go either, but it's too cold. You can't stay. It's Lacey, her father, and Beau. They're here for you; they'll get you where it's warm. Go. I'll call you in the morning."

I protested through chattering teeth, acutely aware of the temperatures now that I wasn't curled up next to Drake. "I'm-m-m-m n-n-n-not leaving you alone."

"I'm built for this. You aren't. Lacey's the seer who sent Beau and Daniel to warn us about Phineas. You can trust her. Don't let them see me like this. I don't know her father, but I'm sure his reaction would be bad. If you love me, you'll go."

I worried that if I left with them, Drake would disappear again and I'd never find him. "When will I see you again?"

"I'll be here. I promise. Go, quickly. If they come through that door, I'm a dead man."

"I don't understand?"

"I promise I'll explain tomorrow. Please, Cami. Go." The urgency in his voice was something I trusted. I squeezed his hand and made a dash for the door just as the trio was an arm's distance away from the structure.

Lacey's voice was the one I heard as I pulled the door open, "We found you!" Her voice sounded excited.

Beau scooped me up in a bear hug and twirled me around as I

answered, "Yeah, thanks."

When Beau put me down, he asked, "Are you nuts? We've been looking for you for hours! There's a blizzard coming! Why were you out here by yourself? Why didn't you answer your phone?"

"There isn't much of a signal here, and you know why I was out here."

Beau shook his head, "Did you find him?"

I hated lying to Beau, but Drake seemed really worried about anyone finding him. "No, but I felt like I was getting closer this time." I felt like my world had been rocked all over again. How could I leave Drake alone, here, with a blizzard on the way. I'd never been in one but had seen them on the Weather Channel. What would happen to him?

Lacey stepped in between me and Beau. She took my hand to reassure me, and whispered so low, nobody but me could hear, "He'll be fine. He wants you to go." She gave my hand a gentle squeeze, silently telling me what I already knew. Lacey reminded me of Bianca, and I had to trust that she would keep Drake's secret for me.

Beau had his phone out and was dialing as the four of us walked to the gravel driveway where they'd left their SUV rental. "Dad, we found her. She's okay." I couldn't hear William's side of the conversation, but Beau answered him, "Yeah, we'll be back at the hotel in thirty minutes. We'll fly out after the weather passes. It's supposed to be a pretty bad storm." Another pause where William was talking, then Beau answered, "Okay. I don't know why you sent Bart back, but we'll get him from the airport on the way back to the hotel. I'll tell her. See you in a couple days."

I didn't care what message Beau was going to pass along from William. I wasn't getting on any plane without Drake.

CHAPTER 27

Drake – Abandoned Barn, SD

I watched the taillights pull away from the house and drive down the dark road. She was gone. I could feel the emptiness in my chest returning. Cami had filled the hole while she was here, but she took my heart with her when she left. Since the night I stole the arrow, the night of my transformation, I was sure I'd never see her again. Her reaction puzzled me: it was almost as if she were blind to it.

I loved her. I really loved her. I had convinced myself the only way to prove my love was to let her go, to shove her toward Daniel. He could give her what I couldn't – a normal life. The night I called him begging him to take care of her, I destroyed half an acre of trees after I hung up with him.

I'd believed my life was over; then she started looking for me. At first I was a little surprised; then I realized she was tracking me with uncanny accuracy. She had had me on the run for two full days. Tonight when she caught up to me, I didn't have the strength to run away from her again.

I expected her to see me and that would be it. Either her brothers would come later and hunt me down, or she'd spread the word and let my family take care of it. Having a living, breathing Centaur walking the earth would prove to be too much of a risk for our whole race. We'd lived undetected with humans for millennia; no one would let me live if they knew.

Until tonight, I guess I wasn't convinced she felt for me the way I felt for her.

When I shut my eyes, I could remember every moment, every conversation, every. . . touch we had ever shared. I believed the day she chose me could never be topped, but tonight, when she said the words about not letting me take back my betrothal pledge, I fell in love with her all over again. There is nothing I wouldn't do for her, no sacrifice I wouldn't make, and no risk that would ever be too great. She was mine.

I remembered seeing an electrical outlet in the pumphouse. It was the only place on the property that had electricity. I loped over to it with my cell phone and charger. I wanted to make sure it would have a charge when she called.

Looking at my watch, it was almost 1 a.m. I was running low on food. There was a farmhouse twenty acres from here, where they had a deepfreeze on their back porch. I'd make a midnight run. I didn't need a place to preserve anything that I took; according to the forecasts, it wouldn't be over thirty degrees for at least the next seven days.

I counted out some cash from my wallet and put it in an easy access pocket in my backpack and threw it over my shoulders. Grocery stores were out of the question for me, so leaving cash in place of the food I took seemed the best I could do.

I made my way slowly along the tree line. Then I realized I liked the way the earth felt under me. Everyone was fast asleep by now, and it would be hours before anyone stirred. I ran at a full gallop, the earth pounding under my hooves, wind blowing against my face, sweat beading on my chest, my muscles welcoming the challenge.

I could run as fast now as I ever could when I was in a human form, but feeling the earth beneath me, I slowed my pace to a horse's gallop. I'd run nearly a mile when a sharp pang of fear sliced through my chest. I stopped abruptly, stepped into the camouflage of the trees, and tried desperately to slow my labored breathing. I listened hard, trying to hear the sound of anyone or anything that may have alerted me.

I took in a deep breath and silently let it release. I noticed my surroundings. It was too much of a coincidence. I was too close to the place I'd hidden the arrow. Zigzagging through the trees, I retraced my steps.

When I'd hidden it away, a fresh blanket of snow was falling, hiding my hoof prints from others. As I approached the little church, I saw fresh footsteps that couldn't have been there longer than an hour. It was only one set, and they led into the structure.

Whoever it was, they were still in there. Maybe it was someone like myself, someone who had heard about the blizzard on the way and was simply looking for shelter. There would be no better place to wait out the gods' wrath.

I stayed in the tree line in a position where I could watch the exits, where it would be nearly impossible to see me from the inside. I waited for hours. As dawn began to approach, it struck me as odd that whoever had gone into the long forgotten church hadn't started a fire. I'd been in this form for a week, and the temperature normally didn't bother me, but the wind had to be blowing at close to thirty miles per hour, and the air was well below zero.

I wanted to get a better look inside. Maybe whoever had stumbled into the structure was hurt and needed help. If I was going to peek through the window, I'd need to do it now, before the sun came up.

A large oak tree obscured the window's view, and I did my best to stay off to the side of it. Anyone looking out the window wouldn't see me. Unless they were directly in front of it, I'd be in the tree's blind spot.

When I peeked through the window, I saw a woman lying still on a church pew. I took another step closer to the window to see if she had any obvious injuries.

She sat straight up, her voice booming, "I thought you would make me come looking for you, Drake. Come in so we can get this over with, and I can get out of this disgusting place."

I froze. I didn't know what she was or how she knew who I was. She was not a Centauride, but magic coursed through her veins. It was not any magic I had come in contact with: it was powerful, all-consuming – immortal magic. I argued with myself about what I should do, and then I saw it in her hand: the arrow. She was twirling it like a high school baton. My heart stopped; my blood forgot how to move through my veins.

"You can come in here out of the cold. I want to talk to you. I'm taking this arrow back to whom it belongs: Hercules."

The thought of losing the arrow overwhelmed the fear that I would come face-to-face with an immortal. Without the arrow, I'd never get Zeus's curse lifted.

I stepped up to the doorway of the abandoned church, "Who are you?"

"I'm Harmonia. I've asked my mother to help you."

"Harmonia? Your mother? Wait. . ." recognition flooded my mind, ". . . your mother is Aphrodite! Is she going to help me?"

"I'm not sure. I hope so. The fruit basket at the hotel got her attention. This arrow has caused nothing but pain and death since the day Hercules put it in his quiver. I mean to take it back with me. I don't want anything else to happen."

"Wait! No. Look at me. Zeus's curse transformed me. I won't be able to get the curse lifted if I can't get it back to its rightful owner."

"Hercules is its rightful owner. It was given to Chiron. While his family possessed it, no one would take it back. Now that they no longer have it, it needs to be taken back where it belongs."

"Can Hercules lift the curse?"

"And override his father? I don't think so."

"How can I get my body back?"

"That's the body you were meant to have. Maybe you should embrace it." My plight didn't move her to help me, but what did I expect from Goddess Harmonia? Of course, she would tell me to embrace it. She helps people get along; she seeks harmony.

Frustrated with her reaction, I asked, "So, that's it? You waited around in a dilapidated church for hours to tell me you were taking the arrow, and I'll have the honor of living out the rest of my life as half a man. Thanks for nothing!"

"No. I waited to share with you that my mother is aware of your circumstance. She is considering whether to lobby Zeus on your behalf, but you must be worthy. The last time mother asked Zeus for a favor she ended up with my brother Priapus, so she needs to be sure you're worth it."

"Priapus? Who's he?"

"Priapus is the god of livestock." I couldn't tell if she was trying to be funny, but she continued, "Look him up and see what Hera did to him when she got jealous of my mother's conversation with Zeus. You'll understand why my mother won't lobby for you unless it's really worth it."

I winced. I didn't need to look him up; I had heard the stories of what Hera had done to him. I flinched at the fact that in Harmonia's eyes, maybe I was merely livestock. A plan started to take shape in my mind. I took several steps in her direction, only a mere arm's length away. I wanted to snatch it from her, take back my life.

Harmonia's tone was contemptuous when she answered, "Despite your new physique, you are but a mortal. Do not attempt to take the arrow from me. Crossing me would not be wise."

Ashamed she had so quickly seen my plan, even before I could commit to it, I bowed my head and answered, "I beg your pardon, Goddess Harmonia. May I plead my case to you?"

"I have what I came for, and I have left you with some hope. There's nothing more I can offer you."

I had to delay her, come up with a way to keep her from making off with the arrow. "How did you find the arrow?"

"It was built by immortal hands. Think of it like a plane's little black box. It gives off a signal so immortals can find it."

"But why did you wait for me?"

"I could have located you, but I'm an immortal, so time doesn't have the same meaning to me. Waiting for you reduced any chance of running into a human."

"But, you didn't just take it. Is there anything I can do to convince you to leave it with me?"

She smiled, "I'm afraid not, Drake. Things have a way of working out. As I've said, hope is not lost." She didn't leave me with hope. She was carrying what little hope I had in her hand. It felt as though she had wielded a sword that sliced my soul into pieces. My head stayed bowed as she walked past me, through the door, and out into the forest.

All of my hopes vanished with her into the storm. The arrow was lost, and with it, the life I had hoped might still be in my grasp.

I abandoned my plan to raid the deepfreeze of the farmhouse. Food was no longer important. Instead I returned to the barn where just hours before I had held Cami – maybe for the last time. I remembered my promise to call her in the morning. I had made her promises I would no longer be able to keep, but this was one of the few I could.

I walked to the pumphouse to retrieve my cell phone, now holding a full charge. A voice mail was waiting for me. It was from Cami; my hand shook as I stared at it. I wasn't sure I possessed the strength to listen.

When I got inside the barn, I closed my eyes, pressed *play,* and braced myself for what I was about to hear. Her voice was beautiful, much as I'd imagined an angel's might sound like, "Hey, it's me. I know you're freaked out. I wanted you to know, I'm not. You know when I was freaked out? When I didn't know where you were or if you were okay. I can handle anything as long as I'm with you. Don't disappear again. I'm pretty sure losing you one more time would kill me." There was a long pause before she added, "I love you, Drake."

The voicemail ended and I pressed "play" a second time. Then a third. Finally a fourth.

I looked down at myself. How could she love this? How could she willingly give up her future for me? The ache in my chest began to intensify. I couldn't tell if my heart was swelling or breaking. I listened to her voicemail a fifth time.

A single tear rolled down my cheek. She wouldn't abandon me, but what kind of a life would it be for her? Hiding in shadows, sleeping in barns, for what? Without thinking of the repercussions, I began shouting into the night. "Dammit! Damn Zandra for making us believe we would never be safe. Damn Chiron for holding onto the arrow to begin with. And Damn Zeus for letting this whole situation happen!"

The barn began to shake; snow fell in through a hole in the corner of the roof. I could feel the ground rumbling underneath me. I squatted down, wondering how often earthquakes happened in this part of the country. I'd been wrong: the earth wasn't shaking, just the structure. A booming voice echoed through the barn, "Be careful, Centaur. Be mindful of the seventh tenet."

Without thinking about which god the voice could belong to, I shouted, "Go to Hades!"

The same booming voice made the walls vibrate again, "Drake of the Nash herd, be mindful of the seventh tenet!"

The seventh was one of the easiest to avoid: *Never speak ill of the gods.* With more rage than I could ever remember coursing through me, I shouted, "Strike me down. Take away my Centaur blood, do whatever the hell you want. My life's over anyway!"

The booming voice responded, "You are not worthy of my gifts. You have broken the seventh tenet."

The words: *my gifts* echoed in my head. Zeus was talking to me? I had just told the father of the gods to strike me down? I had more than broken the tenet; I had thrown it in *his* face and told him to strike me down. Before I could do anything else stupid, I came to my senses and forced myself to be quiet.

"You have nothing to say in your defense?"

Oh right, let's see, maybe he didn't notice I have hooves or a tail. Yeah, right. I needed to get it together. I was a mortal. I knew better than to provoke the gods. Asking him to strike me down would accomplish nothing, and if he did, what would happen to Cami?

I swallowed what was left of my pride, "I humbly apologize for my outburst. I meant no disrespect, only that I . . . only that. . . my circumstances are dire."

I stood motionless, waiting for him to take his vengeance on me. Whatever he decided would be over soon. I couldn't imagine anything he did would be worse than me telling Cami what happened with the arrow. His voice was still strong and unyielding, but his volume much lower, "Drake of the Nash herd, I am aware of your plight. It was not my curse that transformed you into the shape of your ancestors."

Not his curse? Was this Zeus? It couldn't be. Zeus didn't deliver messages to mortals. He had lesser gods and demi-gods to deal with us. If it was Zeus, he must already know as soon as I pulled the arrow from the book, I transformed into a real Centaur. Of course, it was his curse. "Will you tell me how I was transformed, if not at your hand?"

"My dear friend Chiron was immortal, were you aware?"

"Yes, your grace."

"When he took his place in the stars to watch over his children, all the remaining magic he had was put into the arrow. The arrow has protected his family ever since. I can transform you into what you were before you touched the arrow, but that transformation carries a price."

"Anything, your grace. I'll do anything."

"Let me finish before you agree. I am not unfeeling and believe you should know the repercussions before I set things as they were. You have been chosen by Chiron's last Centauride heir, Camille."

I nodded my answer and he continued. "You are aware that not only does she belong to Chiron, she is also part of the Tak family. The Tak bloodline was cast out by me with a death warrant placed on their heads. Until recently, I believed they had been expunged from existence. Once again, I had been deceived when I learned the Tak bloodline still roamed the earth. Their powers are too dangerous. They are deceitful and my order stands. A Centaur Council meeting will be held soon: a messenger of mine will attend and will reiterate my decree."

Forgetting who I was addressing I blurted out, "But Cami isn't dangerous! She would never hurt anyone, she . . . she. . . she didn't even know she was a Centauride. She grew up as a human. You have to spare her life!"

"I will not make the distinction." A long pause echoed loudly in the silence of the night. "But out of respect for Chiron and his attempt to save his last remaining female heir, I share with you what will happen soon, so you may make an informed choice now. I can transform you into your human form, just as you were before you touched Chiron's arrow. Or I can leave you as you are now, the fierce warrior who is capable of defending Camille should she be attacked."

"I was a warrior in my human form. I would lay down my life protecting her."

"Ahhh, that is exactly the choice. You were recently in a situation where you were attacked by four Centaurs and your strength and determination were not enough to save her. Do you remember? What happens when you are attacked by eight, or ten, or twenty? You do not stand a chance to protect your beloved if you are human. Chiron still watches his children, and your transformation is his way of protecting his daughter."

"You are offering me my old body back? No strings?"

"Yes. I have watched your every move since your transformation. You have proven your worthiness. Should you wish your previous form, I will make it so."

"But if you change me back, you don't believe I'll be strong enough to protect Cami?"

"I know you won't, son. When I reiterate my decree with the Centaur Council, Camille's life will be in danger. She will require a true warrior at her side. Out of respect for my friend, Chiron, I leave the choice up to you."

I thought back to the morning in the hotel room and the helplessness that I felt when Phineas and his goons took her away. After Cami had been kidnapped, not knowing where she was or what they were doing to her, I thought I would go insane. My gaze fell onto this body, this *form* Zeus had called it. He was right. I was strong, powerful, and the diluted warrior I had been as a human had been reconstituted when my body morphed.

If I told Zeus to change me back, I wondered if Cami and I could hide. If we could find an obscure home away from all Centaurs and humans, we might spend the rest of our days wrapped up with just the two of us both in human form. As much as I savored that thought, I knew it to be unlikely under normal circumstances; if every Centaur on the planet were after her, it would be impossible. We would never be able to start a family as our children would also carry the Tak blood and would be targets, as well.

"I need your decision, Drake of the Nash Herd."

"Thank you for the choice, your grace. I choose this form. I must remain a warrior."

"Very well. You are a noble warrior and when the time comes, I promise you a warrior's death." I don't know why, but talking to thin air felt odd, and I kept expecting a body to materialize in front of me.

Instead I heard his voice growing distant, "May the Fates be your friends, and may death always be a stranger to you."

A ferocious *BOOM* let loose. If there had been an aircraft overhead, I would have sworn the sound barrier had just been broken. Instead the walls gave one final quiver, then folded in and the structure came down on top of me.

I lay buried in the rubble. I felt around in the dark, my fingers grasping at the dirt floor while hundreds of pounds of weathered wood lay on me. When I didn't find my backpack, I scooted another few feet to the left. The lantern I had used was still lit; I turned it off before it could catch the old wood lying atop it on fire.

I fanned my hand out again, and found the canvas of the backpack – it was all I had in the world. Clutching the backpack in one hand and my lifeline to Cami in the other, I used the massive strength in my legs to kick the fallen wall away.

Splinters of wood flew in all directions as what was left of the wall holding me gave way. I righted myself and stepped over the pile of rubble. I walked a few feet into the tree line; the wind blew hard and the snow nearly blinded me. The blizzard had arrived. I had no arrow, no shelter, and would now never have Cami the way I longed for her.

I stood there in shock, hearing the words from Zeus echo over and over in my mind. I would live in this form for the rest of my life. I wanted the words to stop playing in my head, but I couldn't drown them out with thoughts of anything else. I tried to concentrate on the memory of Cami, not anything specific, just the warm memory of her love engulfing me. Even the memories I carried with me would not drown out the knowledge that I'd just chosen this form for the rest of my life. I would remain this half a person until I died.

I pressed "play" on my voicemail and tried to listen to Cami's message again. My eyes began to burn, and my body felt numb. I couldn't tell if it was from the cold or if it was adjusting to the knowledge that Cami's life would never be the same again. Over the howling wind I could barely make out Cami's words from the voicemail. I pressed play again. And again. The burning in my eyes refused to leave, no matter how many times I listened to Cami's words of love.

I couldn't make a call from outside. She'd never hear me over the wind. I staggered through the gusts, back to the pumphouse. After I wedged myself inside the little structure, the air was still frigid, but it felt warm without the blowing snow pelting me. I pulled a string hanging from a light fixture; a little twenty-five watt light bulb glowed to life. I went to press play one more time but dialed her number instead.

Cami's voice answered right away, "Drake? Are you okay?"

No, I wasn't okay. I'd never be okay again. "I just wanted to hear your voice."

"I was worried. You didn't answer when I called last night. I thought . . I mean. . . never mind. I'm glad you called me."

"Lacey didn't tell the others about me?"

"No. Not a word. They all think we're leaving after the storm blows over. I've been trying to figure out how to break it to them that I'm staying here. I'm going to call Cameron and see if I can stay at his house until we can figure out how to get you and the arrow to Zethus."

Her voice was so full of hope, how could I tell her?

Cami couldn't read my thoughts, and I didn't interrupt her. "I saw Zandra. She told me that Cameron's guardian left him when he turned eighteen. But she's lied about so much – I want to talk to him to find out if his house is really vacant."

How do you break it to someone that there's no future, at least not the future you've dreamed of your whole life? I needed to come up with a plan, find a place where I could keep Cami safe. I filled my lungs with air, released it slowly and said, "It might be better for you to spend a little time with William and Gretchen. Recover. You've been through a lot."

"I'm not leaving you, Drake." Her voice was quiet and slow when she continued. "We're going to be fine. Just think, we'll be telling our kids this story some day."

I could feel the muscles around my heart constrict. No future. No happily-ever-after. No kids. No Cami. The thoughts came to me as if shot from an automatic weapon. "I'm not saying to leave forever. But you may need to rest somewhere, you know, to be safe."

"I'm safe with you, Drake. Besides, we've got to figure out how we can fly you out of South Dakota and into Ireland. Have you ever been to a country where you didn't have to pass through customs? I found a charter that will transport horses internationally, but I'm not sure how to get you through the customs inspection."

The muscles holding my heart constricted harder – livestock. That's what I was now. I knew she didn't mean anything by it. Cami was being practical, trying to think through the situation. But that was me: I had hooves and a tail to prove it. Maybe I could buy half a Halloween costume to put over my torso to hide me from prying eyes.

"Drake, are you there? Did I lose you?"

She could never lose me. I could never have her the way I wanted her, but as her sworn guardian, I would never be away from her. Her voice was more urgent, "Drake, can you hear me?"

"I'm here, Love. No. I don't know how to fly into another country and avoid customs."

"Okay. We'll figure something out. The storm's supposed to blow through by late afternoon today. Do you remember how to get to Cameron's house?"

"Cami. . ." I needed to see her again, but the more time I spent with her, the harder she would be to give up. I needed to find a place where she'd be safe, and it would be better for her to go back to San Diego with Beau for a few days.

"Listen, Drake. I can hear it in your voice. Don't. Whatever you're thinking – you're wrong. We're going to get through this. We're going to work it out. Everything's going to be fine. The only way it won't be fine is if you disappear again. Promise me you won't take off!"

I didn't answer right away. Her voice was angry when she said, "You promised me, Drake! You said if I left with them for the storm you wouldn't go anywhere!" She was crying. I didn't need to see the tears, her voice gave her away.

"I'm here, Love. I promise, I'm here."

"You'll meet me at Cameron's later today?"

I needed to tell her what was about to happen. For the first time I realized my sole focus had been on Cami, but her entire family was in as much danger as she was. I'd meet with her at Cameron's, tell her what needed to be done, and get her on the first flight out with Beau to warn the others. "As soon as the weather clears."

I traveled to Cameron's place right after I hung up with Camille. I couldn't tell her what had happened over the phone, but I vowed that I'd tell her the truth as soon as she arrived. I was sure she'd be furious with my decision, but if it came down to my happiness or Cami's life, I wouldn't gamble with her life.

Luckily, Cameron didn't keep his house locked. I had been at his house for hours when the storm finally let up. I tried not to pace, but I wanted to keep an eye out near the highway. The little road that Cameron's house set on had been drifted over by snow. Cami wouldn't be able to drive much past the highway.

Just after three p.m. I saw the little car's headlights turn down onto the road. The car made it onto the road, but the blowing snow created a drift that a monster truck wouldn't have been able to plow through. When I saw the car stuck, I ran to her. I didn't worry about anyone seeing me from the highway. Anyone passing by would be focused on the road in front of them and not the little side road. I loped up to her before she could even turn the engine off. The car would look abandoned if anyone saw it from the road, but it was far enough in, passing snow plows wouldn't bother it.

She fought with the drift to get the door to open until I gave it a quick tug from the outside. She hadn't seen me in the daylight, and I caught her staring.

When she was free of the car, she climbed over the snow drift and leaped into my awaiting arms. She felt so tiny as I held her off the ground. She was bundled up in a ski jacket, gloves, a hat, and tall leather boots. I set her down so we could get her out of the cold and into Cameron's house. As we walked, her strides were so much shorter than mine; it was clumsy to walk beside her. I had considered throwing her up over my back and giving her "a ride" to the house, but the thought repulsed me. Instead I reached down and picked her up with both arms and carried her to the little house.

We arrived at the front door that led to an enclosed porch, then into the kitchen. I had gone over how to break it to her hundreds of times in my mind. When we were inside the warmth of the house, she took her jacket off. I was absolutely speechless. I couldn't look away. I couldn't breathe.

Cami stood before me wearing a simple pair of blue jeans, a long sleeved t-shirt and tall leather boots – a practical outfit considering our environment, but absolutely gorgeous. Last night I had been so shocked by her words that I hadn't given myself a chance to appreciate her beauty. Before I could say a word, she held up a finger as I stood in the kitchen and said, "Wait right here."

She emerged from the living room with a small step stool, positioned it directly in front of me, and climbed it so we were eye-to-eye. Her brown eyes looked directly into mine. Cami's voice was determined when she said, "I made a pledge of my own."

"What?"

"When I told you that I chose you, you made me a promise saying I'd never go to bed angry or wake up alone. With everything going on, I want you to hear my pledge to you."

"Cami, it's the betrothal pledge. It's made by the Centaur to the Centauride. There've been a few developments since last night that we need to talk about."

"Okay, but after."

"It's important."

Her voice was stern, "In a minute. You're going to listen to this, because this is my promise to you. I promise to love you without conditions. I promise always to look on the bright side of things regardless of the situation. I promise to find a way to make this work. I promise never to give you up."

Cami wrapped one arm around me and the other behind my head; beautiful milk-chocolate eyes closed slowly as I saw her lips coming toward mine. My lips moved on reflex as I deepened our kiss and pressed her against me. My hands longed for the suppleness of her skin and slid under her t-shirt to find it. I gently caressed the skin on her back as our kiss showed no signs of ending.

As we stood there in the kitchen locked on each other, I heard her words echo in my mind: *I promise to find a way to make this work.* She was serious.

The fact that I was no longer a man didn't give her a moment's pause. This was the love no Centaur before me had ever known. They couldn't. Arranged marriages, or selections by Centaurides who knew nothing of the Centaurs they chose – none were ever given the chance to fall in love with the other in the beginning.

Then it hit me, Unice had felt this kind of love from Winfield. Maybe it was a curse, but this curse had a silver lining. I would never doubt Cami's love for me.

When we finally pulled away from each other, I knew that I'd been looking at the situation the wrong way. I had missed what was most important because I was blinded by my circumstance.

I wasn't a Centaur as a punishment from Zeus, I was in this form by my own choice. I was this way because Cami needed me to be a warrior for her. Cami accepted me without even knowing the reason. The late afternoon sun shone through the window in the kitchen behind Cami, giving her a heavenly quality. "What was so important that you wanted to tell me?"

Without hesitation, "Only that I am the luckiest Centaur ever to walk the earth." I wouldn't push Cami away. If she ever tired of the situation, I wouldn't guilt her into staying with me, but I now knew the depth of her love was as endless as mine. She was more than my love, more than my Centauride or soul mate – Cami completed me.

A thought occurred to me that had evaded me before. Even if Zeus had not spelled it out for me, I knew in that moment why the arrow had given me this form. This is how I could best protect her from her own curse she carried with her every day.

I was strong and fast in my human form, but my skills before paled in comparison to now. Had I been in this form when Phineas came after her, the outcome would have been much different. Those four Centaurs wouldn't have stood a chance against me.

I considered the events of last night, before Zeus appeared. Even if Cami had seen me and rejected me, there is nothing I wouldn't have done to protect her. The arrow had offered better protection to the Chiron family than anyone could ever have imagined. I'd learned of the arrow when I was just a child and had been told that it carried immortal magic. Until I held it in my hand and it transformed me, I had no appreciation for the magic pulsing through it, and now that same magic pulsed through me.

CHAPTER 28

Drake – Cameron's House, SD

Camille opened the refrigerator, "Are you hungry?"

My plan last night to raid a farmer's freezer in the middle of the night had been abandoned. Today was the first day I had been inside, out of the elements, in five days. I unconsciously let my guard down and allowed myself to feel hunger, not just for food, but the hunger for Cami, too. I'd be able to eat and appease my appetite, but I knew the hunger I felt for Cami would never be satisfied. I reached into a cupboard, found a crumpled up, half-eaten bag of Doritos and did my best to satisfy one of my appetites.

Cami shook her head, "I was thinking eggs."

"You can make eggs. I'd rather have these." I didn't want to own up to the fact that I'd eaten at least two dozen raw eggs the last few days, so they had little appeal for me now.

Cami followed me into the living room, taking a seat on the couch as I took a place on the floor beside her. She abandoned her plan to make eggs and shared the bag of Doritos with me. I didn't want to bring it up, but I needed to know. "So, what did Phineas do to you?"

She shook her head. "Nothing really."

I took both her hands in mine. I had imagined horrific things. I needed to know what the emotional scars were before I could understand how long it would take for her to heal. "Tell me. I need to know."

"It wasn't as bad as I had expected. He's really not that bright." I didn't interrupt, so she finally began, "He took me to Florida. I don't remember anything of the trip there: they'd knocked me out. Once I was there, they kept me sedated. I came to before they had expected me to, and I simply convinced them to let me go."

I shook my head. That didn't make any sense. Why would they go to all the trouble to take her, then just release her after she awoke? Cami was part of the Lost Herd. Had they done it to bring attention to her? To my knowledge, the Centaur Council had not been notified. Zandra chaired the Council, but even she wouldn't have wanted Cami's circumstances to come to light, would she? "How did you convince them to let you go?" Horrible images of Cami begging for her life filled my head.

She smiled at me. In that instant she had read my thoughts, and answered, "No, it wasn't like that. I said I convinced them to let me go; I didn't say I turned into a helpless little girl."

"Show me."

"I thought Centaurs couldn't read minds? Only Centaurides?"

I took her hands and brought them to my lips; there was so much she still didn't know. "I'm your Centaur, Cami. From the moment you chose me, you established a connection with me. I should be able to see any thoughts or images you want me to see."

As I lay there holding her hands, I saw the whole image of what had happened play out in detail in front of me. She was much stronger than I had given her credit for and more cunning than any Centauride I had ever known. I felt her rage.

After she had shown me the whole thing, I was stunned by how she had "convinced" them to let her go. "You can give someone a stroke? That's pretty lethal."

Her smile grew. "I needed to show him that I wasn't playing around."

"Phineas won't give up."

"Now that I know you're fine, I couldn't care less about Phineas." I knew how Centaurs thought. He wouldn't let it go, no matter how frightened he might be of Cami. She had put an enormous target on her back. Centaurides weren't the warriors of our race; they were the advisors. When word spread of Cami's abilities, the Centaur Council could decide she was enough of a threat to extinguish her themselves. Add Zeus into the equation, and we were running out of time. I was still holding her hands as we sat there in silence. I was careful to keep my concerns for her safety hidden behind my mind's wall. "Has anyone told you of the Centaur Council?"

"I've heard of it. You mentioned that they meet in Africa every year. What do they do?"

"Sometimes, it's merely for festivities. Sometimes they act as a tribunal. Zandra is the chairman of the Centaur Council."

Cami's eyes widened, "Someone elected her? What'd she do? Threaten everybody?"

"No. It's always chaired by a Chiron. Until you, Angelo was the only heir to take her seat when she was ready to step down."

I felt her hands tense. She thought little of her uncle, Angelo. Cami had told me about meeting him at Zandra's while we were walking the pastures in Ireland. Her opinion was shared by every other Centaur I knew. It's customary for a Chiron to lead the Council for twenty-five years, although it is at the Chairperson's discretion when he or she is replaced.

Zandra had been in power for nearly forty. As little as I thought of her, I couldn't help but be grateful with all the other Centaurs for her never having passed her position onto her son.

"What about Zethus or one of his sons?"

"I don't know how the Council decided between Zethus and Zandra, but I think you or Cameron are more likely than either of Zethus's sons." Cameron was just as likely to take over the Council as Cami, but the Centauride twin was usually selected because of her skills. Unfortunately, he was also in danger because of his shared lineage to the Tak bloodline.

"But why?"

"Judging by what you did to your captors, you are more powerful. If either of Zethus's sons could do anything close, we may never have gotten this far."

"Do you think Cameron can do what I do?"

"I don't know. I only met him briefly. No one knows much about the Lost Herd because, up until I met you, I didn't even know it still existed. As far as your Centauride abilities, I've never heard of the Chiron Centaurs having any special skills."

"But Phineas and William can't do what I can."

"Maybe they can and they don't know it."

We were interrupted by Cami's phone, "Hello?"

"Oh, hi, Will." She made a sour face. "No, I've decided to stay." Silence. I wanted to interrupt, to try to convince her I agreed with Will that she should go to South Carolina for a few days, but she didn't look my way.

"Because it's my choice." Silence. "I'm an adult, Will. I don't need to run my decisions past you. At least not the ones about staying here." I needed to warn Will, too. He and his family would all soon be targets if they weren't already.

"Fine, but they'll be bored at the hotel. I'm staying out at Cameron's." He must have told her that Bart and Beau were going to stay on. "There is one thing I need you to do for me. I want you to call Drake's parents. Tell them I've chosen him."

A short silence while Will responded to her request and then her voice fired back, "I don't care if you think it's a bad idea or not. Either you call them or I will."

More silence. Her eyes met mine. Will was still on the phone while she told me, "Your father knows my bloodline's from the Lost Herd."

I needed to talk to Will, and given Cami's frustration with him, now was the opportune moment. I reached over and squeezed Cami's knee. "Can you put Will on speaker?"

"Hold on, Will, Drake wants to talk to you."

She pressed the speaker button and laid the phone on her lap. "Will, it's Drake. Can you hear me okay?"

He gave me a frosty response, "Yes, Drake. As I was telling Camille, I'm not sure how welcomed a betrothal to Camille will be with your father right now."

"So, it's true. Centaurs are aware you are from the Lost Herd?"

"I'm afraid so. So far there haven't been any attacks, but we think it's just a matter of time. I've told Beau and Bart I want them to stay up north with Camille."

Camille cut in, "Attacks?!"

Will's tone was soft, "Yes, Camille. I'm sorry to tell you this over the phone. Long ago, when all the herds were still at the pasture of Thessaly, Zeus became angry with our bloodline. He decreed that the Tak line be extinguished. His decree has never been repealed."

Cami was shocked into silence. I took a deep breath. There was a good chance Will wouldn't believe me, but it was more important that his family be ready than it was for them to think I'm sane. "Will, I'm a Centaur."

"Drake, that isn't a secret."

Cami shook her head at me. I hadn't wanted anyone to know initially, but that was before I had made the choice, before I had willingly given up my human form in an effort to save her from the dangers ahead. "No. You don't understand. I've been transformed into a real Centaur. I have hooves, a tail, and I tip the scales at more than nine hundred pounds."

Frustration seeped into his voice, "I don't know what game you're playing, but it isn't funny. Camille, I want you to go back to the hotel. Now."

This time Cami interrupted, "No. Will, it's true. I found Drake last night. When he touched the arrow at Cameron's house, it transformed him."

"What?"

I took a deep breath, "Zeus intends to send a messenger to address the Centaur Council. He plans to remind them about his death warrant on the Tak family."

Disbelief colored his response, "Zeus? Zeus, the father of gods intends to go to the next Centaur Council meeting? The weather on Mount Olympus isn't to his liking these days? That's what you're telling me?"

"Will, I know it's hard to believe. He spoke to me last night. He offered to make me human again," I paused feeling Cami's eyes on me, "but the price was too high." My hand was still on Cami's knee; I gave it a reassuring squeeze. This was not the way I wanted to tell her. "He also shared that he was not pleased that the Tak bloodline was still intact. He intends to remind all the Centaurs on the Council of their responsibility to extinguish the bloodline."

"This is Phineas's fault. If he hadn't pulled that stunt, everything would have been fine."

"I think you're past the point of assigning blame. Will, you need to get you and your family to safety. I'll find a place for Cami and me, but I don't want her worried about all of you. You need to go into hiding – now, before any more people know about you."

Silence. "All right, thanks for the warning. Where are you two going to be?"

"I haven't figured that out yet, but I promise you, no harm will come to her as long as I live."

"Drake, has anyone seen you?"

"No. Just Cami. I think Lacey knows, and I have to assume Zandra is aware, but no one else."

"I'm going to call Beau. I'll have him bring an account number to you. When you two went on the run to Ireland, I had one set up in the Caymans in case you needed it. It should be enough to start a life together. Camille?"

"I'm right here, Will."

"Cami, if this is the last time I talk to you, I want you to know I. . . I would have been better. I would have been there for you your whole life if I'd known. My only regret that I'll take to my grave is I was never able to make it up to you."

Cami's eyes got glossy. She pursed her lips together as if that could discourage the tears that wanted to let loose. I saw her hand start to shake and her voice trembled when she answered, "Dad, you have nothing to make up to me. In the short time we spent together you gave me more than I'd ever wished for. Gretchen even gave me Mom back for a little while. I don't regret calling you or anything that happened after I came to your home. We'll get through this. We'll find a way to make it right."

"Camille, say it again."

"Say what again? We'll get through this?"

Will's voice was full of emotion when he answered, "No. You just called me Dad."

Even my eyes clouded when I heard her whisper, "Take care of our family, Dad. We'll find you when it's safe." Cami handed me the phone and left the room; the good-bye was too much for her. I wasn't even a part of her family, and it was almost more than I could be an audience to.

"Will, I've got an idea how we can keep in contact with each other. I'll run it by Beau when he comes by. If you need us or if we need you, it'll be a safe way to contact each other."

"Take care of her, Drake."

"I will." He shared a few more tidbits of information with me, and we said our good-byes, as well.

My heart ached for Cami. She had been through so much in the past few months. No one would blame her for shutting down. Once again, she surprised me by emerging from the kitchen, eyes red and swollen, but dry. "Did he say anything else?"

"He called my parents to tell them of your choice. He said my parents know about the Lost Herd. My mother gave us her blessing."

"And your father?"

"I don't know. I didn't ask. He also said Zandra notified the Centaur Council that the Lost Herd had kidnapped her Centauride heir. She called a special session. Will thinks since you've made your choice clear, she may turn her sight back on you, maybe telling the Council that you had a hand in your own kidnapping."

"Will they believe her?"

I shook my head as if I didn't know. Absent anyone to tell them otherwise, they would absolutely believe Zandra. I couldn't bring myself to tell Cami. "He also said she'd tried to convince Kyle Richardson for another arranged marriage, this time to Gage's little brother, Brandon. Kyle refused, said you'd already made your choice."

A small part of me was pleased to hear Will say Zandra was trying to arrange a marriage to Brandon. If she were married to Brandon, no one would question her lineage. No one would dare. Instead of saying it out loud and taking Cami's wrath, I thought the words she wouldn't want to hear. "*Brandon's a good kid. You'd be safe if you chose him.*"

"Are you insane?! I told you this whole horse thing is temporary. We get the arrow back to Zethus and have him lift the curse, end of story."

I shook my head. It was time to share the whole truth. She needed to know I'd never be human again. I told her everything about my meeting with the Goddess Harmonia and with Zeus. After she heard it all, she sat still on the sofa, looking as though she were in a trance. I waved my hand in front of her face, worried that this had been the final straw and she would shut down. Without breaking her concentration on the wall opposite her, she murmured, "I love you, Drake. Wherever we go, you'd better find a house with big doorways, because I'm not sleeping in a barn for the rest of my life."

I didn't know what to say. Had she just cracked a joke? Was she delirious? "Cami, are you okay?"

Her eyes left the opposite wall and fell on mine. "You made the right choice. If Zeus knew our days were numbered with you as a human, I'd much rather have a long life with you like this, over a short life with you as a human. But I'm not sleeping in barns forever."

I pulled Cami off the sofa and into my arms. She wasn't angry, or hurt, or numb. She was keeping the promise to me she made the moment she arrived here today. She was looking on the bright side.

CHAPTER 29

Drake – Cameron's House, SD

Beau knocked on the door; Lacey was with him. I noticed Daniel was still absent, probably for the best. He had been angry with me the day I tried to get him to take Cami back to San Diego, then furious with Cami for refusing to go. She told me they weren't speaking to one another, but he refused to get on a plane until he was sure she didn't need him.

I hoped that one day I'd get a chance to know Daniel. There was never a more faithful and loyal friend a person could hope for, and I wanted to make sure Cami never lost him.

Beau had to get over the initial shock of seeing me. Will had already prepared him for it, and I was sure Lacey had confirmed it was true before they arrived – but seeing is believing. I understood the shock he was feeling, as I got the same surprise every time I walked past a mirror.

Cami and I had made two bogus Facebook profiles. There were only a few countries in the world that didn't have access to Facebook, and we didn't intend to go to those. She would be able to go to an internet café and check the messages. We all agreed we wouldn't post any actual pictures of ourselves or where we were, but if we needed to contact each other, we would be able to access these profiles.

I'd known Beau my whole life, and I hoped it wouldn't be long until we saw each other again. Beau held out his hand. I shirked it away and grabbed him in a warrior's embrace. "Take care, old friend. I hope we see each other again, soon."

"Take care of Cami," he turned his gaze to his sister, "and, Cami, don't let him get away with anything just 'cause he's got hooves. There isn't anything says a man's got to have toes to help with the dishes."

The three of us laughed while Lacey stood awkwardly a few feet away and cringed at Beau's comment. I'm sure she must have thought it callous, but it was far easier for all of us to look at the situation with humor, even if it was a dig on me

Beau would be the safest of the Strayer sons, since he was quickly approaching the end of his eligibility. The Centaur Council might choose to ignore him entirely in favor of rooting out members of the Lost Herd who could still cloak themselves as one of the other families. I hoped at least *he* would be safe. Bruce was the Strayer son who was closest to my age, but Beau had always been the big brother I wished I'd had.

Cami grabbed hold of Beau, "Thanks for dropping everything to come to our rescue. We'll do the same for you if you ever need it." Lacey and Cami had spent very little time together, so I was a little surprised at Lacey getting teared up.

Lacey said, "You two are going to be fine. I'm sure of it." It warmed my heart, whether it was a true premonition she'd had or just hopeful thinking.

Cami smiled, took Lacey in a quick hug and answered, "Lacey, thank you isn't adequate. I'll never forget you."

Beau held the kitchen door open for Lacey. It hadn't occurred to me until she passed under his arm through the door to their awaiting car; she had to have sneaked out of the hotel to accompany Beau here. No way would her father have allowed her unescorted in a car with Beau.

I wondered if there was something between them, but dismissed the idea. Beau had already made his decision to leave Centaurs behind and had broken it to his family. Her father must have considered Beau and Daniel safe escorts for her.

We watched their taillights disappear down the road. It would be a rough few weeks ahead of us, and I wanted to enjoy what little time we had left at Cameron's place without the stress of being on the run. I lit a fire in the fireplace, and joined Cami in the living room. Conversation was sparse, our time together to relax was limited, and neither of us needed to fill that time with words.

CHAPTER 30

Beau Strayer – Hotel near Crazy Horse Mountain, SD

We returned to the nearly abandoned hotel. Dad had rented the place for the month, so it looked like a ghost town. The eeriness of the quiet gave me goose bumps. As we walked into the empty lounge, Lacey's expression was tentative. I knew it was time for her to go. She was a sweet girl who dropped everything, putting her own grief on hold to help strangers; I'd never forget her. I wanted to tell her I'd see her back in San Diego, but that was a lie.

My decision had been made. When I returned to San Diego with Daniel, I would start my life over – no longer a part of the Centaur community. Being a descendant of the Lost Herd would be dangerous for my family, but Centaurs seeking the Lost Herd would not pursue me. My decision to leave Centaurs behind me and to live the remainder of my life as a human made me less of a target.

Lacey fidgeted with her purse, absently opening it, looking for something, then closing it. Lacey was a seer: she already knew what lay ahead of me. Her voice was soft when she said, "So, I guess there's nothing left but to go to the airport and to go home."

I could feel the smile stretch wide on my face, "Thanks, for everything. I mean it."

Lacey had been a few feet away from me. She walked over to me and put her hand on my forearm. Her touch was warm, and warning bells went off in my head. I'd been raised never to touch a Centauride, and except for few, if any, missteps in my life, I hadn't. Her gesture had caught me off guard. Electricity shot up my arm and straight to my heart.

I needed to pull my arm from her hand before I did something I'd regret later, but I didn't. Her touch was tender. The initial electricity I felt gave way to a warm sensation just before her words sliced me wide open. "Beau, you know it's your right to claim me."

I felt my heart picking up speed. She couldn't be serious. I'd already told her I wasn't carrying on my bloodline. I had decided to live as a human; I was doing it on my terms. She had her whole life ahead of her; why would she bring this up?

Lacey was just a kid – a stupid kid who was playing with fire. She didn't know the beast raging just under the surface, fighting to be free and make that proclamation.

I looked into her green eyes staring into mine, the delicate lines of her face – she was the most enchanting Centauride I'd ever seen. It would be easy to claim her as mine; it would be more than the answer to a prayer – but I had already resolved to that dream's death. I refused to sentence her to a marriage out of obligation. I simply responded, "I know."

Her eyes continued watching me; she waited for me to say something else. I refused to claim her, to force myself on a Centauride, even as every fiber in my being screamed for her. The turmoil in my head was unbearable; a weaker Centaur would crumble, but I held strong. I'd made my decision. When I didn't answer, her soft voice prodded, "Beau, you saved my life. I wouldn't be alive right now if it weren't for you. You only have to tell my father that you're taking what belongs to you."

I shook my head. Nothing would make me happier than to spend this life and eternity with Lacey, but I couldn't think of an action that would be more selfish. Of all the Centaur laws, the third Centaur tenet was the one I disliked the most. Having seen it invoked on an unwilling Centauride when I was young, the image of her protests still haunted me.

Evangeline and I had known each other most of our lives. It was the summer before our junior year of high school. A group of us were spending the day on Folly Beach, surfing, sunning, playing volleyball – everyone enjoying that perfect beach day.

Evangeline had just turned sixteen the day before and was waiting for the DMV to open Monday morning so she could get her driver's license.

The waves were enormous that day; a summer storm was brewing in the Atlantic and would hit the coast the following morning. None of us should have been in the water, but we were all stupid. While Evangeline was surfing, the undertow pulled her under the water and out to sea. We saw it happen, and every young Centaur on the sand went into the water after her. The current was too strong, and we lost her.

Word spread like wildfire, and Centaur rescue boats started arriving from all directions; a couple helicopters were even brought in. Several hours went by without any word. Her family paced the shore with the rest of us, looking for a glimpse of her.

Five hours after she was pulled out to sea, an older Centaur found her and radioed back to let everyone know she was alive. Evangeline had been found clinging to her board: dehydrated, burned from hours in the sun, and terrified. The Centaur who found her had been days from his thirtieth birthday, and he invoked the third tenet.

An unbetrothed Centauride whose life is spared forfeits her choice to the Centaur who saved that life. The tenet treated Centaurides as property, stating that because they were given a second chance at life, it was their obligation to repay their life to the Centaur.

That day on Folley Beach has haunted me for thirteen years. I can still hear Evangeline's screams when her father gave her to the Centaur who was nearly twice her age. Every race has their undesirables; Evangeline's Centaur had been a beast. I never saw Evangeline after that day. Her Centaur forbade her return to school. I heard she was rewarded with a horrible existence and bore eight children before she died at his hands a year ago.

I'd seen Centaurs purposely put young Centaurides in danger in the hopes that they could be the rescuer. It turned my stomach.

Lacey took a step closer to me – I distanced us with another step in the other direction. I shook my head, gritted my teeth, and told her, "I can't do that to you, Lacey."

The hurt registered on her face. I'd seen the expression many times on my own; she believed I was rejecting her. Lacey reached over and touched my forearm a second time. "You've already proven that you'd put your life in jeopardy for mine. I'm yours to take."

I shook my head. "No. I don't want to marry you because you've got some misplaced obligation you feel you owe me. I would have done the same thing for anyone: Centauride or human."

Her head was bowed. She gazed up tentatively and gently argued, "But you didn't do it for anyone. . . you did it for me."

"Lacey, you're an incredible Centauride. You're going to make a Centaur very happy. I'm too old for you."

She wouldn't let it drop. Did she not know that I was a hair away from doing what I had detested in so many others over the years? She didn't relent and answered, "Only eleven years. My father was nine years older than my mother was."

"Lacey, I'm not unhappy. I don't begrudge my destiny. My family won't disown me, and I'll be free of the Centaur restrictions. Don't pity me for not having been chosen."

She shook her head, "It's not pity, Beau. It's your right. You only have to decide what is yours and take it."

I stood looking into her eyes, unable to believe what I was hearing. I couldn't afford to live in this fantasy, and I wouldn't let her convince herself it was okay. "It's not fair to you, Lacey. I won't take that choice away from you. Whatever obligation you feel you have to me for pulling you from the car wreck, I release you." In that moment my mind was screaming to take back my foolhardy words, screaming that she belonged to me. As difficult as it had been for me to accept that I would never be chosen, I would never forgive myself if I stole her choice from her.

Lacey looked at me with her soft green eyes; her expression disarmed me, as if she weren't looking at the failure I felt I was. "So, you've made up your mind. You won't seek a Centauride for a wife?"

I took in a deep breath. "That ship's sailed. I've made peace with my decision. My family has accepted it."

"What if a Centauride chose you?"

I felt a surge of the same energy from before when she touched my forearm. I could hear my own heart beating. My palms were sweating. Lacey couldn't possibly be considering choosing me?

I swallowed a large gulp of air; my throat was dry. I felt light-headed and could see tunnel vision coming on. My eyes narrowed when I asked, "Hypothetically. . . or are we talking about you?"

Her eyes held mine, "Me."

My words were barely audible when my resolve began ebbing away. "Lacey, don't do that."

She couldn't possibly understand. I needed to walk away before I enacted the tenet which said she was rightfully mine. I tried to make her listen to reason, "You're young and beautiful. You've got a heart as big as a Volkswagen. Don't settle for me." My eyes dropped from hers as I mumbled, "Find a Centaur worthy of you."

Tears had already welled up in her eyes, her voice no more than a whisper, "So, you don't want me?"

I closed my eyes. I couldn't look back into hers, and I couldn't admit the truth. If I told her how I felt, she would choose me. I couldn't let her give up her future for me. For the first time, it hit me: if we were to become betrothed, regardless of who made it so, both our lives would be in serious danger. I would willingly accept the risk, but I couldn't let her squander her future. "I didn't say that. I said I've made peace with my decision. You don't have to feel sorry for me. I'm going to be fine."

"Beau, I don't feel sorry for you. I don't have a misguided sense of duty. I don't have an obscure obligation that I feel I owe you. Don't you see? I care about you."

"You hardly know me."

Her hands went to her hips, her brows furrowed; her voice was strong and unyielding, scolding me. "I know more than you might think."

I hated it when people assumed they knew me. We'd spent very little time together. How could she claim to know me? I challenged her without meaning to. "Really? What do you think you know?"

"I know your father tried to pay another Centaur for his daughter's choice." I'd never told anyone that. The only people who knew were my dad and me. I'd refused an arranged marriage for the same reason I hated the third tenet. "Her father accepted the bribe, and when you found out, you called her father; you told him to keep the money and his daughter. You knew he needed the money, and you knew his daughter would have married you out of obligation to her family."

She paused waiting for me to say she was wrong. She wasn't, but it made me uncomfortable that she could have known about any of it. "I know your friend Daniel didn't start out as your friend. The only reason you ever spoke to him was to keep him safe from your father. You moved out to the west coast to prove to him that not all Centaurs are unfeeling and pre-programmed to be jerks. I know the day you pulled me from the burning car, you were furious that my betrothed died, because you felt he had more to live for than you did."

I shouted, "Enough!" I couldn't listen to her romanticizing my decisions or my thoughts. "Lacey, I'm not going to force you to marry me. You're free. Your life is your own." I put my back to her and walked away.

The strength in her voice never wavered, "You see, Beau, that's the part that sucks about this gift I have." Her words stopped me in my tracks, and without wanting to, my body involuntarily turned back to hear her, "I can see visions of things that are going to happen. I can read minds as easily as I can read the written words in a book, but I can't see how you feel about me."

I mouthed the words because my voice refused to work, "Lacey, don't."

"I've made my choice, but if I say it out loud and you decline, it will break my heart." She closed the distance between us as she spoke, "I cared for my lost betrothed. He was a good Centaur and would have made a fine husband. But he didn't have what you have. He wasn't noble."

Shaking my head, I felt my shoulders slump. "I promise you, I'm not noble."

Her hand softly cupped my face, as her voice quieted, "More noble than you may think. The pettiness of the Centaur ways are beneath you. You won't grovel. You won't oblige underhandedness. You're better than that."

I didn't know what to say. My voice wouldn't respond, and even if it worked, I wouldn't have known what to say. My hands started to tremble. I couldn't walk away a second time. I heard my own voice echo in my head: *Do not give up the gift, that which is due you*. The seven tenets were drilled into us from the time we could speak. I winced when I realized I was a breath away from claiming her. If she said another word, I wouldn't be able to stop myself. I *would* claim her as mine.

Her nervous smile eased, her lips opened, and I heard the words I believed I would never hear, "I choose you, Beau."

Her words echoed in my mind as if she'd spoken them in the Grand Canyon. I could feel my chest swell, a heat radiated from me inside out, and I fell to my knee. Lacey offered me her hands as I knelt next to her and gave the sacred betrothal pledge. "Lacey, you are mine. I promise to protect you. I promise always to put your needs before mine. I promise I'll never let you go to bed angry, and you'll never wake up alone. I promise to love you the rest of my life, and when this life is over, I'll spend my eternity in the pasture with you."

She smiled, and I felt as though I needed to shield my eyes from her beauty. Lacey gently tugged on my hands, letting me know I should stand. When I did, I realized it had been more than just the two of us in the dimly lit hotel lounge. Her father, along with my brother Bart, had just witnessed the whole thing.

Bart is the next oldest eligible Centaur in our family, and although we'd never openly discussed it, I got the distinct feeling that he understood my desires to leave Centaur life behind and start a new life as a human. My decision to leave allowed me to escape the state of perpetual waiting. Bart was twenty-six and had another four years worth of potential rejections.

Bart had always been a Centaur of few words. We five brothers looked strikingly similar, so when people described him, it would always be, "You know, the quiet one. . ." He came to me with his right hand extended. As we clasped hands, he reached around with his other arm and pulled me into a bone-crushing embrace. In the previous twelve months, I'd heard Bart speak fewer than thirty words. I was surprised when his embrace was accompanied by, "Beau, you can come home. None of us could stand to be apart from you. Come back to South Carolina with us. Bring Lacey."

I wasn't sure which one had surprised me more: the choice by Lacey that I couldn't have seen coming if it were written on the Sears Tower, or the heartfelt congratulations from a brother who cared more about my decision to leave the Centaur way behind than I would ever have guessed.

Lacey's father was affronted by our exchange. "What have you done?"

His gaze fixed on his daughter, but his hollow words were directed at me. "You've just sentenced her to death."

Without thinking, I leaped in front of Lacey. I could feel the muscles near my eyes flex and my nostrils flair, "She is mine."

Her father pleaded, "Beau, don't do this to her. They'll be looking for you. You won't escape them."

I understood his painful words. He was right. By choosing to remain a Centaur and accepting Lacey's choice, we would now be targets of those seeking the Lost Herd. The blaze that had radiated in my body turned to embers. I turned to face her to try to find a speck of regret looking back at me.

I only saw her unshakable strength, "Beau, I knew the risks. I chose you. You are mine." My upbringing taught me to keep a distance. Touching, even while betrothed, was frowned upon – but I couldn't stop myself. I gathered Lacey in my arms and cradled her head against my chest. I willed the world to spin without us, to let me stand here in her embrace.

Her father interrupted us, "If you care for her at all, you'll let her go. You'll break your pledge and never set eyes on her again. Do it now, before anyone finds out." Lacey looked up into my eyes: my heart was hers. It would always be hers.

If I broke my pledge here, now, she had a chance of a life with another. As a Centaur, I could only make that pledge once. There were no do-overs for Centaurs. Centaurides could accept a betrothal pledge and change their minds after, but the Centaur would never be able to force the pledge a second time. The bond was once in a lifetime.

I had asked Drake about it when we were searching for Cami. He told me he had accepted Bianca's proposal, but he never gave her the pledge. Centaurs were never psychic, but he knew his best friend Gage wanted to give her his pledge.

I considered her father's words. If I broke my pledge, I would still be tied to her for eternity and could protect her on earth. It was the only responsible thing to do. I had to let her father take her home, give her a chance at life. I opened my mouth, but the words refused to escaped me.

Lacey, no doubt reading my thoughts, pushed back away from my embrace, "Don't you dare!" Her words startled me, and whatever words I was trying to form vanished in front of us all. She continued, "Beau Strayer, you are my Centaur. If you break it, I will never forgive you. You are mine."

She stood straight, fists balled at her side, and in a ferocious voice I never wanted to hear from her mouth again, she shouted "Daddy, I've made my choice. Be happy for me. For as long as I live, Beau is my Centaur. I don't want to waste time. Call Uncle Norman, find a priest, we're getting married today before either of you," she pointed her finger menacingly at both her father and me, "tries to stop it."

Her father was the first to recover, "Lacey, there's no rush. Even with Ted you planned a long "

Lacey cut him off, "Dad, today. Stop arguing. Set it up or I will." She turned her attention on me, her voice much softer, and the furrowed brow holding the glare for her father abated, as well. "Beau, you left your family because you couldn't take the rejection. You don't want to be human any more than the river wants to run still. I'm not afraid of marrying you or joining your family. The only thing that frightens me is you getting a hair-brained idea to try to save me by breaking your pledge and disappearing. I want this. I want you. I want it today."

CHAPTER 31

Drake – Cameron's House, SD

I thought we would have weeks together before we needed to make any more permanent plans. After just days together, we'd received a call that the Centaur Council would meet in Centauride, South Africa at the end of the month. It was a special session, and we already knew the topic.

I was still awkward as half a man. I'd never been vain, at least I tried never to be, but I would catch my reflection in the glass of a window or the large mirror hanging in the living room – I couldn't get used to my new form. Cami had moved most of the furniture into the bedrooms; the small living room felt much bigger when the only piece left was a well-worn recliner. At night she lay with me on the floor of the living room, and throughout the day, I did my best not to destroy the place.

How long could we continue like this? I asked myself this question hundreds, maybe thousands of times. I tried to comfort myself knowing I was in this form by my own choice. But that fact gave me no comfort.

I doubted it ever would.

"Stop it, Drake."

Cami was standing in the door frame between the kitchen and living room staring at me. I forced a smile back at her after looking around the emptied room. "I'm not doing anything."

"Yes, you were. I can hear your thoughts, remember?"

I nodded. "Cami, I'm your Centaur. Nothing will change that. I think it's time we look at this from a practical perspective."

"I've made my choice, Drake."

"There's no future with me, Cami. We aren't even the same species anymore. You have an obligation to our race. You are the last Chiron Centauride."

"So?"

"So, you have to. . . you need someone. . . you can't. . ." I couldn't finish the thought. Daniel's face flashed in my head. I may not be able to get the words out, but I knew he loved her. He'd loved her for longer than I'd known her, and I understood why her mother believed the two would end up together. They were compatible; they were comfortable friends, trusted allies, and shared a mutual respect. Under the right circumstances, it could be more.

She remained in the doorway. She knew what I was thinking; I didn't need to spell it out. My thoughts wounded her, but if she were to have any kind of life at all, we needed to stop thinking about just surviving and come up with a plan for her: a life she could live with.

"Drake, I can't keep being the strong one. You can't keep doubting us. . ." Cami was still talking, and her words were heartfelt, but a strange feeling came over me. Voices, no. . . thoughts, swirling all around me – danger was near. I could feel the danger encircling us, not the threat of what could happen weeks or months from now, but a tangible threat just outside the house. Centaurs were here. They were stationed at each exit, all with weapons: guns, knives, one carried a mace.

She was still talking when I cut her off, "Cami! Get in the basement, now!" I was across the room and lifting the trap door before the words were fully out of my mouth. "Get in, don't come out." I tried to count the warriors outside in my head, at least ten, a perimeter around the property, another thirty. Damn it! How had they gotten so close?

"Drake, I don't under. . ."

"Down, now! I'll be back for you. I promise. Not a word and don't come out. Do you understand? Don't come back up!"

I slammed the trap door, heaved the single reclining chair that still remained in the living room over the access panel to camouflage the entry. The doors burst open and windows were smashed into the house. Centaurs leaped in through each opening.

Shock, outrage, and disbelief shone on the faces looking at me. I didn't recognize any of the Centaur faces staring back at me, and no one moved. Lacey, Daniel and the Strayers had kept their word: no one knew of my transformation. They lost their element of surprise when no one knew what to do against a living, breathing Centaur with hooves. I towered over all of them, rage emanating from every pore on my body. I was ready for them and they were ill-prepared for me.

The ten men stood, mouths agape, only one holding a gun. I put my back to him and kicked him with every ounce of strength I had, which, funny enough, was almost too much. He sailed through both sheets of drywall separating the living room from the kitchen and ended up sprawled out across the kitchen table. I reared up, my head a fraction of the inch from the ceiling as my front hooves pawed two more attackers to my front. When these two went down, the very real danger registered with the remaining seven in the room. Weapons were drawn, but my reaction time was swifter than theirs.

A stout muscular man lunged at me with a knife. I easily moved out of his path and delivered a heavy blow to him as his forward momentum was helped along by the strength within me.

Another carrying a dagger came at me from my other side, trying to bury it deep in my back. I caught the knife in my hand before it could sink into my flesh, did a quick turn and had it aimed squarely at his heart. Before I could sink the knife into him, I felt another approaching me from behind. My hoof caught him in the jaw as I heard his body sail several feet back and plant hard in a corner. I easily disarmed and knocked the other five unconscious.

The brute force this body was able to deliver was astonishing. I stood alone in the room, bodies laying in all corners. I hadn't killed any, but that wasn't my goal. I merely needed to keep Cami safe. Their deaths would serve no purpose.

After the battle this evening, I doubted any would come after us again. There was still a concern over those guarding the perimeter. How could I get Cami away from here? Knives, daggers, and handheld weapons were of no consequence to me, but bullets were another matter, and I couldn't tell who outside held guns.

I wouldn't risk even a whisper but knew Cami would be listening to my thoughts, "*I'm fine, Love. Stay where you are while I find a safe way out of here.*"

Her answer was immediate in my mind, "*I trust you, Drake.*"

An outside light shone brightly. I wanted to keep whatever element of surprise might be available. The broken windows would allow someone to see directly into the place. I turned off the light switch in the living room, the kitchen, the hallway; I stood in the pitch black willing my mind to locate all the remaining warriors around the perimeter of the property. All had held their position until the lights went off.

I had to have stumbled onto a predetermined signal because as soon as the house was completely dark, I could feel them all sauntering toward the house. Their confidence radiated from them; they believed the house was secure and the occupants were restrained.

A voice called from the yard, "Geeze, Rosco, what the hell happened?

It sounded like a bar brawl from out here."

I didn't know Rosco, but could only assume he had been the leader of the assault. The voice called again, "Rosco, everything's okay, right?" I felt him stop his advance.

To keep my element of surprise, I had to do something. If I answered and I sounded off, I didn't know how many guns might fire in through the windows. If I didn't respond to the question, it could be the same response. I searched my mind trying to remember any accents, but none of the attackers had muttered a single word. I needed the Centaurs outside to believe it was safe; I needed them in closer. I took a deep breath and yelled, "Clear! We got her!" I didn't dare say another word and worried that my shout may have just given me away.

It didn't. I was so attuned to this man that I actually heard his footsteps separately from the others who were advancing. We really were a warrior race because this was better than any military technology that identified friend or foe. Not only could I identify him, I knew his position and could determine which footsteps were his from at least fifty feet away through the walls of the house.

"What, are ya,' havin' a séance or something? Turn the lights on already. It's like the arctic tundra out here! Get the girl in the van and let's go!" I heard a vehicle pull up the driveway, the engine running.

I needed them on my turf; I needed them off-guard. Taking out ten Centaurs at once was better than I had hoped just moments before their assault, but thirty was a different matter and would require more than just a few seconds of shock to gain the advantage. I looked around the room and picked up a dagger and a hunting knife. I believed my hooves were better weapons, but putting one in each hand gave me an option if anyone got close.

"Rosco, turn on the damn lights!"

I saw the fuse box in the hallway. In the blink of an eye I was at the panel and had shut off the power to the house. I bellowed back, "Can't!

Guarding her!"

I heard his heavy steps stomping the snow off his boots onto the floor of the kitchen. He was in the pitch black house after emerging from the front yard that was lighted by the bright light. His eyes hadn't adjusted when he said, "Guarding her? Just tie her up and let's. . ." He was out cold in one blow. He hadn't seen the man still sprawled out on the kitchen table beside him, the one I believed was most likely Rosco. I boosted the second man off the floor and on top of Rosco and waited for more footsteps.

Cami's thoughts came to me quickly, "*Drake, there's no one at the back of the house. It's safe. I know it.*"

The warrior part of my brain told me to stay and fight the others so we couldn't be pursued, but the betrothed part of my brain argued that it was more important to get Cami to safety. My pledge won out. I moved the chair from the trap door, lifted the hatch, and reached my hand as far down as I could to lift Cami out.

When we reached the back door, I looked in all directions. Footprints etched in the snow showed feet had gone toward the front of the house. She was right: this was our best egress.

I took a second to catch her gaze, the adrenaline still pumping hard in my veins, "Cami, you're going to need to hold on. We're going to race the wind tonight." A thick comforter was balled up near the back door with our backpack and Cami's coat. It hadn't been strategically placed there, but when Cami was rearranging the house to accommodate me, this was where the blankets, pillows, and our personal items were kept during the day. Neither of us felt right about disturbing Cameron's things in the bedrooms.

I lifted Cami easily into my arms and galloped out the back door, through the back yard, along the river's bank that bounded the property and into the night. We didn't hear a voice of any kind, and as I put distance between us and the house, the Centaurs who had surrounded us became more fuzzy in my mind as their potential for danger diminished.

I had run for at least forty miles, through streams and over rocky terrain where my hoof prints couldn't be detected, when we came upon a boarded-up motor lodge. The sign in front indicated it was closed for the winter and would open again on Memorial Day. The place was far better than the barn I had spent a few nights in.

It felt safe, as the place had no ties to anyone we knew. We tried several of the doors, and all were locked tight with curtains drawn. We found one that was on the back side, opposite the abandoned parking lot that nestled into the forest behind it. Seeing our footprints would be next to impossible in this remote area. I thrust the door handle hard, and the lock gave way.

Cami walked into the dark room. The electricity hadn't been cut and the heat was on, not warm, but enough so that the pipes wouldn't freeze. Cami went to the thermostat and turned the temperature up to a balmy sixty degrees, then flicked on the bathroom light. It didn't light the entire room but gave off enough of a glow that we could see where objects were in the room.

Cami asked the question I didn't have the answer for. "Who were those guys?"

"I wish I knew."

"You didn't recognize any of them?"

"No. They weren't there for me."

Cami nodded. "You didn't kill any of them. Once they recover, they'll tell. Everyone will know about you." She looked sad, and I wished she would share her thoughts with me, but she held them in, blocked from me.

I walked to her. I had felt so awkward around her in this body until tonight. I understood Zeus's words; I understood why Chiron's magic had done this to me. I was better able to protect her in this form. That was what she needed now more than anything. More than a lover, more than a confidant, more than a friend, Cami needed a warrior if she were to survive.

I was pleased that it would be me. I wondered selfishly if I would ever be given my old body back. I wondered if I'd grow old like this. Would Cami ever find peace, and if she did, would she share that peace with someone else? My mind tumbled in a free fall, until I felt two delicate hands placed on my cheeks.

I looked down into Cami's milk-chocolate brown eyes. She had heard my concerns and answered, "It isn't permanent."

I shuddered under her touch. "You can't know that, Cami." I took a breath and added, "If it is, I have no regrets." I pulled her to me, nestling her head against my chest. One arm held her to me as the other caressed her cheek with my thumb.

She whispered, "These men, whoever they were, won't stop. They'll find us again. They'll use a Centauride to locate us."

"I know."

"We'll never know peace." Despite her words, the warmth of her body calmed me. I remembered the rage I felt when the men surrounded me while Cami was safely tucked in the basement. A rage I had never known consumed me and with it a single goal, to keep her safe.

With more confidence than I felt, I answered, "We'll find peace. We'll find it together."

Her resolve was strong, "Not unless we take the fight to them."

My arms tensed so I loosened my arms as I was worried I'd crush her. "What're you saying?"

"I'm saying we go to Centauride. We meet with the Centaur Council. I'm saying we let the world know I am the last Chiron Centauride, and I am of the Lost Herd."

"Cami, that would be suicide."

"If we don't and a stupid Centaur decree, or whatever they're called, gets passed down to hunt all the living Tak descendants, it's a death sentence for my family. We've got to try to stop it. I can't lose my family."

"I can't lose you. Even if I'm stuck like this forever, I can't stand the thought of losing you."

She was still snug against my chest, "You won't lose me. If we can't have this life together, you already promised me eternity in the pasture. If we don't do this, now, while we can, this life will be spent on the run, being hunted. No. We take the fight to them."

"There's a good chance we won't make it out alive."

"But there's a chance we will. Plus I have my secret weapon."

"Your secret weapon? You're able to plant ideas in other's heads?" We hadn't discussed it before, but I'd been told this was the Centauride skill which had infuriated Zeus to begin with. If she had the skill and planned to use it, there would be no escape for either of us.

She shook her head, "No. I have the strongest magic in the universe." I thought of the arrow, the way it had transformed me, and the fact that it was lost to us forever.

Cami had read my arrow thought and answered before I could protest that the arrow's magic was never going to be ours. "No. Before my mother left for the pasture, she told me the strongest magic was love. You've proved her right over and over again. Tomorrow we make our plans to travel to Africa."

"You're forgetting Zandra is the chairman. We could fly all the way there and never address anyone."

"*You* are forgetting the effect you will have on them. Remember the astonishment on the men's faces who saw you tonight? You are a living, breathing Centaur – no matter what they're told to do, they'll listen."

I hoped she was right. I hoped we wouldn't be walking into more of an ambush than we had found tonight. I hoped a lot of things, but one more so than anything else. There was a chance that she was right. If we could make the Centaur Council see reason, we had a chance at a life together.

I thought back to the few short weeks before when the only thing I had to protect Cami from was Zandra. I silently wished she were our only threat, but Cami was right. Looking over our shoulders for the rest of our lives was no life.

I picked her up and laid her gently on the bed. "Get some rest. You're going to need it." I gave her a whisper of a kiss as I watched her heavy lids close. I held her hand with mine and used my other to gently stroke her hand.

I watched her drift off to sleep as I had so many nights before. Once she was sound asleep, I let the words escape me. "Aphrodite, I feel you watching."

The only sound was Cami's soft breathing. I let my eyes wander to her for a second then took a few steps to the window and looked up into the night's sky. "I have felt your watchful eyes for days."

I don't know what I expected, maybe for Aphrodite to materialize and acknowledge the only reason I still looked like this was my love for Cami. Maybe if we survived, Aphrodite would make me human again and let us have a normal life.

I found Venus set close to Virgo in the sky; this was where Aphrodite watched from the heavens. When no voice spoke and she didn't appear in front of me, I made one final request. "If anything happens to me, convince Cami to seek Daniel. He's the only one on the planet I would trust to love her." Venus twinkled brightly, acknowledging my request.

After I said the words, I caught myself staring into the clear night sky through the gap in the curtains. Sagittarius is a summer constellation; there would be no hope of seeing it this time of year in the northern Hemisphere. I saw Orion, the hunter with his bow. The three stars in his belt shone more brightly than I had ever remembered seeing. Something clicked inside my head: it was Orion who I would want helping me protect Cami at the Centaur Council.

CHAPTER 32

Drake – Deserted Hotel, SD

I felt my own eyelids growing heavy and gingerly backed away from the window. The room was the size of any budget rate motel I'd ever seen, so movement was restricted. As I was easing myself onto the floor, my phone began to vibrate.

I looked at the caller ID and couldn't believe my eyes: Gage Richardson.

Gage was my best friend growing up. So much had happened since I talked to him. I didn't worry about the danger of my cell phone signal being traced; I wanted to talk to him. The last I'd heard, he and Bianca had gone into hiding after our escape from Zandra's.

I could hardly contain my excitement when I answered, "Gage? Is it you?"

"Yeah, how's it going?"

Loaded question. I looked at Cami sleeping peacefully a few feet away and answered without hesitating, "Never better. So what happened with you guys? I heard you left town."

"We're back. We went to Cancun after we left you and Cami."

"Cancun? I thought you hated it there."

"It's a popular wedding destination."

"No way! You two are married?"

"Yeah, like the day we got there."

"Congrats, man. I'm really happy for you both."

An awkward silence hung when Gage said, "I . . . uh. . . I heard what happened."

The kidnapping? Our trip to Ireland? My transformation? There were too many possibilities to guess. "Yeah, it's been a busy few weeks since we saw you."

"I haven't told Bianca. She's been driving me nuts wanting to call and talk to Cami since we few south, so I called William's house tonight when we got back to see if she was there."

"William told you?"

"He said they're part of the Tak bloodline and they're going into hiding. He said you and Cami are already to the winds."

"What else did he tell you?"

"He was really cryptic, but said you might need me. I don't care what Cami's bloodline is, if you're with her, we'll do whatever you need us to. Just say the word."

He didn't know about my transformation. "Thanks. So what happened with you two? No more sneaking around, her parents were okay with it?"

"Yeah, that was amazing. The night we left Zandra's we went straight to Bianca's house to grab her stuff for the trip. Her parents still thought she was dead, so when we got out of the car and they saw us walking toward the house, her mom told us we had her blessing before we even got a word out!"

"That's awesome."

"What about you and Cami?"

Pride was loud in my voice when I answered, "She chose me."

"I knew it! I told you she would. So have you set a date?"

I looked at her sleeping body just a few feet away from me, "With everything that's been going on it hasn't been a big priority."

"Man, I saw the way you two looked at each other. I know you two have been traveling all over without an escort. How are you keeping your hands off each other?" I could hear the humor in his voice when he added, "Or are you?"

I thought of Gage as more family than friend, but I wasn't sure how much I could tell him without putting him and Bianca at risk. "So far we've been able to keep the brakes on."

"You're a better Centaur than I am. Once I saw Bianca was alive. . . let's just say it's a good thing the Bahamas are only a couple hours away."

Cami was still sound asleep in the bed while I was on the floor beside her. I touched the back of my hand to her cheek and felt the suppleness of her skin when I answered Gage, "I'll wait as long as it takes. She's mine."

"You pledged her, right?"

I laughed, "Yeah, that was funny. You know how she's never been around Centaurs? She'd never heard the pledge before. She woke up the next morning and wanted to hear it again."

"What?"

"Yeah. Cami had no clue that I was tying my soul to hers. She thought I was just being sweet."

"That's a riot. Did you tell her?"

"It kind of gave it away when she found out I could hear her thoughts."

The humor in Gage's voice diminished, "So, this Tak stuff could get bad. Where are you two going to go?"

I cringed, hating to admit it out loud. I'd been through enough with Gage, there was no sense hiding the truth. "Centauride."

"Centauride! Are you nuts? You can't go to Africa! They'll kill her!"

"Cami's pretty sure about it. She wants to address the Council."

"The Centaur Council? What's she going to say? 'Never mind Zeus's decree, leave the Taks alone.' Tell me that's not her plan."

"I'm not sure what she's going to say, but yeah, that's probably pretty close."

"Come back to South Carolina. I'll hide you both. I owe you both my life, because without Bianca I was pretty much dead."

"I'll let her know you offered, but I doubt she'll change her mind."

"You're okay with it? Drake, it's suicide."

"I love her. If she wants to address the Council, I'll be standing right beside her when she does."

"I can't let you go by yourselves. How about Bianca and I pick you up tomorrow. It'll be like the old days. You can pilot and I'll co-pilot for you."

Gage's parents had a plane, but he'd never gotten his pilot's license. I had a license but it wasn't commercial and I had almost no hours logged flying a jet. Our "old days" consisted of renting small commercial planes from the local airports and flying a few hours away for an afternoon excursion. Even if I could pilot his dad's jet, trying to fit into the cockpit looking like this would be impossible.

"I appreciate the thought, but I'm not licensed for your dad's plane."

"Where are you? Bianca and I'll be there tomorrow, and we'll figure out a plan from there."

Gage and Bianca could make all the difference for us. I trusted them both with my life, and more than that, I trusted them with Cami's life. "It's pretty late here. We're near Rapid City, South Dakota. Call me in the morning after you've had a chance to lay everything out for Bianca. If you two are still up for it after she knows everything, call me and we'll figure out where to meet from there."

"I know she's going to be up for it. She's dying to see Cami." Gage paused for a minute and lowered his voice. "She told me those weeks that you two were locked up at Zandra's, you kept telling her everything was going to work out. You told her you knew how much I loved her and that I'd find a way to get you both out of there."

"Hope was all we had. Neither of us knew what was going on, only that we were locked up and guarded."

"She said you told her no matter what happened, she could be with me."

I swallowed hard. I knew there was a chance Bianca and I wouldn't escape until after Gage and Cami's wedding. If that had happened, Bianca and I had already decided we'd find a way to be with the one we loved whether it went against the seven tenets or not. "We knew there was a chance we'd be locked up until after your and Cami's wedding."

"You're the only Centaur I know who would take the wrath of the gods over a beautiful Centauride."

"No. I'd take the wrath of the gods for the love of a beautiful Centauride. I'm glad it didn't come to that."

"Yeah, me too." I heard the shame in his voice when Gage admitted, "I wasn't there for Cami the way you were there for Bianca. I left her alone."

"You thought we were dead. You were grieving."

Gage's voice lowered, I couldn't be sure if he was talking to himself or me. "I shouldn't have left her. I want to make it up to Cami. She needed me then and I failed. I want to be there for both of you now."

Cami stirred on the bed next to me. There was no one I wanted in our corner more than Gage. "Sounds good. Give me a call in the morning; we'll figure out how we can hook up. Tell Bianca we said congratulations. We're really happy for you both."

"I will. I'll see you tomorrow."

As I hung up the phone, a huge weight lifted off me. Gage and Bianca were fine. We'd see them both soon. Gage was one of the most cunning Centaurs I'd ever met. With him helping us, we had a much better chance of coming out of the Centaur Council alive.

Cami's family had gone into hiding, so they should be safe. Daniel was probably already in San Diego, so Cami wouldn't have to worry about him getting caught up in any of this. He wasn't a pure-blood and he wasn't part of the Tak bloodline; he'd be safe as long as he was home.

My transformation into a real Centaur kept Cami safe today. Zeus had been right. If I were in human form, I'd never have been able to fight off the thirty Centaurs who stormed Cameron's house tonight.

Chiron hadn't cursed me with this transformation; it was a better gift than I would have ever thought to ask for. My transformation saved the Centauride I loved.

I leaned over and brushed my lips against Cami's cheek. Her lips turned up in a content smile while she slept. Even if my days were numbered walking the earth, I knew what she'd said earlier was right. We could always count on eternity together.

FROM THE AUTHOR

I hope you enjoyed *Centaur Legacy*! I would love for you to write a review on Amazon. It doesn't have to be long, just let others know what you thought of the story. Here is the link: www.amazon.com/review/create-review?ie=UTF8&asin=B00AB77ZTG.

I am an independent author, which means I do not have an agent, a publicist, or a publishing company backing me up. I DEPEND on word-of-mouth advertising. If you enjoyed *Centaur Legacy*, it would mean the world to me for you to recommend it to a friend (or ten friends!). If you recommend it to someone who tells you they do not have time to read, let them know it is also available as an audiobook!

If you would like to chat with me, here are the best places to find me:

Amazon author page: www.amazon.com/author/nancystraight

Facebook: www.facebook.com/nancystraight.author

My blog: www.nancystraight.com

Twitter: www.twitter.com/NancyStraight

Goodreads: www.goodreads.com/NancyStraight

Email: nancystraight@gmail.com

I read and respond to every message I receive. (Sometimes a day or two late, but I do respond to everyone who reaches out to me). I hope to hear from you!

If you wish to receive free promotional items, notification of book signing events, and upcoming book releases, you can join my subscriber's list here: http://eepurl.com/bDtmDL

Happy Reading,

Nancy

ACKNOWLEDGEMENTS

Centaur Legacy would not have been possible without the support of several incredible people. Linda Brant, my aunt, has painstakingly edited and polished *Centaur Legacy.*

Rebecca Ufkes, Kris Kendall, Charles Young, Melissa Balentine, Suzanne Finnegan, Amber Gest-Troyer, Christie Rich, Shannon Dermott, Bart Soucy and Jennifer Nunez volunteered to be Beta Readers – their feedback was invaluable.

The beautiful cover was designed by Amber McNemar at eTHINK Graphic Solutions.

I wish there were a way to single out each of the independent authors out there who has helped and inspired me along the way, but a thank-you to each one would be a book in itself. A few that I cannot leave out are: Shelly Crane, Rachel Higginson, Charlotte Abel, Amy Bartol, Christie Rich and Shannon Dermott – each one has been an incredible inspiration to me and I highly recommend all of their books!

Book bloggers are the unsung heroes for independent authors. There have been many that I feel indebted to. One book blogger who deserves a special place on this page is Heather at www.supagurlbooks.blogspot.com. She has become a dear friend and is a true indie advocate.

Finally, my husband, Toby, has been supportive of my every adventure. Thanks for all the nights you made dinner and did homework so that I could follow my dream!

All my love,

Nancy

www.ingramcontent.com/pod-product-compliance
Lightning Source LLC
Chambersburg PA
CBHW070636310726
48982CB00001B/301

* 9 7 8 0 6 9 2 7 9 8 6 0 7 *